Sign up for our newsletter to hear
about new and upcoming releases.

www.ylva-publishing.com

# Other Books by Jenn Matthews

Hooked on You

*Rob & Ros*
*Enjoy reading!* ♡

# The Words Shimmer

## JENN MATTHEWS

# Acknowledgements

This book would never have been written without my lovely wife, who helped with medical-type things and the emergency care practitioner course information. She, amazingly, has completed the course with flying rainbow colours, and now has her dream job in a GP surgery!

Thank you to my parents, the great Paul and Ann, and my Grandma Kathleen, who, at the age of ninety-one, is writing her memoirs.

To my wonderful friends Ceri and Sara, who helped greatly with the dyslexia aspect of this book. Thank you for the interviews and for being so open and honest about your experiences.

# Dedication

To all those who struggled to read before dyslexia was widely known. To all those who have yet to obtain a diagnosis and continue to find it difficult to get through a book. Take your time. Ask for help. Don't give up.

This book is also dedicated to Whisper, my mixed-breed dog. I had to include a brown stripy mutt in one of these stories; I'm just sorry it wasn't the first. Love you forever, however bad you smell.

# Chapter 1

Mel Jackson stepped into the busy canteen. The smell of chips made her stomach rumble and her mind slip backwards to her school days. *I didn't realise I was so hungry.* The sounds of trays clanking, chairs scraping, and people chatting were just short of deafening when combined. Her ears slowly became accustomed to the cacophony, however, and she was able to focus on the students, lecturers, and for today, members of the public that milled around her. The crowd didn't bother her—she was quite used to winding her way through busy areas, usually carrying heavy equipment. She squared her shoulders with her chin lifted to create the outward appearance of someone used to maintaining their own personal space.

She lurched forwards as someone shoved past her, a dull pain spreading across her back at the impact. Mel spread her hands, trying valiantly to stop the momentum, but her palms hit the glass counter with a *thwack*. Further pain shot up her arms and she only just contained a whine. She squeezed her eyes closed for a moment, then turned in time to see her assailant grabbing the last sausage roll. He shouldered his way toward the till, not giving her a second glance. Anger roiled inside her, but she shook herself and tried to smile apologetically at the server. The look she got in return stank of disapproval. *It wasn't my fault. I didn't ask to be bowled over by some kid wanting the last pastry!*

Mel shuffled down the line and muttered under her breath, but then turned as she heard someone shouting.

"Hey! Mel!"

It took her a moment before she caught sight of someone she recognised stepping up to her in the line. "Sarah."

"Hey." Sarah held out a hand, which Mel shook warmly. "Weird seeing you without your greens." She glanced up and down Mel's body.

Mel's cheeks burned at the scrutiny, but she tried to ignore the feeling.

"You look so different with your hair like that too. No ponytail today?"

"No." Mel laughed. It was too hot, really, for her hair to be down; the July heat was filtering into the large buildings of the university and making it stick to the back of her neck. She felt like she was going for an interview somewhere, all posh clothes and shiny shoes.

"You looking to do the Masters?"

Mel shrugged. "Maybe."

"Brilliant. Well," Sarah said, cocking her head to one side, "be great to have you. You're exactly the kind of person the course is aimed at, and your experience will be invaluable." She winked and strode away.

Her laughter continuing, Mel waved as Sarah disappeared into the crowd. She then looked over the choices on offer, not immediately sure what she wanted to eat. The queue was long and moved slowly, with quite a few people before her. She looked around again, people-watching.

*Please, let no one choke on anything. I'm off duty today and not really wearing appropriate clothing for resuscitation.*

She caught sight of a young man in his twenties, his black hair neat and proper, eating a sandwich with delicate precision. *If only everyone would eat like that.* With a sigh, she turned back to the queue and waited her turn.

Once she'd selected a meal and drink and had it settled on her tray, she turned back to the room to find somewhere to sit. She'd decided on a toasted sandwich and chips, regrettably not something she could carry outside. She tongued the inside of her lip for a few heart beats, her gaze pulled magnetically towards the sensibly eating man, and his dark-haired female companion.

The man stood, his lunch apparently finished, and he made his way through the busy tables, leaving his seat unoccupied.

Mel shook her head so her hair fell behind her shoulders and scanned the canteen for another seat. Nothing. A few other people were looking too, so she scooted towards the vacated seat quickly, approaching with what she hoped was an apologetic look. "Sorry. Nowhere else to sit. Mind?"

The brunette looked up from behind large black-rimmed glasses and showed no suggestion of disagreeing or that she was even interested. Mel gave her a tight smile in response and slid into the seat, her tray landing haphazardly on the table in front of her.

The woman looked at Mel, then at the tray, and back at Mel.

*She's pretty.* Mel flicked her eyebrows up once in acknowledgement of the fact. "I suppose as we're spending lunch together," she said, chuckles bubbling up in her throat, "I ought to introduce myself." She held out a hand. "Melissa."

The other woman stared at her, the fork that held a mouthful of salad hovering by her mouth.

Mel cleared her throat awkwardly, but continued to hold her hand out, with the opinion that sometimes one needed to wait a little while for another person to find their manners.

"Ruby Clark." She put her fork carefully into the plastic box in front of her and took Mel's hand. "Nice to meet you."

*Northern accent.* Mel tried not to grin too widely. Ruby's wide eyes suggested that she wasn't the most outgoing of people, perhaps unused to having complete strangers introduce themselves. Mel did it every single day in her job, and it was therefore a matter-of-fact issue for her.

"Call me 'Mel' though." Their hands fell away. "Sorry, should have said." She tried to add lightness to her voice and lowered her gaze to her food. "Have I made a terrible choice or are the chips here as good as they look?"

"They're not bad. Not that I advocate fried food in any sense." Ruby eyed Mel's food with disdain, so Mel plucked a chip from her plate and munched cheekily. Ruby's gaze lowered back to her salad.

"Well, it's not a normal day for me." Mel shrugged. "I'm here for the open day."

"Are you?" Ruby seemed mildly interested now, and Mel was pleased. *She's intriguing; I might as well include her in some topic that takes her fancy.*

"Looking at doing my ECP training. Oh." She stopped talking with her mouth full and swallowed, patting her finger against her plate. "ECP stands for Emergency—"

"Care Practitioner. I know."

"Oh good. Saves me explaining."

"I'm an anatomy lecturer, not a moron." Ruby's clipped words held a trace of humour, but they made Mel catch herself all the same.

"Do you teach any of the ECP modules?" Mel asked politely, pushing away the desire to tease and joke. *I don't think she's that kind of person.*

"No. Mostly nursing students. If you can call them that." Ruby carefully speared a tomato piece and ate it, her mouth working slowly.

Mel shifted her gaze to her own food, not wanting to stare.

Ruby placed her fork down and took a paper napkin, pressing it to each corner of her mouth. Her large dark eyes seemed to study Mel, her thick eyebrows pushed down just a bit. "So, you're from a nursing background yourself?"

"Nope. Paramedic through and through."

A flutter of something akin to disgust shot across Ruby's features, and Mel felt her hackles rise.

"What's the matter with that?"

"Nothing. Nothing at all." Again, with the clipped words.

Mel folded her arms and sat back in her chair, deciding to regard Ruby with an air of aloofness and scrutiny. "Oh, come on, spill."

"I just come across a lot of gung-ho, thrill-seeking paramedics. You're all fast-driving, crisis-loving, ego-maniacs, are you not?"

"What? Course we're not." Mel's stomach was starting to ache. Maybe she hadn't eaten enough yet. She leaned back over her table and shovelled chips into her mouth before picking up her sandwich, the crusty edges feeling harsh against her fingers. "We're not like that at all." She considered the statement, then grimaced around her sandwich. "Okay, well, perhaps one or two…"

"You're all like that." Ruby sounded completely sure.

*Who made you the boss of judging everyone on the planet?* "I'm guessing you're an RGN," Mel said, meaning a Registered General Nurse.

Ruby nodded. "Yes."

"Well, I can't say I've seen eye-to-eye with every single nurse at every single A and E. Most of them seem to think all we do is scoop and go. Who needs proper assessment skills when you can drive fast?"

"Who indeed."

"Okay, you know what? You're really starting to get on my wick." Mel balled a fist and held it steady on the table top. When she realised how that looked, and that Ruby's gaze was trained on her hand, she consciously loosened her fingers. "Have you any idea the skills we have to have these days?"

"So you can do a manual blood pressure." Ruby's eyes were narrowing.

"Yeah. And an ECG, and interpret it, and we administer around thirty drugs, all independently without a medic."

"Patient Group Directive," Ruby stated, with a piercing and amused look in her eyes.

*Is she enjoying pissing me off?* Mel took a slow breath in and let it out, rolling her shoulders back to allow some of the tension to drop. "PGD is still independent."

"Anyone can give a bit of paracetamol to someone with a headache."

"We give controlled drugs, without supervision. Are you able to do that?" Mel decided to give as good as she was getting, so set her jaw. "I suppose it's been a while since you even did a shift on a ward."

"Yes, a whole week." Ruby's accent made the word 'whole' sound so different to how Mel would say it. It was long, drawn out, with more than a little sarcasm pushing it into the cavernous canteen. Ruby seemed very satisfied with this. "I do a shift a month."

"Must be hard, working under all those doctors when you're so used to having hundreds of student nurses looking up to you like you're some kind of deity." Mel focussed back on her plate and began to eat again, an air of forced nonchalance in her movements. "You obviously think you're the boss of everything."

It was a cheap shot, but Mel felt overwhelmingly satisfied when Ruby scraped back her chair and gathered her things, nearly dropping the water bottle that appeared to be full of something purple. Slinging her bag over her shoulder, she stuffed her hands into her beige jacket pockets and pushed her glasses up her nose and into place. "I really wouldn't sign up. From what the ECP lecturers have told me, paramedics rarely do well on the course. Something about not being focussed enough for the workload." She looked Mel up and down. "You seem a bit long in the tooth anyway, don't you?"

Mel screwed her face into a frown and her gaze followed Ruby as she sauntered off, easily picking her way through the crowds of extra people.

Sitting back again, Mel allowed herself to seethe. *How dare she make such assumptions about me!* She tapped idly at her plate with her fingertip, then pushed her hand under her own leg to stop herself from fidgeting. She was pretty sure she'd only ever see Ruby in passing again. But Mel was one hundred per cent sure she was signing up to the course now.

# Chapter 2

Ruby strode away from her Mini Cooper, pressing the button on the key behind her, locking it with a bleep. She walked purposefully towards the main entrance, her briefcase swinging from its long strap, her handbag atop it.

Wednesday was her favourite day, mostly because she only taught during the morning. The afternoon was supposed to be for extra-curricular activities for the students. Therefore, she used the time to catch up on essay marking, lesson plans, and whatever took her fancy once she was done.

Before she could get to the short path that would take her in through the front doors, a taxi pulled up close by. The back door opened and nearly fell off its hinges with the force at which it was pushed. Two rubber-ended crutches thumped onto the tarmac before one trainer, then a thick-socked foot joined them.

Leaning forward to get a proper look, Ruby noticed the passenger had a plaster cast on her lower left leg, and a frustrated frown on her face.

Like someone in an old people's home, the woman in the plaster cast rocked forwards once, then twice, and then used the momentum to haul herself onto her good foot. White knuckles gripped the car door, which swung towards her with the force of her pull.

Ruby's nursing instincts kicked in and she lunged towards the taxi, grabbing the door before it could swing back into the passenger and cause more harm. It was then that Ruby recognised the woman attempting to, now successfully, get out of the taxi.

Mel pushed her hands into the crutches to steady herself before looking up with a relieved smile. The smile fell away as their gazes locked and Mel realised who her knight in shining armour was. "Oh." She looked around the sunny car park, perhaps hoping for someone else to take over so that she didn't have to deal with Ruby. "Thanks." The reluctance flowed from her entire body.

Ruby decided to continue with her nurse persona; something caring and non-judgemental. *Maybe we got off on the wrong foot three months ago.* "No problem." She couldn't help eyeing the plaster cast with a chuckle of amusement and was pleased when Mel rolled her eyes with a snort.

"Don't ask."

"Actually, I wasn't going to."

Mel began to shuffle slowly towards the front entrance of the university and looked back at the taxi as Ruby closed the door for her. The taxi drove away, and they were left alone. A few students gave them a wide berth as they too went about their day.

Ruby walked next to Mel, her hand hovering at the small of her back in a gesture so familiar to her. *The number of patients I've taken to the toilet or to the snack machine in this way.* When Mel smiled up at her, she smiled back.

"I'm fine once I'm going." Mel gazed determinedly at the double doors, and the relief that crossed her face when they reached them was endearing.

"You decided to do the training, then?" Ruby asked, holding the door open for her, and then returning to her slow walk next to Mel, her hand behind her once again.

"Yeah. Well." Mel chuckled and indicated her crutches. "Seemed logical, especially while I'm off work. Can't sit around all day waiting for my bones to heal."

"Eight weeks?"

"I've done one week, so, yep seven more to go." She sighed. "If only I was, perhaps, a decade younger. It'd only be six."

"You don't look like you're in the age group to require more than six weeks."

"A compliment?" Mel's eyes were good-humoured. "That's refreshing."

Ruby pursed her lips around a grin and fixed her gaze in front of them. Mel was heading towards the eastern area of the university, where Ruby knew they taught most of the ECP modules. They'd need to exit into the central, outside area, which contained benches and a small fountain containing fish; and that would require a small step down. Ruby's internal nurse couldn't quite allow Mel to attempt this on her own, so she remained close.

"How old are you?" Ruby put a hand to her throat and looked away. "Apologies. I haven't had my morning coffee yet."

Mel laughed. "I don't know why people are weird about their age. I'm forty-seven."

Ruby looked up at the tall woman, whose crutches were on one of the top settings. She took in the strawberry-blonde hair that was pulled back into a ponytail, the green piercing eyes, and the striking cheekbones. Her gaze travelled downwards, resting on strong arms encased to the elbow in a red chequered blouse. *Bare below the elbow.* She blinked and shook her head at her own thought.

"How old are *you*?" Mel asked.

Ruby felt her cheeks reddening. Had she been caught staring?

"It's only fair." Mel stopped in front of the door to the central garden and frowned at it, so Ruby reached to push it open for her. "Thank you."

"Forty-two."

Mel seemed to look her up and down, and Ruby indicated with a shaky hand that she should go out of the door first. Her hand floated at Mel's back again.

"I'll parrot the compliment back at you."

"Please, if you could tell my girls that, it would be great. They seem to think I'm ready for the grave."

Mel wobbled on her crutches, and Ruby's hand automatically lay flat against her spine, the belt of her jeans hard against her fingertips. Mel steadied herself, then stepped down and out.

The sunshine caught the long straight hair clasped tightly in her ponytail as it swung like a pendulum, and Ruby smiled. *Such a pretty colour.* She followed her out and removed her hand once she was secure in the knowledge that Mel wouldn't fall. They began a slow but continuous journey along the concrete path and rounded the block towards another door.

"This is me." Mel stood still, her mouth pulled to one side. "Thanks for the... support."

"That's all right. Make it up to me at some point." Ruby took a chance and swished her hair back. "I love a nice Zinfandel."

"I'll keep that in mind."

Mel winked, and Ruby lowered her head so she could hide behind the top rim of her glasses. Mel's feet shifted towards the door, and she hesitated before practically jumping through. It swung closed behind her, and Ruby touched her chin as she watched her go.

*I wonder how she fractured her leg. Probably tibia fibula.* She considered Mel's predicament. *She's going to end up struggling. I know they have practical lessons.*

# Chapter 3

The minute Ruby saw the email, she locked her computer and raced out of her office and down the corridor. Skidding into the staff meeting room—which, thankfully, was not far away—she took in the sight of the whole department beginning to pack up. Her unexpected foray into patient handling with Mel had made her late checking her emails, and therefore late to a spontaneous staff meeting.

Alexander sent her an apologetic look and then looked around, a stack of papers in his hands. He seemed unwilling for her to read what they contained even as he held them out to her. "You weren't here. You got the last thing on the list."

"What're you on about?" Ruby looked down at the collection of papers and read the words *Gardening Project* across the top of the first page. "What's this?"

Ruby's head of department, Christine, approached them, a large grin on her face. "Lucky you. You get the kids."

"Excuse me?"

Christine flounced away, indicating that Alexander should explain.

His blue eyes followed Christine desperately, but he held a hand out towards the door. "Let's go back to your office. You're going to have to sit down."

Ruby followed him with an air of trepidation. Kids and gardening. *Oh bugger.* She sat when Alexander tapped the back of her worn leather desk chair.

"It's a project. All the lecturers got one. The university wants to implement a general rule that everyone must use their free time to help out charities. Andy got a painting project with the older adults at the nearest care home; Sonya got a youth offender's charity." He scratched the back of his neck and leant a hip against her desk. "You got a gardening project with Year 4s."

"And I'm supposed to do this when, exactly?" Ruby pressed the papers into the wood of her desk, rolling her eyes as she scanned what was written.

"Wednesday afternoons."

She glared at him. Not her beloved Wednesday afternoons.

He cleared his throat. "It, erm… starts in March next year. So you've got tons and tons of prep time."

She glared at him some more. Just for good measure.

His Adam's apple bobbed as he swallowed hard. "It's all detailed in the paperwork." His voice was little more than a squeak.

"What charity is this in aid of?"

"Air Ambulance. They're run completely by charitable funds, with minimal NHS involvement." He relaxed, knowing he was on much safer ground now. "Good cause, don't you think?"

"Suppose. Was it a 'first come, first served' type of situation?"

"It was."

Ruby groaned and stuck her fingers into her hair. "Painting and old people I would've been happy with."

"I did try to get you that one, but Andy was insistent."

Ruby groaned again and let out a dry sob. "I love my Wednesdays."

"I know." Alexander fidgeted. "I'm sorry." He eyed her curiously when she looked up. "Why were you late, anyway? You're usually so prompt for your first coffee." He pointed to the slightly steaming cup on her desk.

She lifted it gratefully to her lips and sipped. The taste, as always, made everything feel better, even before the caffeine hit her bloodstream. "Somebody needed help getting in from the car park. Someone on crutches."

"Hmm." He studied her, and she rolled her eyes. "Not your usual reaction. Had they not brought their own support?"

She finally lifted her coffee in the air. "Thank you for this."

"You're welcome."

"I met her in July. She's a paramedic, doing her ECP training."

Alexander scrutinised her, but his eyes also held a teasing sparkle. "Even more baffling. You hate paramedics."

"I don't hate them, exactly." Ruby huffed at him affectionately. "I suppose she seems like one of the good ones."

"You reckon?" A smile tugged at his lips.

"Anyway," Ruby said, swerving the conversation away from the reasons why she'd run to the aid of an attractive woman, "I'm hoping you know at least *something* about gardening."

He shook his head. "I've never been the sort of person that enjoys getting their hands dirty."

"Fantastic!"

"Hey, *you* were late, not me."

"Yes, I'm well aware of that." Ruby grumbled again and sipped from her coffee, hoping it would ease the ache that had started in her gut. *Fabulous. Just what I need: extra-curricular activities. As if I don't have enough to do.*

# Chapter 4

Mel rocked her plastered leg from side to side as she sat on the low wall outside the front entrance; tapped the Call button on her phone, and held it to her ear.

"Apple Taxis."

"Yep, I've been waiting a while now for my taxi. Melissa Jackson, I'm waiting outside the uni."

"Let me just look for you." The woman on the end of the phone paused as she tapped away. "I do apologise, the next free taxi will be an hour."

"An hour?" Mel's heart fell into her feet. She sighed. "I'm kind of battered and broken here. I can't sit outside for that long."

"I'm really sorry. One of our drivers had to go home, his wife's in labour." The woman sounded like this made up for everything. Or perhaps Mel was supposed to feel elated that someone she didn't know was about to be a father.

"Right. Well, in that case, shall we make it from the Landing Light Pub? I reckon I can make it to there."

"No problem. Sorry for the delay."

Mel hung up without saying good-bye. Her leg was hurting, although she'd managed to sit still in her first two introductory lectures, and lunch too. She needed some painkillers, and she needed a drink to take them with.

Hauling herself to her feet, she made her achy way across the car park, along the road, and crossed over to the yellow-lit pub. A few other students, most of them half her age or younger, were gathered around. Afternoon pub goers, even students, didn't seem to be there to get drunk; that was what the union was for. She'd already seen one eighteen-year-old tottering about outside the small bar at the university, hugging all her new friends and promising she loved them.

*Kids.*

She didn't mind so much. She'd missed out on that element of her teenage years, going straight into work after her A levels. She'd got a good job in retail that she worked up to, before deciding upon a different professional track. She remembered being a young adult, being fun-loving, happy, and free. She liked where she was now though.

*At least I will once I get something juicy and paracetamol-based inside me.*

The barmaid, luckily, noted her crutches and rounded the bar to collect her drink for her once she'd handed over the money. Mel gave her an appreciative nod and led the way to a quieter area, away from the younger students. She stopped and nearly lost her balance as she spotted Ruby, who had her head in one hand, a glass of something pink in front of her. She looked as if she was searching for something in the rosy depths of her wine.

Twisting her lips against a smile, Mel indicated to the barmaid the table Ruby occupied and awkwardly dropped into the seat across from her. Her juice landed on a beer mat close to hand. "Thanks. You're a star."

The barmaid nodded, then left.

With her hair hanging over her face, Ruby looked up and blinked at the appearance of her new drinking buddy. "Hello." Her voice held no friendliness, only dejection and depression.

Cautiously, Mel leaned forward and tilted her head to one side. "You okay?"

"Not really, no." Ruby played with the stem of her glass before sitting up straight, apparently realising the company she was in. "Oh, it's really annoying."

"What's really annoying?"

"Long story short, it looks like I'll be in charge of thirty kids from March onwards."

"Blimey, that's quick work. You should let me know the name of your fertility specialist."

Ruby rolled her eyes. "Not funny." She sipped her wine and sighed as it slid down her throat. "I've been *forced* into running a gardening group for a class of Year 4s. All in the aid of charity."

A slow grin spread onto Mel's face as she imagined being in Ruby's situation. "That sounds like so much fun."

"No. No, it won't be fun. It'll be a disaster." Ruby continued to look like the world was ending. "I did not sign up for it willingly."

Mel gave her time to continue and took the moment to shift her broken leg around a bit, trying to get comfortable. She opened her bag and took out the painkillers the hospital had given her.

"Bloody Alexander—who is usually rather a good personal assistant, I might add—managed to sign me up to the worst possible activity he could."

"Gardening with kids?" Mel swallowed the pills with her juice and set her glass back on its mat. "Doesn't sound too bad."

"I hate children. School-aged children, anyhow. They are not my idea of fun."

"You don't like kids?" Mel asked, unabashed surprise in her voice.

"I really don't. They're snotty and small and annoying." Ruby stretched her head back and sighed. "I don't have the first clue how to handle them. And I am not one for gardening either."

"Oh dear," Mel said into her glass before she drank. The juice was tart and fresh and just what she needed after a morning of information-gathering. "Didn't you say you had girls? The ones who think you're an old-aged pensioner?"

"Yes, I do," Ruby said, and a flicker of affection passed over her face. "Two fantastic, irritating, intelligent daughters. They're teenagers now, almost grown up, really. Not kids anymore."

"Did you hate them when they were?"

Ruby chuckled, some of the tension in her shoulders dropping away. "I didn't hate them, no. I suppose you don't, do you, when they're your own?"

"I wouldn't know," Mel replied. "I like kids—wish I'd had my own."

"Why didn't you?" Ruby inhaled sharply. "Sorry. You barely know me, do you?"

"It's fine. I just never had the opportunity."

"Ah. No one good enough to have kids with?"

"Something like that."

Ruby pouted just a bit, and Mel got the impression she felt bad for her. Despite her aversion to children, she felt bad that Mel had never experienced motherhood. *How strange. She's a walking oxymoron.*

"So, we've tackled kids. What about the gardening?" Mel swirled her juice, mixing the bits in the bottom with the rest of the drink. *Mmm, proper juice.*

"I've not the first clue about anything garden-related," Ruby admitted, her hand going back into her wavy dark hair. It fell over her shoulders and was so long that it nearly touched her elbows. It looked glossy and thick, not like Mel's own hair, which was thin and had streaks of white in it.

"Well, you know how to research, don't you?" Mel asked, a little incredulously.

Ruby sighed. "I'm no good with plants. The only reason the orchid in my kitchen has survived is because I don't water it."

"Yeah, you're supposed to leave them be."

Ruby blinked. "You know about plants?"

Mel felt her cheeks redden and stared into her diminishing drink. "Um, I may know a thing or two."

"Would you help me?"

Mel looked up at the brazen request.

"I know we barely know each other, but I'm serious about this. I could kill a weed without even trying and I could use all the help I can get."

"Not exactly a compliment of the highest order."

"Sorry, I didn't mean it like that. I just, well, like I said, I don't know anything about gardening, I don't know anyone who does, and I'm terrible with kids. As I said earlier, this is going to be an unmitigated disaster."

Mel sipped her juice. "What happened to the 'all paramedics are gung-ho ego-maniacs' rule?"

Ruby blushed too, her hand going to her cheek. "You seem to be the exception."

Mel shook her head. "No, I'm the norm," she stated, pushing her backside away from the chair. She huffed and smoothed back her hair in its ponytail. "You really are infuriating."

"I'm stubborn too." Ruby's eyes were forlorn.

The waning pain in her leg shifted upwards into her temples. She sat back down slowly, carefully, and placed her hands on the sticky table in front of her. "I see that."

"Every paramedic that I've met—"

"That literally cannot be true," Mel interrupted, one hand in the air, palm up, in a half-shrug. "How many have you actually met? Recently, I mean."

"Since the degree came in?"

Mel nodded.

"A few."

"You do bank shifts in A and E?"

"No, I don't."

"Just on the wards, then?"

A pause. "Maybe."

"So, you only see paramedics making scheduled transfers. Which is, what, once in a blue moon?"

Ruby shrugged.

"Did you have a bad experience with a paramedic?" Mel lowered her voice, and forced herself to offer a non-judgemental tone.

"I may have."

She squinted, laced her fingers together on the table, and sat back. The ache in her head continued. "So your one bad experience has made you prejudiced." It was a statement, not a question.

Ruby closed her eyes briefly, and when she opened them, she couldn't seem to look at Mel. "Maybe."

"Definitely." Mel gave her more space, hoping she was the kind of person who would talk if you gave them a silence to fill.

"We had a male patient transferred from Queen's—spinal and head injuries. They were made worse by the manner in which he was transferred."

"Severe trauma? Probably an ECA driving; the paramedic would have been in the back with the patient."

Ruby nodded. "I suppose so."

"The ECA was a bit heavy-handed? Perhaps a bit careless?"

Ruby shrugged.

"You weren't there, in the truck." Again, another statement.

"Of course not."

"Then you've no idea about the condition of the road, other road users, or the weather at the time?"

"No."

"So you placed the blame on the crew transferring, as if they'd done it on purpose."

Silence from across the table. Very slowly, Ruby lifted her glass and stared into its depths, then took a sip. She placed the glass on its coaster and returned her gaze to Mel.

"Sounds like prejudice to me." Mel couldn't help expressing that opinion, especially as Ruby had expressed so many already.

Ruby sighed heavily and asked, "If I admit it, will you help me with the bloody garden?"

*Cheeky so-and-so.* "No."

"Why not?"

"Because we'd kill each other. You're arrogant. And I don't like that."

"I know I am." Ruby sounded like it shouldn't be an issue.

Mel huffed again and stretched her arms above her head, the crack in her shoulders feeling wonderful after a whole morning using her crutches. She rolled her wrists, relished the pops they made too. Then she wiggled her shoulders and relaxed. "What'd be in it for me?"

"You love children. The opportunity to work with a…" Ruby bit her lip. "An adorable bunch of young people."

A laugh shot out of Mel's mouth, unwelcome but inevitable due to Ruby's desperate attempt at talking about children like they were an asset to the world. Mel shook her head in amusement. "You're a real piece of work, d'you know that?"

Ruby barked out a laugh. "I may have been told that once or twice."

"I'm not surprised."

"So you'll help?"

"No, sorry. I really don't have time."

Lines appeared in the corners of Ruby's eyes as she narrowed them. "There's something else. Something that might sway you."

"I doubt anything would make me want to work with you when I have a choice."

Something akin to sadness flashed across Ruby's eyes before her mouth pulled into a smirk. "It's all in aid of the Air Ambulance Charity."

Mel blinked.

"We're to raise money for them; hold a tombola; sell the plants the kids grow—that sort of thing."

A twisting in her gut made Mel forget momentarily about the ache in her leg. "You can do that by yourself."

"I can't. Everything will die, the kids will be… upset. And we'll make no money. And the air ambulances won't get anything. The helicopters'll all rust for want of the oil our charitable donations would have bought and—"

Mel held her hand up to stop Ruby's over-exaggerated, totally fabricated story from going any further as an image of her most recent patient, his leg turned at an angle and his face screwed up in pain, slid into Mel's vision. The helicopter had landed on the coastal path, a few feet away. They'd managed to get the truck off the road for a minute or so before the terrain had become too treacherous. The walk to the patient had taken half an hour.

*We need more HEMS crews, more specially trained individuals, especially when there's so much countryside.* Mel sighed, patted her thighs, and glanced up at the ceiling. "Fine—"

"Amazing!"

"It's for a good cause."

"How much do you know about tending plants?"

The thought of working with Ruby for however many weeks made Mel gather herself inwardly. But the glint of making money for the Air Ambulance tamped down the flames somewhat. The thought of being around to watch Ruby struggle with the children was quite pleasant, as well. "My dad had an allotment the whole time we were growing up." Mel drained her juice, feeling a little bit like she was being interviewed for a job. She supposed it wasn't far from the truth. "He taught me most things. Vegetables, flowers, fruit. He had a greenhouse and heated propagators on the window ledge in the spare room."

The smile that spread over Ruby's face was full of relief. "Then I reckon you're just the woman for the job."

"Once I've got this cast off, I guess I'm all yours."

"You really mean it? You'll help?" Anxiety swam through Ruby's voice.

Mel reached forward and patted her fidgeting hands. "Yes, I will."

# Chapter 5

James brought their coffees through into Mel's conservatory, his eyes glinting with excitement. "There's a reason I come here for coffee: real proper coffee, from grounds."

"And all your girlfriend gets is instant?" Mel smirked and closed her eyes at him in an expression of thanks.

"There's something luxurious about proper coffee."

"Maybe you should do the shopping? Rather than leaving it to her?"

"Then there'd be no point in me coming around to yours."

"Apart from the fantastic company?"

James flopped back into the wicker chair and sighed. "Apart from that."

Epione sauntered in, her tiny white paws silent on the tiles of the conservatory. She meowed and stretched at Mel's feet, then hunkered down and hopped softly next to her on the chair. Mel stroked her head with her other hand, and the cat closed her eyes in contentment.

They sipped in silence for a while; their comradery continuing even when they weren't at work. They'd had a few tough shifts together recently, and Mel felt like they needed a long holiday together, somewhere sunny and warm. But her conservatory, and good, *real* coffee, would have to do for the moment.

James hummed into his mug and set it down, folding his hands over his podgy belly. "Uni okay? How are you finding the lectures?"

Mel knew why he was asking and nodded. "Yeah. They gave me a laptop and I'm making sure to use my Dictaphone every lesson.

When I get home, I listen back to it and amend anything I've missed or written down wrong."

"That's good. So it's not too much of a struggle?"

"I have been to uni before, you know." Mel glared at him and wiggled her head.

"I know, I know. Just checking they're supporting you enough."

"They are. Thank you."

Apparently appeased by this, James moved on. "So, what are you going to do with those tickets?"

"I've no idea." Mel tapped her fingertips against the arm of her own armchair and watched a sparrow flitting back and forth from her bird feeder in her garden. *He's probably trying to get fat for winter. Don't worry, little guy, I'll keep putting seed out.* Epione watched the birds too. Mel grunted, realising her brain was avoiding the question. "Can't you come with me?"

"Can't. It's Jade's birthday. You literally couldn't have got theatre tickets for a worse day."

"Well, there's no way I'm going by myself." She wiggled her cast about on the footstool James had pulled over for her earlier. "Those steps would kill me, and you know my track record with falling over things." She indicated her mangled leg. "Hence the cast."

"If you will go cycling into park benches."

"I swear, it sprang out of nowhere." They grinned at one another, and James went back to his coffee.

"So, what? Give them to someone else." He raised his eyebrows. "You do have other friends, don't you?"

"You are my one and only," Mel whined, pushing her bottom lip out.

James chuckled. "Wouldn't your dad like to go?"

"Even if he could, he wouldn't enjoy it."

"Why not?"

"An all-female version of *A Midsummer Night's Dream*?" She shook her head. "He's accepting, but not that accepting."

"Shame." James murmured his pleasure into his coffee again. "No lady friends on the horizon?"

"Lady friends? What are you, my grandmother?" She poked her tongue out at him, and the cat purred noisily as Mel scratched her between the shoulders. "No. No one I'd take to the theatre."

"You don't have any non-potentially-romantic friends you could take?"

"Everyone's busy." She sighed dramatically. "It's just little old me, all alone."

"Didums."

They snorted into their coffees and continued to relax in the October sun.

Wednesday rolled around again, and Mel found herself alone on her journey from the taxi. She managed it, making sure she didn't pull the door into her legs as she nearly had the week before. She limped through the sunshine into the university and made her way into her block.

There were a few students in her class, and only one was older than her. She felt a bit of a connection with the man in his fifties—a nurse looking for a new set of skills before his rapidly approaching retirement. Mel thought he was fickle, spending so much money on a qualification he would only then use for a few years, but she supposed no one knew how long they had. The retirement age in the NHS was getting older: newly qualified staff members would be hitting seventy before they got their NHS pension.

*I'll be battered and broken before then.* She took her seat, and during the lesson everyone was helpful, handing her things and taking things back. But they still managed to treat her like one of them, not the old codger who needed a nursing home. *Always good.*

She took her Dictaphone with her every week having explained to everyone why she needed it. She wore her glasses when she read, whether it was up close in a book or on the projector. She took her time writing notes and didn't push herself too hard—she knew she'd have time later to rewrite or complete anything she'd missed.

At lunchtime, Mel followed the rest of her class into the canteen, her lunchbox securely stowed in her backpack. She went to get a coffee and left the younger students to it, looking around for somewhere quieter to sit. Her brain needed a break; the information was starting to whirl in her mind and give her a headache. The medications for her leg would help with that.

When she spotted Ruby sitting alone by the window, she changed her mind. Perhaps a little company would be okay.

Ruby saw her a few feet away and smiled, reinforcing the notion that she might be wanted.

Mel sat and took her lunch out of her bag, setting it smartly on the table in front of her.

"Hello." Ruby peered into Mel's lunchbox. "So your diet doesn't entirely consist of burgers and chips."

"To be fair to me, you last saw me eating a toasted sandwich which contained tomatoes." Mel took the sandwich out of her box and parted the bread slices to reveal the salad within. "Tomatoes are a super food."

"Is that what they are?" Ruby's smile grew. "Listen." She placed her fork down and watched as Mel took a bite of her sandwich. "I want to apologise for last week." She nodded, once. "And back in the summer."

"Why? Because you were an idiot?" Mel spoke around a mouthful of lettuce and mayonnaise.

Ruby's face twisted. "Perhaps swallow before you speak?"

Mel rolled her eyes and obediently closed her mouth.

"I ought to say sorry for my behaviour."

Mel nodded.

"I was, as you would say, an idiot."

"Mmhm."

"If we're going to be friends, as I assume we are, due to our looming gardening adventure, we should perhaps agree to show full respect."

Mel finally swallowed and frowned at her. "'We'?"

"Okay, me… I should." Ruby's gaze held Mel's steadily. "Would that be all right?"

"No more gung-ho comments?"

"Absolutely not." Ruby held up three fingers in a Girl Guide salute.

Mel waited for a few seconds, just to make Ruby squirm, before taking another bite of her sandwich and nodding. "Okay."

Ruby held her hand up over her eyes, blocking Mel's salad-filled mouth from her vision.

Mel put her hand over her lips and tried not to laugh. She swallowed and nodded. "Sorry."

Ruby continued with her salad, stabbing a piece of beetroot with her fork. "So, I suppose we should get to know one another. Make friends properly."

"Good idea." Mel grinned. "What shoe size are you?"

Ruby's amused gaze caught her own. "You're a joker, aren't you?"

"Just like making you smile," Mel said, and then blinked, wondering where the flirtatiousness had come from. She shook her head in disbelief and went back to her sandwich. "So how's the fundraising going?"

"I have a plan. My daughter, Chloe, is going to help me with social-media advertising. Get the project out there. And then, I think, a garden party for the tombola and plant sale at the end of the season. Maybe some food."

"What about some live music, or something? Get a local musician to come play?"

The skin by Ruby's eyes crinkled. "Fantastic idea. I'll do some detective work."

"And send letters to the shops close to uni. They'll often donate items to be used as prizes for raffles and things."

"See, I knew you'd be perfect to help with this."

A few minutes of silence stretched between them as they ate.

Ruby tapped her fork on her plastic container. "I was going to ask you how your course was going, but I suppose it's early days."

"It's tough," Mel admitted, nodding. "So much information packed in, but the lecturers are great, and the way they teach is good. Easy to listen to. Lots of demonstrations and images." She picked up a fallen piece of tomato and gestured with it to Ruby. "How are your classes going?"

"They're okay so far. I have one student I'm a bit wary of, seems to enjoy playing me up." Ruby furrowed her eyebrows, and then shook her head. "I'm sure they'll settle down."

"What do you like to do?" Mel asked. "In your spare time, I mean."

"I walk my dog; housework..."

"They're jobs. I mean what do you really enjoy?" Mel popped the tomato slice in her mouth and chewed. "I like watching old films. I like hanging out with my ECA, James. You'd think we'd see enough of each other in our job, but apparently not."

"How long have you been together?"

"Since I qualified. I've done bank shifts with other ECAs but no one quite lives up to his impeccable skills." Mel touched the side of her neck. "He arrives with equipment before I've even asked for it, even going as far as to get me the correct sized cannula."

"He sounds perfect."

"We're like an old married couple. Without the bickering." Mel drank a large mouthful of coffee. "So come on: hobbies."

"Well, whatever you say, I do *like* to walk my dog. Especially if we go to the beach, which rarely happens as I live in town." Tapping her chin, Ruby hummed a bit in thought. "I like going to art galleries. The theatre. Cinema." She chuckled. "Usual things, I suppose."

"Watching anything good on TV?"

"I like crime dramas and things like that. Things that make you think."

"Medical dramas?"

"God no, are you kidding? The things they get wrong."

Mel laughed. "Yeah. Tell me about it. The number of times I've watched someone shock asystole."

"Why stop an already motionless heart?" Ruby countered, her face alight.

"Exactly." They exchanged a smile.

"Nice to see we have something in common."

"It is." Mel tongued the inside of her bottom lip. "Um, did you say you like the theatre?"

"I do." Ruby looked at her curiously. "Why?"

Mel hesitated. Should she ask? They barely knew each other, but at least she'd be in good hands if she struggled getting in and out of the ancient building. Ruby had already shown herself to be adept in assisting broken people, and she did it once a month when she worked a shift. But perhaps Ruby wasn't the kind of person who liked all-female productions of Shakespeare. "There's this play I have tickets for," she began, throwing caution to the wind, having no one else to ask. "It's at the Royal. Shakespeare."

"I do like Shakespeare," Ruby replied.

Mel nodded. "Well, it's a feminist take on... on *A Midsummer Night's Dream*."

Ruby's eyes narrowed slightly, and Mel found she was holding her breath. Would this be something Ruby would like? Would it be a concept that would shock her, and perhaps put her off being friends with Mel?

*I do like her, despite her flaws.* Mel decided she cared how Ruby felt.

"Sounds interesting," Ruby said, and Mel exhaled, her shoulders dropping. "I saw an all-female Macbeth once. Very well done."

"Okay." Mel nodded, and stared into her yogurt after peeling back the lid. "The thing is…"

"Spit it out, Mel."

Mel took an entire spoonful of yogurt into her mouth and swallowed before continuing. "I have two tickets. And I was going to go alone after... well. But obviously now I can't. The Royal has these big stone steps, and the seats are hell if you only have one leg to stand on…" She figured that was enough. If Ruby didn't fancy it, she couldn't do much more to convince her.

"When is it?"

"This Saturday."

"You've managed to get a Saturday off work?"

"Just how the shifts have fallen."

"Your ECA?"

"Out with his girlfriend." Mel got the feeling she was about to be let down.

There was another long pause. Ruby sipped from her water bottle, filled again with some kind of purple liquid. Mel wondered whether it was wine. That thought made her laugh internally.

"Would you like me to come with you?" Ruby asked, her voice making Mel jump after the previous silence.

"Um…" Mel swirled her spoon in her yogurt and then looked up.

Ruby's face was open, her smile soft but genuine.

"Yeah, that would be great, actually."

"When shall I pick you up?"

Mel's eyebrows rose. "Okay. Um. Seven? The play starts at seven-thirty."

"Shall we have dinner first?"

"Oh, of course. I'll buy you dinner, as a thank you for coming with me."

Ruby had her phone out in an instant and was flicking through something on the screen. "All right. Shall I book a table at Pizza Spice? It's just up the road from the theatre. You won't have to walk so far then."

Unused to having someone take control and decide things for her, Mel blinked at Ruby, until she looked up.

"Earth to Mel? Dinner? Italian? Or would you prefer something else?"

"No, that's fine. I love pizza." *I'll just get it all down myself, but hey, what's new.* She inwardly rolled her eyes.

"Dinner for two at six? Gives us plenty of time to get to the theatre then."

"Okay."

Ruby put down her phone after apparently booking the table online and went back to her drink. Mel ate the rest of her yogurt, wondering what on earth she had agreed to.

*Dinner and the theatre. Isn't that a first date kind of a thing?*

───⚮───

Ruby was bouncing on her feet by Friday. *I've not been to the theatre in months, and not with someone else to keep me company. How lovely.* As she taught her last class of the week—a seminar with a small group of first years—she rubbed her palms together, the anticipation of the night out making her restless.

"If everyone could open their text books to page sixteen and take a look at the diagrams there, that would be lovely."

Everyone did as they were told, apart from a young pupil with dark hair and dark eyes who seemed to think looking out of the window rather than focussing on the aforementioned diagram was the way to go.

"Remind me of your name?" she asked, pointing towards the young woman with her pen.

"Francesca," the pupil answered, waggling her head like Ruby ought to know.

Ruby pushed away the annoyance that was building. "We're concentrating on the top diagram at the moment. The lungs."

"Sorry." Francesca rolled her eyes, and her classmates tittered a bit in amusement.

Ruby gave them all a few minutes to look at the picture before tapping the paragraph next to it. "Could someone volunteer to read this passage?"

As expected, no one volunteered.

"Right then, thanks, guys." Ruby's gaze settled on Francesca. "Francesca? I'm nominating you to read."

"No thanks." Francesca's gaze shifted to outside again.

"Okay," Ruby replied slowly, and chose another pupil.

By the end of class, Francesca had seemed more interested, had joked a few times about some of the diagrams and how they all looked like genitalia—something Ruby was very used to, and had answered a few questions correctly. The class left in little groups, and Ruby grabbed her things, leaving close behind them.

She went via her office to grab her lunch things and caught Alexander on the way out.

"Ready for your date?" he asked as he walked towards the door, his own briefcase in his hand.

"It's not a date," Ruby scoffed, throwing him a random hand gesture. "It's just two people seeing a play together."

"I know you think she's attractive," he stated, leaning against the door-frame, clearly curious.

"Anyone would think she was. She's got the cheekbones of a model and the height to top it off. It still doesn't mean we're going on a date."

"Does she like women?"

"I have absolutely no idea," Ruby said, a little too harshly. She calmed herself with a hand to her chest. "It's also completely irrelevant."

"You're single. She's probably single."

"I wouldn't know, I haven't asked her."

"Does she have a wedding ring?"

"Oh, just leave it, Alexander." She shot him a hard look and he backed out of the office.

"Just asking. See you Monday."

"Have fun at your mum's."

He rolled his eyes, and she felt herself grow calmer. They exchanged an affectionate look. Time with Alexander's mother was never "fun" as far as Ruby could fathom. He lived close by, took her to the gym twice a week, and shopping on a Saturday. She wasn't elderly, but apparently she wasn't convinced of this fact and used Alexander as taxi, carer, and confidant. Ruby wished he'd find friends his own age, rather than relying on his mother and his PlayStation, for company.

She left with a spring in her step but a worry in her mind. Was it a date? *Of course not. We barely know each other.*

# Chapter 6

Mel had exchanged her usual walking boots for a single, sensible but clean trainer for the evening. It wasn't what she'd usually wear to this sort of thing, but needs must as the crutches drove. She sniggered at her own thoughts as she hauled herself to her feet and hopped to the front door to answer the insistent knocking that was making the wood shake.

Ruby stood on the doorstep, fist raised to knock again. Her face was creased in a frown but softened as her gaze connected with Mel's. "Oh. Right. Yep, crutches."

"Did you forget?" Mel laughed as she pulled the door open properly and hopped back to allow Ruby into her bungalow.

"I suppose I didn't connect them with the length of time it would take you to…" She shook her head and laughed. "What a plonker."

Mel took in Ruby's attire—her beige jacket and a pair of smart black trousers. Sensible black shoes. Ruby's hair was neat, the wavy pieces loose and shiny.

She led Ruby into the kitchen and slid both crutches into one hand as she pulled on her jacket; the extra hand tugging at the shoulder indicating Ruby was helping her. "Thank you."

Ruby brushed it off with a shrug. "Are you ready? Do you want anything getting from anywhere?"

"I'm ready," Mel said, slipping the bars of her crutches into her hands and leaning on them. She nodded once.

They made their way out to Ruby's car, a blue-grey Mini Cooper. *Very posh.* Mel twisted her lips against a grin and fit her tall frame into the passenger seat, her crutches sliding in beside her leg.

Ruby drove carefully, her phone plugged in as a navigation device, telling her where to go. Mel would've given her directions, but she was content to allow the phone to dictate their journey. "Thanks for coming with me," Mel said, feeling as if she'd said it a few too many times, but wanting to reiterate her gratitude. Ruby didn't have to say yes; hadn't had to help her out.

"It's fine," Ruby replied, her fingertips tapping the steering wheel as she drove. "Nothing like a bit of Shakespeare to round off the week."

"I got the tickets ages ago." Mel pressed her hand to her jacket pocket and felt the shape of her purse, where the tickets were safely tucked inside. "James was going to come, then it fell on the same day as his girlfriend's birthday, so I was going to cut my losses and just come by myself. See if anyone in the street wanted the extra ticket. Then this happened." She gestured towards the cast, which stopped just below her knee and covered her whole foot apart from her toes.

"Good job I was available." They snuck a grin at one another, and Mel felt warmth spreading through her bones.

They parked close by, and Ruby helped Mel out of her little car, despite Mel's protests. After a short walk in the evening air, they reached the restaurant. Mel swung on her crutches up the single step, feeling the lingering heat of Ruby's hand close to the small of her back. *She seems to like it there. Or perhaps it's simply her inner nurse kicking in.*

The Italian restaurant was small and dimly lit, with low-hanging shades over each table and gleaming cutlery that had been polished to perfection. They were shown to their table, and Mel sat down as carefully as she could, stowing her crutches against the corner.

They were handed their menus. Ruby took hers and immediately pushed her glasses firmly up her nose, her eyes flicking quickly across the options.

Mel looked at her own menu and blinked hard. As usual, the black words jumped about on the bright white page. Touching her jacket pocket, she contemplated getting out her glasses. They would make it so much easier for her to read. *No. We barely know one another, and I don't want to have to answer the inevitable questions my specs will create. I want to make a good impression. I don't want to see that look in her eyes, the one they all get when they realise my... issue.* She could hide it. She'd done it before.

So she stared at the menu, held it casually with a light look of interest on her face, and studied the top item for a good minute. *Margherita. That'll do.*

They ordered drinks and a pizza each, and the waiter took their menus away. *Thank goodness.* She watched the mess of words leave the table with a long sigh.

Ruby was smiling at her, the soft light from the restaurant reflecting against her glasses. "So, do you go to the theatre often?"

Mel nodded. "I used to. Certainly before I went to uni the first time."

"When was that?"

"Seven years ago."

"Ah, so you must've been the first lot to do the full degree?"

"That's right." Mel was impressed. "I suppose you would know, being a lecturer."

"I remember it being a huge thing. I really can't believe it was only a six-week course before."

"I can't believe there are still paramedics working on the road, doing the same job I do, with only six weeks of training."

"Madness."

The waiter brought their drinks—rosé wine for Ruby and a diet coke for Mel. Mel lifted her glass and waited for Ruby to clink her own against it.

"I suppose we ought to toast something," Mel said, looking to Ruby for a suggestion.

"To clean slates," Ruby replied, "and friendship."

"And making a massive wad of money for the Air Ambulance."

"And not killing any plants in the process." Ruby's eyes widened. "Or children."

"I'll drink to that." They sipped.

"So, are you looking to work outside the ambulance service when you get your ECP qualification?" Ruby asked.

Mel nodded. "As you can see, I'm not getting any younger. I'm not going to be able to carry thirty-stone patients over their stylish thresholds forever."

"Good point. Where do you want to work?"

"Minor injuries, maybe." Mel shrugged. "I hear they're starting to employ ECPs in out-of-hours GP services too."

"I read about that." Ruby placed her glass down and fiddled with the stem. "Do you think you'll have the skills required to assess patients at that level?"

"What do you think I do now?" Mel replied, her gut twisting defensively. *Not this again.*

"I'm asking because I'm genuinely interested." Ruby caught and held her gaze. "Not because I don't think you have the skills."

"In that case, yes." Still, she wasn't quite convinced. "We don't just scoop and go, you know."

Ruby held up her hands in a submissive action.

"And with the ECP training, I'll have more specialised assessment skills."

"Sorry," Ruby said, her eyes crinkling in such a way that Mel had to smile.

"Let's change the subject. What's the last play you went to see?"

"*Hay Fever*." Ruby rolled her eyes. "A farce, which, I know, is probably a guilty pleasure in your eyes but…"

"I love a good farce, actually." Mel touched her chin. "Isn't that the one with the fabulous middle-aged actress with the libido of a…" A typical phrase eluded her. "…lion? And the family that all exchange partners several times."

Chuckles reverberated from the other side of the table. "That's it. It's such a scream."

"It is. I've seen it twice."

Something akin to admiration flickered into Ruby's eyes. "Have you?"

"Yep."

"What else have you seen?"

"Some high-brow plays. Pinter." She winced. "Ibsen. Chekov. All the usual."

"Did you fall asleep during any of them?"

"Says the woman who agreed to accompany me to a Shakespeare play."

"Oh, give over." The smile remained on Ruby's face until their pizzas arrived.

Mel looked enviously over at Ruby's meal, something with olives and mushrooms and anchovies. *If you were a normal human being, you could have had something like that.* She squashed the self-critical thought away. The voice in her head sounding far too much like her teacher in Year Four—who had become so exasperated with her slow learning that she had started to ignore her—for her to let it linger. She'd let that inner voice control her actions, her self-beliefs, and her sense of self-worth for far too long. She wasn't that person anymore. She'd proven it wrong. In so many ways, she'd proven them all wrong. Besides, what did pizza toppings matter? Food was food, and an admission that she had trouble reading wasn't worth the more complex tastes she could have experienced.

Was it?

They tucked into their meals. Mel couldn't help chuckling at Ruby's decision to use a knife and fork to eat her pizza. She herself picked up each slice and ate with her hands, smacking her lips when the tangy tomato and gentle cheese touched her tongue. It was herby too, and she realised she was a lot hungrier than she had first thought.

Ruby eyed her as she sucked tomato sauce from her fingers and Mel let out a snort. "You're allowed to eat finger food with your fingers, you know?"

"Restaurants don't serve finger food," Ruby countered, sticking a piece of neatly cut-up pizza into her mouth. It was so small it didn't leave a trace on her lips. The fork emerged looking pristine. "That's a buffet you're thinking of."

Mel continued to eat with her fingers, and Ruby continued to eat daintily with her knife and fork. When Mel sucked another drop of herby grease from her thumb, Ruby rolled her eyes.

With their bellies full, Mel got the bill, and they left the restaurant. Mel fastened the top button of her jacket once they were outside, but it took her so long and she was in such a fumble that Ruby stepped in front of her.

"Let me help."

Mel huffed frustratedly but dropped her arms to her sides. She felt like a child having her coat done up by her mother. Looking at the floor in a determined fashion, she allowed Ruby to button up her jacket, her careful fingers pulling the lapels round and smoothing them flat. Her hands lingered, and Mel looked up, curious to see Ruby's eyes.

"Okay?"

Mel nodded and caught a whiff of Ruby's perfume, something subtle and flowery. It made her think of summer. Time spent with her father on the allotment, deadheading flowers that were drooping, and enjoying those in full bloom. The roses he grew, always fragrant and pale pink, her mother's favourite colour. She could still feel the sun on her face as she sat on the grassy paths between the beds.

They made their way slowly, and with plenty of time, to the theatre. Ruby's hand remained at Mel's back as she ascended the steep steps, and Mel was grateful for it. Once she'd got to the top, she was dismayed to discover she was panting.

Ruby rubbed her shoulder. "Just rest a minute."

"This is ludicrous," Mel said, her cheeks going hot. "I can usually climb a lot more the one measly flight of stairs."

"You're healing." Ruby's hand on her shoulder was comforting. "Give yourself a break."

When they got inside, Ruby bought a programme. They shuffled up yet more stairs and through an archway into the Royal Circle. Mel eyed the fold-down seats with disdain. *Why can't they make them more easily accessible?* With Ruby's hand steadily on her back, Mel lowered herself awkwardly into the aisle seat. She stowed her crutches beside her hip and shifted about, grimacing when the old, lumpy seat prodded at her backside.

Ruby's gaze on her was soft, and Mel wondered where the opinionated, harsh woman had gone. *I like this caring person so much better.* When Ruby offered Mel the program, Mel shook her head and pretended to be highly interested in the stage curtain.

The play, as it turned out, was well worth the toil in getting there. Mel turned her eyes towards Ruby a couple of times, mostly when two female actors were sharing a kiss, and discovered bright eyes and an expression of content on her companion. *No issue with ladies kissing ladies, then.* That made her happy. At some point she would come out to Ruby, and the fact that Ruby didn't seem bothered about the—*let's call it what it is*—lesbian activity onstage went in her favour and would make the revelation much less stressful.

Mel fiddled with the seat arm and found Ruby's hand next to hers, their little fingers brushing. She looked properly at her in the semi-darkness. Ruby turned to her as well. Mel threw caution to the wind and brushed her little finger deliberately against Ruby's. Ruby simply smiled at her, turned back to the play, and returned her own hand to her lap.

*I don't know what she's thinking. She didn't slap me, but she didn't return the gesture.*

After the house lights had gone up, the murmurs of the audience mostly positive, Ruby placed her hand on Mel's knee. "No rush. Better to let everyone else get out first."

"Right." Mel tapped her good foot on the seat in front of her.

"I really enjoyed that," Ruby said as she hauled Mel to her feet.

Mel chuckled, gripping tightly onto Ruby's shoulders as she stood, and then turned to collect her crutches. Their journey out of the circle was slow, but Mel could feel Ruby's hand in its usual place, so she couldn't complain.

"Really enjoyed it." Ruby was beaming, and as they pulled their coats back on, she stepped up to help Mel with her buttons.

"I'm good," Mel said, giving her a suspicious look.

"It's okay." Ruby brushed Mel's protests off with a wave of her hand. "Let me."

Mel stood like a lemon and watched the careful fingers as they fastened her buttons. *Short nails.* She smiled. Just a bit. "I did some drama at school," Mel said as they walked out into the evening hustle and bustle.

"So did I."

"O level was great. We did various excerpts from various things. I think we did *Blood Brothers*."

"Oh, that's such a good play. Have you seen the musical?"

"I have." Mel looked across at Ruby, who was walking a foot away from her, without the usual hand by her back. *She must think I'm okay on level ground. If I pretended to slip, I'm sure she'd grab me.* She shook her head and pushed away the amusing thought. "When we did it at school, I got to kiss my crush."

"Ah," Ruby said, her grin widening and her eyes glinting in the streetlights. "That old chestnut."

"She didn't complain," Mel said, deliberately throwing in the pronoun, and looking quickly at Ruby to gauge her reaction. "She seemed pretty interested in practising that particular scene."

"Lucky you." Flicking her eyebrows up a few times, Ruby chuckled. "I can't imagine having managed to bag one of my crushes as a teenager."

"Who did you like?"

Ruby blushed and stopped walking. She turned to Mel with a tilted head. "I was reasonably picky at school."

*Is that all I'm getting?* Mel scrutinised the brunette standing in front of her, her dark hair reflecting the orange of the street lamps.

Ruby indicated the car park. "Come on, let's get you home."

Rolling her eyes and very much none the wiser, Mel limped across the concrete to Ruby's car. *She continues to be an enigma.*

Sitting in the warmth of the car, Mel considered Ruby as she drove. She was a bit of conundrum: on one hand, a caring and accomplished nurse and lecturer, on the other, an opinionated pain in the proverbial. There were a few moments of silence. *I want to know more about her.* She chewed on her lip as she tried to think of something to ask. In the end, she went for a safe option. "I have a cat."

The soft radio music drifted around them, and Mel's words sounded loud in it. She watched as Ruby's eyebrows flicked upwards once, then as a smile settled on her face.

"What's he called?"

"*She* is called Epione." Mel clasped her hands together in her lap, one finger reaching out to touch the grey plastic of the handle of her crutches. "She's named after the Ancient Greek goddess of soothing pain."

"That makes sense, considering your profession."

"Do you have any pets?"

"I do. We have a dog called Barney." An inscrutable grin pulled at Ruby's features.

"Great name for a dog. What breed is he?"

"She's a girl, and she's some kind of terrier mix."

"A girl dog called Barney?" Mel asked, now understanding the grin.

Ruby's low chuckle rumbled about the car. "My daughters, when we got her, were small, and they had seen some film or telly programme, where the dog was called Barney." She tucked a brown curl of hair behind her ear. "And that was that. Never mind that Barney is a boy's name."

Mel laughed, the back of her head hitting the headrest softly. "That's a much better pet story than mine."

Ruby continued to grin and turned into Mel's road, directions apparently unneeded.

"So, you have two daughters?" Mel asked as Ruby easily pulled into her gravel driveway, spun the car ninety degrees to the right, and backed towards her house. *Impressive.* She switched off the engine.

"I do. Jasmine and Chloe. Sixteen and Eighteen."

"Just growing up, then. Good kids?"

"Not bad. I worry about Jas. She's my sixteen-year-old and she wears these terrible outfits. Short skirts, low-cut tops."

"Early developer?"

"She was." Ruby furrowed her eyebrows and twisted in her seat to Mel. She shook her head. "She's going to get herself into trouble one of these days."

"With a nurse for a mother, you'd think she'd want to be safe," Mel said quietly. "If I had a nurse as a mother, I'd be terrified of all the things I could catch."

That earned a smile from Ruby, and Mel returned it, pleased the joke had gone down well.

"Chloe's my little adult, however. She's eighteen and doing a hundred A levels. All science-based." The proud gleam in Ruby's eye was clear to see.

Beaming, Mel placed her hand on the door handle.

"Look at me sat here chatting while you want to get home," Ruby exclaimed, and practically jumped from the car and rounded it to pull open Mel's door before she had a chance to protest.

Ruby helped her to her front door, the climbing plant over the porch catching a bit in her hair. She caught a tendril of the plant between her forefinger and thumb. "Could we grow this, whatever it is?" The look in her eyes was hopeful.

Mel hummed in thought. "I don't see why not. You like it? It's a clematis."

"It's pretty."

"Then we shall look into getting one." Mel clambered into her bungalow. "It'll need something to climb up."

Ruby put a hand to her temple and groaned. "I really know nothing about it all. It's going to be a terrible mess, I can feel it."

Mel reached to take her hand from her head. Her fingers were warm, her skin soft. "Hey, you've got me to help, and besides, don't make it a self-fulfilling prophecy. It'll be great."

"Even if I manage to kill everything that's even remotely green?" Ruby asked, one eyebrow up.

"I won't let you." Mel realised she was still holding Ruby's hand. She let go. "Anyway. See you. Thanks so much for coming with me."

"My pleasure. See you next Wednesday."

"Fancy lunch?" Mel asked, one hand on her door, ready to close it.

"We could do, couldn't we?"

Mel closed the door and felt overwhelming warmth spread through her.

# Chapter 7

November brought with it crisp leaves that swirled in spirals between buildings, rain that soaked everything you owned, and distracted students. Ruby had a headache: whether it was from the drastic change in weather and temperature, or the more in-depth anatomy she was teaching and her students' inability to concentrate, she wasn't sure.

Another seminar about the human body with the same class of first years. Francesca leant her head in her hand and stared out of the window. Ruby gave them a few extra minutes to read the passage she'd instructed them to, then stood up straight and cleared her throat to signify their attention. Twenty-three faces all turned towards her. The twenty-fourth remained directed out the window.

"Something going on outside?" Ruby gave her the benefit of the doubt, but Francesca only sighed and shrugged, placing one hand flat on her book.

"No." Short and blunt, and absolutely not appropriate for an anatomy lesson.

"Is there a problem?" Ruby asked, trying to sound kind, but she was pretty sure it didn't come across that way.

"Problems all over the world. Problems in America, problems in Africa, problems over here." Francesca shrugged again and smirked around at her classmates, some of whom tittered back at her flippancy. "If you're asking whether there's a problem with the lesson, then, yeah, actually, it's boring."

"It may be boring, but it's necessary. For your course." Ruby placed her hands together, palm to palm and rested her chin on her fingertips. A lump threatened at her throat. *How dare she call my lesson boring.* "You wouldn't get very far with little knowledge of the human body, now, would you?"

"It's just IVs and blood pressures and temperatures. And bed baths. I think I know which bits of an old lady need washing."

The lump pressed, but Ruby swallowed it away. *This is not the time to allow your emotions to get the better of you.* "You'll be responsible for much more than that," Ruby said, suddenly reminded of Mel arguing with her about the role of a paramedic. "You'll need to work out dosages of medication, make sure the doctors don't kill anyone by noticing symptoms early, and you can't do that without a good knowledge of anatomy."

"Whatever, *Miss*," Francesca said, spitting out the four-letter word with all the derision of a curse, and the whole class snorted and sniggered.

*Students don't call lecturers 'Miss'.* The name was very much for school, not university, and Ruby was concerned. This kind of silly discussion had no place in her lessons, and she wished Francesca would simply get on with her work and get the most out of the knowledge Ruby was imparting on them all. They'd need it once they got a job.

"That's enough, now." Ruby tried to keep her voice light. "Let's turn to page sixty-four." The rustling of books being manoeuvred was pleasing to her ears, but Ruby noticed that Francesca hadn't moved.

"Heads, shoulders, knees and toes, knees and toes," Francesca sang, just loud enough that everyone could hear.

Ruby's cheeks became hot, and she pressed a palm to one, embarrassed. "That's enough." She folded her arms, her heart rate quickening.

"All right, don't have an aneurism," Francesca said with a smirk.

Everyone laughed, and Ruby felt a little like sliding underneath her table. She huffed and sat up straight instead. *Professional.* "Maybe you'd like to read the top paragraph on—"

"I've said before, no." Francesca's voice had lost the playful tone and now had a dangerous edge to it.

"Why not? Everyone else is perfectly happy to—"

"Because I don't want to," Francesca said, her own arms folding in a stance similar to Ruby's. "And you can't make me do anything without my *informed consent,* Miss."

Ruby left it a few heartbeats before lowering her voice. "Don't call me 'Miss'. That's for school."

"Feels like school, being here."

Ruby gave up, rolled her head on her neck, and picked someone else to read out the passage. *If she won't co-operate, I'll just have to ignore her behaviour and spend time with the people that actually want to learn.*

―✦―

On arrival at the canteen, Mel nearly limped into Ruby. "Fancy having lunch in my office?" Ruby asked, her fingers toying with the strap of her briefcase.

"Oh, um, okay. If that's okay with you."

"I've just had a stressful morning, and I would prefer somewhere a bit quieter."

"No, no, that's fine."

Mel followed her at her slow pace down the corridor and towards the biology block. The office, when they entered it, was warm and inviting, with a large painting of a beachscape to one side of her desk and a small sofa with a coffee table.

Mel caught Ruby eyeing the sofa, which was sunken in the middle and therefore quite low down. "Risk assessing the chances of me getting up again if we take the sofa?" Mel asked, grinning. She indicated her crutches. "I'm getting quite good with these, you know."

"No." Ruby's gaze met Mel's and her face relaxed. "I wasn't," she insisted, and perhaps to prove her point, she strode over to the sofa and plonked herself onto it.

"Comfy." Mel ran her hand over the worn leather of the sofa as she sat beside her. "Very nice."

They got out their respective lunch items, and Mel set her flask of coffee on the table. She grabbed a cushion from the corner of the sofa and placed it over her knee, to make a better surface to spread out the foil her sandwiches were in. She could feel Ruby's gaze on her and turned her head to grin.

"So, why the change of location? Something bugging you?"

Ruby sighed. "My first-year class."

"Is that the one with the student who's…an issue?" Biting into her sandwich, Mel leant over the foil so as not to drip on her trousers.

"That's right." Ruby made a long noise in her throat. "She's getting worse."

"In what way?"

"She's rude, combative, and today she tried to humiliate me."

"Well, that's not on, surely?"

Ruby shrugged and stabbed a little too aggressively at her salad. "She refuses point blank to contribute, won't read out loud, and won't answer questions properly." She crunched her salad, swallowed and rolled her head on her neck. "And she won't stop calling me 'Miss'."

"Oh dear," Mel said, a small chuckle in her voice. She put a hand to her lips and quietened. "Have you asked her what the problem is?"

"Oh, several times," Ruby replied, playing with her salad, poking it around inside her plastic box.

"And you say she won't read out loud?"

"I think she's rebelling against my authority. Not that it's really like that at uni, is it? I mean, you know, *you're* here."

"I am." *Won't read out loud; disruptive in class? Sounds like my own childhood at school. Sounds far too familiar.*

Mel watched Ruby as she continued to stab and munch on her salad, taking regular drinks from her bottle. She had an inkling what was wrong with this student. The similarities to her own past were stark and a bit frightening. *But it's none of my business. She hasn't asked me for advice. I'm just here as an ear to moan at. And I don't mind that at all.*

Mel looked at her hands. The spaces between her thumbs and forefingers were getting sore. *Damn crutches.* She ate her sandwiches as Ruby continued to complain, happy that Ruby could come to her, and happy that Ruby felt comfortable and relaxed enough in her presence. They knew each other fairly well now; not the details of favourite colours or family histories exactly, but Mel thought she knew Ruby's personality and what made her tick.

Ruby was passionate about her subject and wanted to impart that passion on to her students. Ruby was caring and gentle, but also fiery and opinionated—often to the point of rudeness.

The desire to hide, however, reminded her that Ruby didn't know everything. She didn't know of her *affliction,* of her *abnormality.* The special glasses she wore, the coloured Perspex she held over a book so that the words didn't jump around like grasshoppers. She didn't know about the extra time she was given for exams, the special allowances she had when her assignments were marked. She didn't know about her diagnosis, if one could call it that.

Dyslexia.

Putting a name to it was a reasonably new thing and still didn't sit well in the list of things that made up Melissa Jackson. *I think Ruby's pretty, and I think she's intelligent.* Perhaps that was why Mel didn't want to relinquish that part of herself to Ruby. Right now, Ruby thought—she hoped—that Mel was clever and found it easy to learn. Especially considering she was tackling her ECP training, which was hard-going and required academic prowess. At the moment, Ruby saw her as normal, as someone who was just like her. What if she told Ruby of her difficulties and Ruby changed her mind? Mel didn't even want to contemplate that possibility. She didn't want to be... less in anyone's opinion. But mostly she didn't want to be less in Ruby's mind.

Mel finished her sandwich and sucked her fingers clean. She grinned as she saw Ruby's look of disgust. "Finger food is the best," Mel said, drinking from her flask and brushing her hands against one another.

"What d'you think I should do about Francesca?" Ruby looked sincerely upset about her pupil.

"I think... maybe just leave her to it." Mel sucked on her bottom lip as she took out her yogurt. "She'll come around to thinking you're the bee's knees when it comes to everything anatomy."

Ruby threw her an appreciative look, and Mel hoped right inside her chest that she'd skirted around the issue for now. *She'll work it out on her own. She's not stupid.*

# Chapter 8

December was colder still, with ice on the ground even in the middle of the day, and on Ruby's windscreen every morning, without fail. She was enjoying the lunches she and Mel shared, and the permanent swap to her office offered them more privacy to really talk, too. Mel seemed to like it in there: it was more comfortable, and there were less people to knock her as she made her way across the room.

They'd taken to sitting together in the quiet and chatting. Each week, Ruby thought she should explain to Mel that she was attracted to women—it was only fair; Mel had come out to her weeks ago—but every time she tried, she lost her tongue… or her nerve. Perhaps it was the easy friendship they had settled into, the jokes and light teasing that were now staples in their lunchtime conversation.

The Christmas holidays came around more quickly than Ruby had ever remembered. As she and her daughters sat down for coffee on Christmas Day, she realised that, although she had Mel's number, she hadn't phoned her once since they had finished university. *I'll text her, maybe, to wish her a happy Christmas.* Nodding once and determinedly, she sipped at her coffee and watched Jasmine and Chloe open their presents. Barney lay on her back, her feet kicking in the air occasionally, as she languished with a belly full of wet food and dog biscuits.

Chloe, the more affectionate but less exuberant of the two, sat beside her mother—her lap covered in all the cartoon T-shirts and new accessories she'd asked for—and put an arm around her. "Love you so much, Mum."

"Love you too, sweetie."

"Yeah, thanks, Mum," Jasmine echoed, her gaze already trained on the number on the iTunes voucher, typing it into her phone so that she could use it as soon as she wanted.

"Open yours," Chloe insisted, thrusting an envelope into her hands.

"Oh, it's not a blooming facial again, is it?" Ruby slid her finger under the flap of the envelope and pulled the contents from inside. Her eyebrows rose as she took in the slim tickets. "Aquarium tickets." She wasn't sure whether she felt surprised or amused.

"You've been talking about it for ages," Chloe said, her corduroy-covered knees bouncing a bit with excitement. "And this way, you have an excuse to go."

"But there are two tickets," Ruby said, holding them up. "Don't tell me one of my dear sproglets would like to come with me."

Barney made a groaning noise, and her ribs expanded as her biscuit coma apparently became too much.

"Not gonna happen," Jasmine said, followed by a derisive snort.

"We were thinking…" Chloe looked down at her sister who was sitting on the floor, now perusing her music options. "Jas?"

"Why don't you take that Mel you keep going on about?" Jasmine finally looked up and put her phone down.

Ruby planted an arm around Chloe's shoulders and squeezed her. "I'm sure she wouldn't want to come with me to see a load of fish."

"She likes animals, doesn't she? You said." Chloe looked like it was the best idea she and her sister had ever had. Even better than the pasta pictures they had made as small kids. "She's got a cat, so chances are she'll like fish too." Chloe shrugged.

"And you *so* like her." Jasmine was smirking, her arms folded over her front, so her boobs squished together above the low-cut neck of her top.

Ruby rolled her eyes at her youngest and stared back down at the tickets. "I *so* like her as a friend."

"Clearly bollocks."

"Language." Her sharp tone dissipated as she looked back at Chloe, who had a sickly-sweet smile on her face. Ruby rolled her eyes.

"I know when you like someone, Mum," Chloe said, her tone careful and kind. "And you definitely like Mel."

"She is very pretty, I must admit." Ruby looked over at her dog, the expanse of fat belly with four legs sticking up at odd angles.

"You've literally only had lunch with her, what, a handful of times, in your grotty office."

Ruby opened her mouth in indignation at the criticism of her working space, but snapped it closed again at the glint in Chloe's eye, which meant she was joking.

"Not particularly romantic," Chloe said.

"What if I don't want to be romantic with Mel?"

"Every time you talk about her you get that dreamy look in your eyes," Jasmine said, her voice taking on a sing-song quality.

Chloe giggled and gave her mother a look. "You should try to woo her somewhere out of the work place."

"'Woo her'?" Ruby laughed incredulously and shook her head. Her hair swiped her forehead as it swished around. "What is this, a fifties film?"

"Might as well be." Jasmine's cutting tone made Ruby frown at her. Jasmine rolled her eyes and went back to looking at her phone.

Something inside Ruby started to flutter about. The thought of taking Mel on an actual date was making her palms sweat and her mouth dry. *What if she doesn't want to go on a date? What if she does? What would I wear? What does one wear on a date to the aquarium? A fish-printed dress?* That thought caused her to press her lips with her fingers. She forced a look of faint interest back onto her face.

"I just mean that you should take her somewhere nice," Chloe said, holding one hand up, palm to the ceiling. The brightly coloured silicon bracelets, of which there were many, slid up her thin arm to her elbow.

"And the aquarium is somewhere you'd consider 'nice'?" Ruby asked, really wanting to know.

Chloe snuck under Ruby's arm again and laid her head on her shoulder.

A mass of blonde curls brushed Ruby's face and made her splutter. Ruby pushed the hair back so she could breathe.

"Just see what happens, please?" Chloe squeezed her mother warmly. "I love you and it's been far too long since you had a date."

"*I* have a date, like, every weekend," Jasmine murmured.

"Will it stop you nagging me? If I invite Mel to the aquarium?"

Chloe's grin was so wide she didn't have to answer.

"Are you actually suggesting I ask her *now*?"

"No time like the present."

"It's Christmas Day. She's probably out with her family or…" Ruby bit her lip and played with the knee of her trousers.

"Just do it." Chloe shrugged. "Maybe it being Christmas will mean she's in a romantic mood. More likely to say yes."

With a strangled sort of snort, Ruby found she didn't have enough energy to argue. So she grabbed her phone and the tickets and scooted out into the hallway. She stared at one of her watercolour prints for a minute—her favourite, with the deer and countryside—before bringing her phone up and scrolling to Mel's number.

She had the phone to her ear, her eyes squeezed shut and her breath held, before she had the chance to lose her nerve. The thought of returning to the living room, and the critical but affectionate gazes of her children, was worse than the potential rejection Mel might give her. Just.

"Hello." Mel's tone sounded somewhere between pleased and very surprised.

"Hiya. It's… it's Ruby."

"Yes. I know." Mel chuckled.

Everything relaxed just a bit. Mel didn't seem bothered that Ruby had rung her, or that it was Christmas. Ruby wondered if she was on her own but threw that idea out. A sociable and outgoing woman like Mel would not be on her own, surely?

"Um… hiya."

"You definitely already said that. But hey, twice is better than not at all."

Ruby set her jaw but found humour pulling her lips upwards. "Yeah, all right, clever clogs."

"Merry Christmas."

"Oh, yeah. Merry Christmas. Are you... I mean..." Ruby stamped her foot, the noise of which was luckily muffled by her slipper and the thick carpet. "Right. My daughters have badgered me into giving you a ring."

"Have they?" A teasing note.

Ruby's confidence grew. "Yep. They've given me tickets for... for the aquarium."

"That's an... interesting present. Nice though. If you like that sort of thing."

Anxiety lifted its terrible head again and made Ruby ball a fist. "Is that... Is it something you'd like?"

A pause. Ruby perched on the telephone seat and wound her finger into the curly wire of the landline phone while she waited. *Oh God, now I've really embarrassed her. Or confused her. She'll probably hang up.*

"I like animals. I think my cat would prefer it, but I'm not sure the aquarium is feline-friendly."

"No, I can assume it wouldn't be."

Mel still hadn't really answered the question.

"Are you sure you don't want the ticket?"

"Oh." Ruby pulled the cord so hard the receiver bounced onto the floor. A growl passed her lips as she bent to retrieve it, settling it back in position. She grimaced as she realised the clattering might have made Mel more confused. "No. Actually, I was going to ask if you'd come with me. There are two tickets."

"Oh!" Something seemed to click on Mel's side of the line. "Oh, I'm sorry I thought..."

"Yeah. Sorry. I wasn't clear. But yes, I'm asking you to the aquarium." The word 'date' seemed to rattle the walls around her, but Ruby couldn't bring herself to use it.

"That'd... Wow. Okay. I'd like that."

"You would?" Ruby's finger was encased in curly wire again.

"Of course. Like I said, I like animals. Usually more of a mammal type of girl, but hey, who am I to discriminate when it comes to species?"

Ruby hummed out a giggle. "Well then. That's brilliant." She clamped her mouth closed. "Um… I mean it'd be really lovely to go with you."

Another chuckle, broken slightly by static, as if Mel was currently somewhere that the signal wasn't great. "You too."

Heat flushed across Ruby's cheeks. She toyed with the collar of her top. "The only thing is…" Ruby checked the tickets. "It's not actually until March."

"What isn't?"

"The tickets. They're specifically to go see the new rays. They don't get them until March."

"Really?" Mel's voice had lowered. Ruby thought she could detect disappointment.

"Yes, I'm afraid you'll have to be patient," Ruby replied, pressing humour between her words. *I hope she doesn't forget. Or that we don't fall out before we go.*

"I think I can manage that."

"Oh, good."

Yet another silence; more uncomfortable this time. Ruby supposed she should say good-bye; make sure Mel didn't think she was hogging her at Christmas time when they should both be spending it with their families. She cleared her throat, ready to speak, but was beaten to the post.

"How's your day going?" Mel asked.

Ruby cleared her throat again and dropped the phone cord, settling more comfortably on the seat. "It's fine. The girls seem pleased with the things I got them. And the things they got each other."

"You're at home?"

"Yes. Just me and the girls. Mum'll be joining us later, with my sister in tow, I'm sure."

"That's nice."

"What about you?"

"Seeing Dad this afternoon. But currently being stared at by my crewmate."

"You're spending Christmas morning with your colleague?"

Mel laughed. "Strange, I know. But he just finished a night shift. And his girlfriend is with her family, his folks are away. So he's stuck with me."

Ruby tried to keep the disgust out of her voice. "Oh dear. A night shift? Not the best start to the holidays."

"It was nice, apparently. He came to mine armed with snacks. Charitable funds delivered a big collection of food and drink to the station, and he mostly gorged himself for the whole shift."

"Aha. Not many people to save, then?"

"Not too many. He's off now for a couple of days and the majority of proper poorlies happen after everyone's consumed far too much food or alcohol. And that's usually the day after Christmas."

"Good for him."

"Good for me that I'm off sick this Christmas." Ruby glanced towards the door, remembering her daughters. *They're probably amusing themselves with their new belongings. No need to rush back.*

A squeak and various expletives from the other side muffled whatever Mel tried to say next.

"Are you okay?" Ruby asked, laughing.

"Currently being poked and prodded by James. Bloody hell, dude, enough!"

Ruby put a hand over her mouth to smother her remaining chuckles.

"I'd better go. He's getting jealous."

"Oh right. That sort of friend, is he?"

"Very much."

"Fair enough. Bye, then."

"Enjoy your Christmas Day."

"And yours."

The line went dead, but not before more squirming noises and swear words flowed down the phone in abundance.

Mel hung up her mobile and stuck one finger in her mouth, grinning around it. James grinned back from his now relaxed position on her sofa. Even Epione appeared smug, sitting with her tail curled primly around her white feet.

"Was that Ruby?" James asked, lifting his coffee in a salute. He'd stopped prodding her when she had hung up and adopted a nonchalant exterior.

"Might've been." Mel slid back around the sofa without her crutches, having dropped them both when her phone had rung and then given up retrieving them in case Ruby had hung up while she was waiting. The edge of the sofa had seemed a perfect place to perch.

"Just wishing you a Merry Christmas?" James asked casually. There was an evil gleam in his eye, however, and Mel knew she could hide very little from him. *He had heard the entire conversation, anyway.*

"She did say that. But she also invited me to go with her to the aquarium."

"That's... nice?" James said, obviously a bit confused by the location of the proposed outing. "But I thought you said she wasn't into women?"

"I didn't... I mean... I'm not sure." Mel huffed frustratedly. "I expect she's straight and just being kind."

"Or your gaydar's wonky."

"Shut up." She jabbed his ribs with a finger, and then turned her head to contemplate. "It sounds very nice, actually," Mel replied defensively. She sipped deliberately from her coffee and threw her head back in a gesture of nonchalance. "She wants to go in March; they have some special rays being added to the collection, so..."

"A date?" James leant forward, his elbows on his knees. "Like an actual one, rather than one where neither of you actually know if it's a date or not?"

Mel put a hand over her face and groaned a bit. "I've no idea."

"Didn't you ask?"

"No, of course not." Mel flicked her eyes from side to side, as if someone could be listening in. "That's not the kind of thing you ask."

James sighed dejectedly. "It's been a couple of months."

"I know."

"And you haven't even established whether she's gay?"

"She has children."

James let out a "pfft".

"She's quite a private person. I don't want to ruin it by making it all awkward if I ask her out."

"Aww, didums." He leant to poke her good leg and she kicked out at him.

"Leave it out."

Resting back in his armchair, James regarded her with affectionate eyes. "You won't ruin it by asking her out."

"I will. I'm no good at relationships."

"We seem to have a good thing going."

"Aha, yes, but we're not sleeping together."

"Aren't we? Why have I not noticed that?"

She threw the television remote control at him.

Epione stared at her with critical eyes and slouched off over the side of the sofa to find a warm spot to curl up in. She flopped down by the radiator, and the rumble of her purr was audible from across the room.

"You're really good at friendships, mate," James continued, apparently going down a route that did not include teasing his friend.

"But I'm no good at romance, or dating, or keeping a girl for longer than five minutes."

Again, he softened. "Rach was a bitch."

"I know. But it terrifies me when I think about how she treated me. I don't want that to happen again." Some of the tension flew from her shoulders as she expressed herself. *I can tell him things I could never tell anyone else.* Mel sighed and put her head in her hand. Her hair filtered between her fingers and hung over her face, brushing the arm of the chair. *I need to get my hair cut.*

"You treated her like she was a goddess." James looked smug. "You're a great girlfriend."

Mel groaned and threw the DVD player remote at him. It actually hit him this time, clonking him on the shoulder. He caught it and threw it back at her. She laughed and folded her arms in protest.

"Ask her out, you big wuss, otherwise you'll die alone and depressed with only Epione for company, and eventually she'll eat your face." At her horrified look, he shrugged. "I saw it on a documentary once."

She threw the remote at him again, and laughed when it bounced off his head.

# Chapter 9

Mel wiggled her toes in her trainer, rolled her foot in a circle, and hummed in happiness. Her leg felt cold and unprotected, sure, but it felt wonderful. The cast now gone, she felt free, happy, and she was just about ready to get back on her bike and ride a hundred miles into the countryside.

She didn't. Her physiotherapist had suggested a less vigorous form of exercise to begin her rehabilitation with, and Mel had agreed—grudgingly. She didn't want to overdo it, especially with her practical assessments at university looming on the horizon. So she'd taken it easy, going for brief walks around the garden, stretching regularly, and trying to relax. She wasn't allowed back to work for yet another three weeks, but she figured she'd find something interesting to do.

When she didn't find Ruby in her office, the first Wednesday back after Christmas, she took a stroll into the middle garden area of the university. There, she stood by the water fountain and gazed at the fish that flopped back and forth in its depths. Taking a seat on one of the benches in the grassy area to the right, she crossed her legs and rolled her foot again, idly. *That feels so good. But I really need to shave my leg.* Her other leg she'd kept in tip-top condition, but not having access to her broken one had meant the whole thing had been rather neglected. *Maybe I'll go for a beauty treatment or something. That'd kill some time while I wait to go back to work.*

A muffled groan from a few metres away made her look up. She caught sight of Ruby, bending over in a dirty greenhouse in the far corner. *What's she doing?* Mel stood and strode across derelict land to the glass house, green with algae and covered in streaks of muck.

"Hey," she called, pushing at the creaky sliding door. It opened—but only after a good shove.

Ruby jumped and whacked her head on a shoulder-height shelf. "Ow," she mumbled as she rubbed it. Mel pushed the door open fully and stepped inside.

The musty smell of old pots and compost hit her, an aroma she found sweet but stale. She wrinkled her nose and wafted the air about a bit in front of her face.

"I know. Blooming disgusting, isn't it?" Ruby sighed and looked around her.

"What're you doing in here?" Mel leant against one of the work benches and regarded her.

"Trying to sort out what's salvageable and what isn't." Ruby shrugged and held up a dirty plastic plant pot.

Mel grimaced and took the pot from her, brushing out a spider that had taken up residence.

Ruby squeaked and put a hand to her chest.

"You are not afraid of spiders, surely?"

"Only when I can see them." She squeezed her eyes closed tightly, then let out an explosive sigh. "And sometimes when I can't."

Mel chuckled and placed the pot down on the shelf. "I'm not sure anything can be kept, to be honest. Otherwise you'll have a job to clean it all."

"Chuck it all out and start again, you mean?"

"I would."

Ruby nodded and then smiled. "Hello, by the way."

Mel grinned. "Hi. How're you?"

"Not bad." Ruby's eyes trailed down Mel's body, and Mel thought for a moment that she was being checked out but then realised she was looking at her leg. "You're good, I see."

"Got it off yesterday."

"I know, you texted me, all excited about it. Good."

They both looked around the greenhouse, and that stale smell struck Mel again. "Could we go somewhere else? It's a bit pungent in here."

They exited the greenhouse and strolled around the little area. "This is what they've given me for the gardening project," Ruby said, scuffling her shoe against the gravel path that surrounded three mucky patches of ground.

"Ah, okay." Mel nodded, tilting her head in interest. "Ideas?"

"None. I was going to ask you." They exchanged an affectionate look, and Mel took in the area: Three rectangles that needed turning over and fertilising if they were to grow anything in them; then off near the fountain, a wooden shed—*perfect for tools and for keeping seeds in*—and finally, a small patio with plastic chairs and a small table.

"So, I'm assuming that the kids are supposed to be learning about where their food comes from? And how things grow?"

"That's right."

"And we need to think about how we can use the space to make money. Things we could grow and then sell on, maybe?"

"I've literally no ideas." Ruby sounded so dejected that Mel stepped up to her and placed a hand on her shoulder.

"It's okay. I'll help you plan it out."

Ruby's smile was warm. "Then what d'you suggest, Ms Titchmarsh?"

After rolling her eyes and glancing about again, Mel pointed to the greenhouse. "Well, that thing needs a good clean. Hot soap and water, inside and out." She considered the patches of ground and folded her arms across her chest. "Onions and potatoes are easy to grow outside, and they show two different parts of a plant that can be eaten. Maybe lettuce too; that's three."

"Yep, okay."

"Tomatoes are a must, of course." Mel pouted in thought and nodded. "And maybe peppers. What about some flowers?"

"Oh, that would be lovely."

"Marigolds, then, definitely. They go well with tomatoes and keep the aphids off them. Sunflowers are very popular with kids. You could have a competition to see who can grow the tallest one."

"Good idea."

"You could harvest some of the produce you've grown and the kids' parents can come and sample some at the party."

When Mel turned back to Ruby after looking around her, Ruby was grinning. Ruby sidled up beside her, reached up to clear the few inches that separated their heights, and kissed her cheek. When she pulled back, her cheeks were pink.

"It all sounds ever so complicated."

"I'll help you."

Ruby's eyebrow rose. "Promise?"

Mel nodded, stuffing her hands into her trouser pockets.

"Thank you," Ruby replied, her voice soft.

Mel held out her hands in a shrug that she hoped said 'it's fine' before returning her hands to her pockets.

"So," Ruby said as they made their way to the bench that Mel had vacated minutes before, "you said you learned to garden from your dad."

"That's right." Mel rubbed both her knees, relishing the fact that she could do that now. It felt strange but wonderful. "He's in a home now, but he still helps out with the garden there."

"What sort of things did he grow?"

"Everything, pretty much, but mostly tomatoes. I don't know a variety he hadn't tried."

Ruby looked at her hands with wide eyes. "I wasn't aware tomatoes came in different varieties." She lifted her head. "Apart from cherry and… normal."

"You'd be surprised."

"I suppose there are different types of onions and potatoes too, and peppers?"

"I'm wondering whether we should do some hot ones for the kids; see what they think of the taste."

Ruby screwed up her face, which made Mel chuckle. "Sounds like child abuse to me."

"Hmm." Mel touched her chin and leant her elbow on the table part of the picnic bench. "Maybe we get the parents to do it."

"So why is your dad in a home?" Ruby's voice was gentle, and Mel wasn't surprised when her hand made its way to Mel's arm.

"Dementia."

"That's sad."

"He's an amazing man, and yes, you're right, it really is sad."

"What did he do, other than gardening?"

Mel looked out to the shed, the image of her father coming out of one very much like it and waving to her, shimmering in front of her eyes. A pale pink rose, freshly cut for her mother. "He was a graphic designer for a firm that made all sorts. Mechanical appliances, mostly, but he ended up designing some car parts and various toys."

"What a great job," Ruby said. "He sounds like he's an intelligent man."

Mel was grateful for the prolonged contact of Ruby's hand on her arm but also for the way Ruby was talking about her father in the present tense. She nodded. "He is. Still plays the organ for the other residents. I don't think he'll forget how to do that until he's forgotten everything else."

"Muscle memory, maybe." Ruby slid her palm up and down Mel's arm, which tingled a bit under her touch.

"So, come on you." Mel slapped her thighs and then gestured around the garden. "When are we to begin?"

Ruby's face lit up, and she laughed. "Um, are you free next Wednesday afternoon?"

"Operation Garden Clean Up shall commence."

---

A week later, Ruby was dressed in waterproof trousers, a long-sleeved T-shirt she didn't mind getting dirty, and wellington boots. She had an entire bottle of green washing-up liquid, two buckets, two brushes, and two cloths. Both buckets were full to the brim with warm water. *I'm not using cold; my hands will freeze.*

The day was bright but chilly, it still being January, and she hoped the students would finish their lunches and dissipate before their task began. She didn't fancy being stared at while she washed the greenhouse and got water all down her top. She'd attached some brightly coloured posters announcing the project and what it was in aid of, to every wall in the university, and around the garden too.

When one o'clock rolled around, Mel emerged from the paramedic science block, walking boots on her feet and rubbing her hands together in glee and motivation. "I saw the event Chloe created on Facebook." Mel gave her a thumbs up.

"I hope you… accepted it, or whatever the phrase is."

"Of course. Any luck on finding some free bits for the tombola?"

"Actually, yes. Most of the supermarkets were reasonably helpful. Got a voucher for a massage from that beauty place on the high street. And a few toys—they'll go down well with the kids."

"Definitely. Well done."

Ruby's stomach tingled. "So, where do we start?" she asked, setting one of the buckets down by Mel's feet.

"What's the shed like?"

Ruby wrinkled her nose. "Full of arachnids."

"I'll tackle that, then. You start on the inside of the greenhouse."

A nod from the both of them, and they set to work. Ruby cleared the greenhouse of debris and old plant pots first, lugging out a huge bag of mouldy compost. She was about to haul it over to the bin bags she'd pilfered from the domestic staff, but Mel stuck her head out of the shed.

"Throw it on the veg patch," she suggested, pointing to one of the oblong areas of muck.

"Really?"

"Yup."

"But it's mouldy."

"But still full of nutrients."

Ruby stared at it, shrugged, then nearly tripped over her own feet as she slid the bag over and upended it on the clay-filled earth. Even mouldy compost looked browner and healthier than the grey-orange stuff that covered the patch. *Okay, point taken.*

She threw all the pots away, bar one: a blue ceramic thing with a shiny outside and a big hole in the bottom. *That's far too pretty to throw in the bin.* She set that by the plastic chairs on the patio and went inside the now empty greenhouse to begin soaping up the glass walls.

The work was tiring but exhilarating. *I do very little physical work these days. Bed baths once a month for a selection of patients, but apart from that it's mostly talking to people and teaching.* She loved walking her dog; the parks around where she and her daughters lived were pretty but very much in the city. She liked the beach and rolling fields. Woodlands and hilltops and fresh air. *I miss the Pennines, and the farms of Yorkshire.*

This was almost fresh. Now that she'd got rid of most of the things causing the smell, all she could detect was the faint whiff of detergent and fresh earth. A worm wiggled its way over the concrete squares that ran up the middle of the greenhouse. She didn't want to touch it, but she did wait until it was out of harm's way before she walked to the end of the greenhouse and began washing the steepled roof. She knew her basic natural history—worms made the ground nice.

She glanced over to the shed and watched as Mel carried tools and large bins out of it so that she could clean inside. The strength in her arms was noticeable, the muscles taught and prominent under her T-shirt. Faint freckles dusted her arms right down to her wrists, where long fingers grasped a huge bin, before she heaved it over the ground towards the rest of the salvaged items.

Ruby blinked. *I'm staring.* She wiped her soapy hands on a spare, clean rag. Then, the perspiration beginning to drip down her back, she gathered her thick hair into a loose twist and secured it with a hair bobble to keep it off her neck. The cool air of the January afternoon swept past her exposed skin, and she sighed.

When she looked up, Mel was looking at her in a thoughtful kind of way. Ruby offered her a small wave and scrubbed hard at a particularly stubborn streak of muck that she didn't care to identify.

Once the inside was finished, Ruby emerged from the greenhouse and swiped at her forehead. "Fancy a coffee?" she called, and Mel's head poked out from the shed.

"Good timing; I'm just done in here." Mel stepped out and held up a hand. "Sparkly clean."

Ruby didn't need to look inside the shed to check, so she sauntered across Mel's path towards her office. As she passed her, Mel caught her arm and pointed to her own cheek. Ruby stopped walking.

"You've got some kind of crap…" Mel swiped Ruby's face and then held her fingers out to show Ruby the bubbly mud.

Ruby put a hand to her face, her cheeks burning but not unpleasantly. "I'll just go… make coffee. I'll bring them out." Mel nodded, and Ruby strode into the building, down the corridor, and into her office.

As the kettle boiled, Ruby sat in her office chair and took out her phone to use the camera to check her face. Just as Mel had indicated, there was mud smeared across her skin, so she wet a tissue and rubbed it clean. She scratched the back of her neck and chose to distract herself by checking emails. It didn't work. The memory of Mel's touch on her face hadn't been washed away by the tissue, and she wasn't quite ready to ponder over the reason just yet.

The click of the kettle broke her out of her non-reverie, and she poured the coffees into large mugs before carrying them back to their little garden area.

Mel was already seated at the plastic table, her feet propped up on one of the chairs. Ruby set the mugs down and indicated which coffee was Mel's. Mel's smile was grateful, and she let out a huge sigh as she leant back in her seat.

Ruby frowned at the walking boots making smears of mud on the plastic chair as she sat in her own, carefully crossing her legs and making sure her wellies were nowhere near the white plastic.

"What?" Mel said, obviously trying not to grin. "I'm supposed to keep it elevated."

"Like bugger you are," Ruby teased, but she moved her gaze deliberately from the mud smears and back to Mel's face. She had dirt on her chin and a happy look in her eyes. "You're having fun."

"I am," Mel replied, pushing up her shoulders as the sun gleamed off her skin. She drank her coffee and hummed her appreciation. "Thanks."

"You're welcome. That's the deal: you help me in this little endeavour, and I provide coffee."

"Sounds fair to me."

"So what's next?"

"Post-coffee break? I suggest we wash the outside of the greenhouse. Need to make sure as much light as possible can get inside, if we're to grow things in there."

"What will we be growing inside?"

Mel indicated the glass house with her finger. "Ah, that is where we shall start things off. All the flowers, tomatoes, and peppers."

"Not the rest of the veg?"

"Nope. You plant potatoes where they are to be harvested. Same with onions. They don't like to be moved."

"Right." Ruby looked over at the three plots they had. "Do we need to do anything with them?"

"Next week I'll get some wood from the recycling project and we can line them. And I have a friend who has some manure doing nothing."

"Manure?"

"Yup."

"Manure as in… poo?" Ruby's face must have been a picture, because Mel laughed, her head thrown back.

"Exactly. You never heard of that before?" Mel's voice was incredulous.

"Of course I have."

"But?"

Ruby sighed. "I thought that was some sort of old wives' tale or something."

Mel smirked. "No such luck, my dear sheltered friend. Poo is essential for healthy crops."

Ruby looked into her half-empty coffee mug and placed it decisively down on the plastic table. Suddenly, she didn't really feel like drinking it.

"It's just horse manure. Maybe a bit of chicken thrown in, if we're lucky." Mel drained her coffee and set her mug down too. "Don't worry, I'll be bringing it in my car."

"You certainly will be," Ruby replied, horrified by the notion that her Mini Cooper could contain anything that had come out of the back of an animal. *I vacuum it after each time Barney travels in the boot.*

Mel laughed again. "We'll get it all ready for the seed potatoes. I assume you have a budget?"

"Two hundred quid."

"Plenty. We'll get all the pots, some seed compost, all the seeds, seed potatoes, and onion sets for half of that easily."

"I don't have to spend the entire lot, I don't think."

Coffees finished, they emptied and refilled their buckets with extra washing-up liquid and started one at either side of the greenhouse. They washed the outside panes of glass, scrubbing gently where they met the metal framework of the greenhouse. When they came together around the front, Ruby accidentally dropped her cloth into her bucket, causing a plopping noise and a bunch of bubbles to fly out and hit Mel on the leg.

Ruby stared in horror at her and was just about to apologise when Mel reached into her own bucket, pulled out a handful of bubbles, and smeared them over Ruby's shoulder.

Ruby looked incredulously at the chuckling woman in front of her and could do nothing but retaliate. Another handful of bubbles landed smack bang in the middle of Mel's T-shirt, right between her breasts.

It was on.

Mel, grinning evilly, gathered another handful and followed as Ruby backed away, placing the bubbles on top of her head.

The bubbles were cold even though steam still rose from their buckets. The fight that ensued was contested with laughter, threats of grievous bodily harm, and Mel getting the upper hand and adorning the entirety of Ruby's face and head in grubby bubbles. Not to be outdone, however, Ruby fought her corner, smacking soapy water wherever she could on Mel's taller frame.

Giggles and shouts from both of them echoed across the garden patch, and Ruby was inordinately pleased no one came to see what on earth was going on.

In the end, they quietened, hanging off one another and panting. Mel was the first to shiver, and Ruby rubbed the bubbles from Mel's arms, admiring the orange freckles up close as she did so. *She looks like she's dusted with cinnamon.*

Mel's eyes continued to laugh with her. They clutched each other with hands on shoulders and smiled through parted lips, their breath swirling upwards in clouds of hilarity.

"I do not approve of foam parties," Ruby said once they both had calmed down.

"Really? Could have fooled me."

Grinning, Ruby patted Mel's shoulder. "Well, I think the greenhouse is pretty much clean."

"Very sparkly." Mel let go of Ruby to take her bucket and drain it over one of the veg patches.

Ruby followed suit, feeling the loss of Mel's hands on her skin like the chilly breeze that was drying out the greenhouse. Mel hooked up the hose to the external tap and began to spray the bubbly water from the glass panes, while Ruby found an old patio brush and swept any extra muck from the concrete path inside the greenhouse, onto the earthy sides. Mel sprayed the glass right by Ruby's face as she knelt to pick up a few twigs, and Ruby stuck her tongue out at her, immediately feeling her face warm at the childish expression.

Collecting up their tools and placing them back into the shed, they made plans to go to the garden centre. "The kids arrive on the second of March."

"Plenty of time." Mel stretched her arms up over her head and backwards, and the pops of her shoulders were audible. "And a perfect time for planting seeds."

Ruby looked over towards the now neat and tidy greenhouse and felt a sense of pride warm her. The warmth intensified when she looked back at Mel. "Thank you for all your help."

"You're very welcome."

# Chapter 10

Their lunchtime meet-ups continued, usually followed by a quick walk around the garden area and a chat about their plans. Ruby loved to watch Mel as her face lit up, her eyes sparkled, and her hand gestures became emphatic. Passion poured from Mel like liquid honey, and the limp in her stride that lingered from her injury seemed to melt away once she got going.

They enjoyed sitting in the cold air with coffee at their plastic table and chair assortment, chatting about this and that. Ruby finally asked Mel how she had actually sustained her broken leg. "You didn't save a puppy from a burning building, did you?"

Mel chuckled. "No. Nothing quite so dramatic." Her fingers toyed with the end of her ponytail, and her cheeks pinked slightly. "I... rode my bike into a park bench."

"You did not!" Ruby knew her mouth was hanging open but couldn't imagine a more suitable reaction.

"Yep." Rubbing the back of her neck, Mel ducked and tried to hide her face. "'Fraid so."

Once Ruby was sure her surprise had continued for long enough, she closed her mouth and stifled her laughter. Head tilted to one side, she lifted her coffee. "Would you say you were a bit accident prone?" Ruby asked, her glasses steaming up slightly as she sipped.

"Sometimes. Not all the time." Mel crossed her legs. "Won't be cycling for a little while though." She patted her belly. "I'm going to have to find something else to do to keep the weight off."

Ruby allowed her gaze to wander up and down Mel's body; she felt a flush in her face, and other places, when she really, truly took in the long legs, wide hips, and small bosom on her friend. *That's it; your friend. So stop ogling.* "You don't have anything to worry about."

"I eat a lot. It's usually healthy but I get low blood glucose if I don't eat well." Mel narrowed her eyes. "What do *you* do for exercise?"

"Walk the dog," Ruby replied, her lips twisting in thought. "I swim on occasion."

"Maybe I should come with you." Mel's gaze was steady on her, but Ruby had to look away as the image of Mel in a swim suit appeared in her mind's eye. "My physio said swimming is good after an injury."

"If you like." Ruby sipped her coffee.

---

It was Friday afternoon, and Ruby's classes would finish at three. Sitting in her office eating lunch, she jumped when her phone buzzed and nearly fell from her desk. She picked it up and saw she had a text from Mel.

*Fancy a drink or something later? Mx*

Ruby's insides immediately flooded with warmth, and a now-familiar tingling began across her skin. So far, except for their drink the day Mel had started university, and the theatre, they'd only met on a Wednesday, when Mel was at the campus for her classes. *This is purely social, nothing to do with the gardening project, or being at the same location just by chance.* Her phone hovered in front of her face as she considered her options. Mel could drive now, so proximity to either her own house or university wasn't important. *Perhaps somewhere in town? Oh blimey, I'd better reply!*

*Sounds great. How about at The Lamb, on the high street? Rx*

Tapping her finger on the desk, Ruby turned back to her computer screen, a forkful of salad half way to her mouth. She was just about to take a bite when her phone buzzed again.

*I love it in there, nice and quiet, perfect for a pint. Shall we say seven? Mx*

Ruby's heart leapt, and she sent a quick reply to the affirmative before wolfing down her salad in a fashion she was unused to, and grabbing the things she needed for her next lesson.

When she entered the lecture theatre, she knew something was up. Her first-year class sat stock straight, all of them with their hands folded, all of them facing front. This was not the usual gabble of disarray she was used to arriving into. *What's going on?*

She caught sight of Francesca and her friends at the front and went to turn on the computer that was set up on the left of the large screen. "Hi everyone," she called as usual, trying to simultaneously figure out what was amiss and act like she didn't care. "Today, we'll be taking a more in-depth look at blood vessels. I hope everyone's read the required chapter."

Still, everyone sat motionless. Ruby tried to rise above rolling her eyes but was finding it increasingly difficult. She brought up the relevant PowerPoint slides and clicked 'Go'. The whole class erupted with laughter, and Ruby shot up from her chair before stepping out from behind the computer.

"What's going on?" She folded her arms, attempting an air of authority, but was met by more laughter and jeering. She turned slowly around to look at the screen, some of which was hidden by her silhouette.

A large, explicitly photographed, depiction of an erect penis met her, the head of it almost bobbing despite it being a very still image.

She slowly and deliberately turned back to the class. Her gaze immediately flickered to Francesca, who was doubled over in giggles, a small laptop on her knee, partially out of sight behind her wooden desk. Ruby stared at the laptop, her gaze following the now-apparent cable that worked its way from the laptop across the floor and to the socket in the wall that usually connected her computer to the projector.

Very slowly, very calmly, although her heart was thumping loudly in her ears, Ruby walked over and disconnected the cable. She rolled it around her hand as she walked back towards Francesca, who had tears running down her face. She handed the cable to the young woman and was annoyed when she didn't take it.

"Not mine, *Miss*."

"It's attached to your laptop, Francesca. Do you think I was born yesterday?"

Francesca put on a reasonable Yorkshire accent when she replied, "Not by t'look of ye."

Ruby pushed down the anger inside her chest as her heart rate rose a notch. She counted to ten in her head before leaving the cable on the desk by Francesca and her friends and walking back to her computer. She reconnected the projector to the computer with the university-issue cable and began the lecture.

Throughout, Francesca continued to giggle and throw Ruby wicked looks—whispering things to her friends, who found equal glee in Ruby's irritation.

Ruby rolled her eyes. *Perhaps that would have caused serious embarrassment in another lecturer, but I teach anatomy and work in general nursing. Do I look like I've not seen a penis before?* She figured the girls would settle, and they mostly did, but Francesca developed that far-off look in her eye once her classmates had begun focussing on veins and arteries, and their properties.

At the end of the class, Ruby took Francesca aside and waited until her friends had left the room. She threaded her fingers together and pulled a concerned look onto her face. "I wanted to talk to you about the joke you pulled today."

"Brill, wasn't it?" Francesca waggled her head and puffed out her chest.

"Not the word I would use. Elaborate, perhaps."

"Whatever." Perhaps aware that she was not going to get an angry shouting-at, Francesca looked at the ceiling and huffed.

"It disrupted the class's focus. And it ate into my lecture time," Ruby explained, her hand on her chin. "Your classmates missed out on an extra five, ten, minutes that I could have used to read through things a bit more slowly." *Does she not understand some of the things we are learning? Is that why she's being so disruptive?* "What do you think about that?"

Francesca snorted and continued to look at the ceiling.

"You need to get your act together and start focussing on the course." Ruby pushed her glasses up her nose and pulled a hand through her hair. She didn't care if it betrayed her frustration. She wanted Francesca to understand how she felt about the long-term effects of missing things in lectures, even if she wished to remain nonchalant about the actual prank. "Otherwise, you're not going to pass and all this time will've been wasted."

Francesca stepped back. "Don't worry. I'm not going to pass anyway."

"Why do you say that?" Ruby reached out to touch Francesca's shoulder, but the young girl stepped back and stared at Ruby's hand like it was going to bite her.

"Because I'm too thick. Anyway"—Francesca flicked her hair over her shoulder and turned her dark brown eyes to the door—"I've got to go."

She turned on her heel and, her backpack thrown loosely over one shoulder, scarpered.

Ruby stared at the door and stood for a while. *What's going on? How do I control her? She's a complete menace.* She combed her fingers through her hair, settling it back into something resembling neatness, and went to collect her things.

---

Mel sipped the cool beer and hummed her approval. *A nice pint, some soft music, and the appeal of a pretty woman about to join me. What more could a girl wish for?*

She'd made an effort, but not too much: clean jeans, a blue tank top, and a red checked shirt with the sleeves rolled to the elbow and fastened with the handy little buttons the manufacturers had provided. She'd brushed her walking boots, and the hems of her jeans fell in a way she liked over the black laces. She'd even managed to put studs in her ears and tie her hair in a neat ponytail.

Facing the main door to the pub, she watched a few people come and go. When a woman with dark wavy hair entered, holding her beige jacket around her from the chill of outside, Mel sat up straighter and held up a hand.

Her cheeks a bit pink, Ruby flopped back into the chair opposite.

Mel chuckled and reached to pat her hand, feeling the difference between Ruby's frosty fingers and her own warm ones. "You look like you could do with a pint."

Ruby made some kind of acknowledging groan.

"What're you drinking?" Mel held up her drink. "Carlsberg okay?"

Ruby just nodded.

*Not just a wine drinker, then. It's nice to see some chinks in that refined armour.* When Mel returned to the table, Ruby looked a little less like she'd died from exhaustion. Mel set the glass onto a beer mat and returned to her own half-empty drink, which had condensation running down the sides.

"So, how was your day?" Mel asked, trying to brighten her voice as much as possible.

The effect was instant: Ruby's eyes met hers and she smiled. She seemed to think hard for a few seconds before saying, "Penis-filled."

Mel spat a mouthful of beer onto the table, her hand flying to her mouth. "I'm so sorry," she said, grabbing a napkin from the little caddy on the table and mopping up. "But *what?*"

Ruby appeared chuffed to bits with her shocking revelation but grabbed a napkin too, to help. "My lovely *student from hell* managed to hack into my projector in room seventeen, and up popped the most *distasteful* picture of an erect penis I've ever seen." Ruby's expression was much more placid than Mel thought her own must have been. "Honestly, it barely looked real."

Mel spluttered and took a restoring mouthful of beer, this time without spitting it all over the table. She swallowed carefully and then looked back up at Ruby, who was smirking. "I'm going to need more detail."

"She thought it was funny."

"Oh, a prank." Mel coughed, some residual beer lingering in her windpipe. "Hope you gave her hell."

"I did speak to her about it, yes." Ruby's mouth became a thin line, and Mel's body felt heavy. *She works hard at teaching others to nurse; she doesn't deserve that kind of joke to be played on her.*

"Did she apologise?"

"Nope."

"Hm." Mel leant an elbow on the table and rested her chin in it. She idly played with a single droplet of condensation that was making its way to the beer mat under her glass.

"She seems to want to humiliate me at every opportunity," Ruby sighed, mirroring Mel's stance and drinking heavily from her pint.

"Good job you're well acquainted with male genitalia," Mel said, but then sat up, biting her lip. "I didn't mean—"

"I know you didn't." Ruby smirked again, apparently amused that for once she was not the one blushing. "And for the record, my 'acquaintance', as you put it, during the last fifteen years has been purely professional."

*Finally, she tells me.* Their gazes locked. The music playing softly in the pub ended and began again, something slower and more peaceful. A slot machine chimed musically from the other side of the room, and a couple more patrons entered from outside, their voices muffled.

*So she's gay, then. Or she is now. Or she's bisexual. Why am I labelling her?* Mel blinked a few times to clear her thoughts before sitting back against the bench back and regarding Ruby with interest.

"That's good to know."

"I thought you might say that," Ruby said, pink blossoming on her cheekbones.

Mel spent a beat longer smiling at Ruby before remembering the topic in hand. "So, this student. She's still being a nightmare?"

"Yep. There isn't a single lesson I have her in where she doesn't do something disruptive. Rude pictures and comments, trying to get me off-topic, making fun of my accent…"

"I like your accent," Mel said plainly.

"Do you?"

"It's nice." She shrugged and looked away for a minute, deciding this wasn't exactly the context to be telling Ruby she thought her accent attractive. *Focus.* "It suits you. Do your girls have the same accent?"

"I moved down here before I met their father, so no, they are very much south-westerners." Somehow, Mel got the feeling this was a bone of contention between mother and daughters.

"She needs sorting out," Mel said, referring to the student.

"You offering?" Ruby asked, and Mel nearly spat her beer out again.

"If you like. You could tell her I know how to kill someone as well as how to save them."

"Is *that* what they teach in the ECP training?" Ruby laughed and lifted her glass in a salute. "Who'd have thought?"

"Those advanced assessment skills aren't just for the poorlies. They come in very handy as assassination techniques."

They ended up clinking pints, just because…and settling into small talk again. By the time eight o'clock rolled around, they were drinking coke and laughing into the cheerful air between them. Mel was warm all over, despite the draft every time someone entered the small pub, and she was feeling a sort of pull toward Ruby that she hadn't felt in a long time.

In the end, Ruby leant forwards on the table, her hands clasped. Mel's gaze tracked from her elbows, down her slim arms that held a scattering of dark moles, to her hands. Her nails were neat; her fingers neither long nor short. She wore a single silver ring on the middle finger of her right hand, and a simple watch adorned her wrist.

Fiddling with her glass for a second, Mel reached out to touch a fingertip to Ruby's silver ring. She had an overwhelming urge to take her hand and fit their fingers together across the table, but she refrained. "Where's your ring from?"

"My mother bought it for me after I got divorced."

"From the girls' dad?" Mel bit her lip and hoped she wasn't delving too deep.

"That's right." To Mel's surprise, Ruby stretched her fingers out to touch them to Mel's. "She said one should always have a ring on, even if one isn't married." Laughing a bit, she gazed down at their touching hands. "I forget what her explanation was, but I like it."

"It's simple, classy," Mel said, and cleared her throat when she heard her own voice was scratchy. She took a chance and tickled the skin of Ruby's finger, right by her ring. Then, with a burst of courage, she reached to gather Ruby's fingers in her own. Her heart pounded and her hands felt sweaty, but she didn't want to pull away. "Listen..." Their eyes locked again, and Mel opened her mouth to ask the question she'd been wanting to ask since October.

Ruby's phone rang.

Mel sprang away, rubbing at her upper arm as she wrapped an arm around herself. She threw her head back and sighed.

A flicker of something that looked like regret moved over Ruby's features, but she took her phone out of her pocket and the moment was lost. Rolling her eyes, she answered the call. "Yes, sweetie?"

*One of her daughters, perhaps. Or maybe her partner? She's told me she likes women, not that she's single.*

Mel stared down at the table as she pretended not to listen to the one-sided conversation taking place three feet from her. She drained her coke and set the empty glass back on the beer mat. She rubbed at her forehead.

"I'm sorry," Ruby said after she hung up. "Jasmine wants some kind of special pasta for dinner. Her friend apparently has it 'all the time' and she's convinced it will help her lose weight."

"She thinks she's overweight?"

"She does. And she's not one hundred percent wrong. She's teetering on the edge."

Mel looked around her, her knee bouncing.

"Sorry, I should go."

Mel's heart fell into her walking boots. "Okay, that's fine." She forced a smile onto her face. "We should do this again. Outside of uni, I mean."

"That would be nice. And, if you have any thoughts about my unruly student, please don't hesitate to tell me." Ruby huffed as she scraped her chair back and pulled her jacket back on. "You don't think she has things going on at home, do you?"

*Something inside her is switched on.* Mel shrugged. "Good thinking, but the only way to find that out is to ask her, and for her to tell you."

"Not blooming likely," Ruby replied, her expression sad. "She thinks I'm the devil, or something similar. I'd be incredibly surprised if she opened up to me." Then she reached forwards to touch and squeeze Mel's shoulder.

Prickles of pleasure swirled down Mel's arm. "See you soon."

"See you after reading week."

Mel's heart fell a little bit more when she realised it would be over a week before she saw Ruby again. *Damn it, why didn't you ask her out earlier? Like the minute she came into the pub?*

---

"Pasta's arrived," Ruby called as she swung in through the front door, shopping bag in hand.

Jasmine's face poked around the door from the living room. "Is it the right one?"

"You'll have to see for yourself, oh loveliness."

Jasmine allowed her mother to kiss her cheek in greeting before pulling the bag from her hands. Ruby followed her into the kitchen, where Jasmine lifted the bag onto the work surface and delved inside. The squeal that travelled up from the depths of the bag suggested that she had made the correct purchase.

"Don't get used to being catered for separately." Ruby shrugged her jacket off and went to hang it in the hallway. Her shoes joined the high heels and trainers already side by side under the coat hooks. She shook her shoulders up and down a few times to loosen the muscles there before sliding her slippers on and returning to the kitchen.

"These are the actual ones," Jasmine said, bouncing rapidly up and down on her feet. "You're brill, Mum."

"And don't forget it, hmm?" She glanced at the wall clock. "Isn't it a bit late to be eating?"

"Carrie says that the best time to eat is at night. Because you're body digests everything properly."

"Not strictly true." Ruby leant against the counter and folded her arms. "A good hearty breakfast is best, and then light meals throughout the day." As Jasmine started to protest, Ruby cut her off with a chuckle. "Healthy ones, missus."

"I'm not eating salad. It gives me wind."

"Charming."

The sound of a huge pair of trousers shuffling along the floor announced the arrival of Ruby's eldest daughter, whose corduroys were at least six inches too long for her, despite her tall stature. Without preamble, Chloe stepped up to her mum to give her a one-armed hug. "Were you out?"

"Just having a drink with Mel," Ruby said, returning the hug and pressing her cheek to Chloe's.

Chloe moved towards the kettle and gave Ruby a questioning look. Ruby nodded, so Chloe filled the kettle with water and flicked it on. "You're spending quite a bit of time with Mel." With her back to her, Ruby couldn't see Chloe's face.

"That's right." She pressed her lips together and tapped a finger against the counter top.

Jasmine sat at the kitchen table, the packet of pasta held in both hands as she read the back of it. "Why?"

"Why what?" Ruby wrapped her hands around the warm cup of tea Chloe handed her.

"Why are you spending so much time with her?"

Ruby cleared her throat and gave both her daughters a stern look. They spoke about their personal lives with each other, but it had been a while since Ruby's personal life had included a romantic relationship, or even something that had the potential to become one. She looked between them, noting Chloe's steady eye contact and Jasmine's more nonchalant attention to her pasta. "I like her."

"What does that mean?" Chloe asked, going to the table and sitting at a right angle to her sister. She placed a cup of tea in front of Jasmine, who didn't even look up. Chloe indicated the chair opposite her, so Ruby slid into it, feeling very much like this was about to become an interrogation.

"It means that I like her company, and I think she's funny and good to talk to, and she's intelligent."

Both girls looked up at their mother, Jasmine's eyebrows raised in adolescent indignation.

Ruby sighed and tilted her head to the side. "I'm aware it's been a little while since I've had a friend, so to speak."

"You'd better bring her round," Chloe said, lifting her tea to her lips and pointing one finger through the handle across the table. "I don't want you starting with someone when we've not even met them."

"Me neither." Jasmine rolled her eyes and wrinkled her nose, banishing the thought away with a wave of her hand.

"I'm not entirely sure if she wants... any kind of... romantic relationship." Ruby thought back to their exchanged glances, and the way their fingers had touched briefly in the pub before her phone had interrupted them. She looked out of the window, trying to collate all the times they'd touched and form some sort of conclusion, like a clinician searching for a diagnosis.

"Maybe she's too busy," Chloe said, her maturity showing through the small huffs and eye-rolls she was getting from her sister. "She works full-time, doesn't she? And the uni course." Chloe sipped her tea and shuttered her eyes thoughtfully. "Maybe she doesn't have time for a girlfriend."

"She's a student?" Jasmine snorted a bit behind her cup. "You're dating a student."

Chloe shot her a derisive eyebrow raise and shook her head in something close to disbelief.

Staring at her cup, a feeling of dread washed over Ruby. *She's a student. I'm a lecturer. How many times have I read about student-teacher relationships in the media? These people go to prison.*

"She's older than me." Ruby allowed the steam from her tea to tickle her nose as she drank.

"She's still a student, Mum," Chloe said, apparently also amused by Jasmine's comment and out to tease her mother.

They sat in silence to drink the rest of their tea. In the end, Jasmine put the pasta in her cupboard, forbidding anyone to as much as think about trying it. Chloe left next, intent on continuing some college work in her room, before bed.

Staring into her empty cup, Ruby just breathed for a while, willing her insides to cease their churning. *Is it inappropriate? She's a student. What if people find out?*

She sank her fingers into her hair as she dropped her head into her hand. The ends of her hair brushed the table, and she stayed in the little dark den for a while, her whole face enclosed. It was the weekend. She had a whole two days of worrying about it before going back into work on Monday and being able to access the university's policies and procedures.

*Even if it is inappropriate, it would be a shame to stop seeing Mel. Perhaps we could just be friends.*

## Chapter 11

Barney sat in the boot of Ruby's car, shifting about as if she knew they were going somewhere exciting. "It's just the beach, you plonker." Ruby turned along the slightly sandy road and onto a small street lined with pretty houses and bungalows of varying size and design.

Barney yipped and wagged her tail, her feet sliding a bit as Ruby turned the car into Mel's small driveway. Ruby turned around in her seat after switching off the engine and gave Barney a look. A pair of big, brown eyes appeared over the top of the back seat.

"Now then, missus. No funny business. No humping Mel's leg, or eating her sofa, or trying to play with the cat. Cats are not like dogs; they don't like to play the same way."

Barney just wagged her tail enthusiastically and turned to the boot door before starting to lick the window.

Ruby rolled her eyes and got out of the car before Mel could appear and see the embarrassing behaviour of her dog. She opened the boot and grabbed Barney's collar before she could jump down and run off. After clipping her lead into place, she scooped the terrier up and deposited her onto the gravel.

Ruby set the strap of her handbag across her body and made sure her jacket was buttoned up properly. Small feet crunched around her as Barney took her time to smell everything, then the lead went taught as she strained towards the house.

"Hello."

Ruby looked up and grinned as she caught sight of Mel holding her front door open and leaning out. "Hiya. Oops."

The dog tugged so hard that the lead slipped from Ruby's fingers. Barney bounded up to Mel, who stooped down to grab the dog around the collar. "Steady on, little one. Let your mum get herself together before you come crashing over here."

Barney's tail was smacking the sides of her hips, and her tongue was hanging out of her mouth in a wide grin. She barked again and settled her backside onto the floor politely.

Ruby made her way quickly over to Mel and chuckled, apologetically. "Sorry, she can be a bit... too friendly."

Barney's nose was trained towards the open door.

"You're pretty desperate to explore, hmm?"

"She will be. New smells, and you have a cat." Ruby scratched her chin. "Is she going to be okay, your cat?"

"She's quite used to dogs." Mel's face pulled into a grin. She let the dog go, watching as Barney raced around her kitchen, then sniffed at the door into the rest of the house.

Looking behind her at the gravel driveway and the row of paving slabs from the front door to half way toward the gate, Ruby furrowed her eyebrows. "What's that about?"

"Ever tried to pull a stretcher over gravel?" Mel asked, and stepped back to allow Ruby into her house.

Ruby wiped her feet on the mat and clasped her hands as Mel sat to pull her walking boots on. "Can't say I have, no."

"Nightmare. If I ever need taking to hospital by ambulance, I want a nice concrete path for my vehicle of transport to take me along before they load me in."

"Very sensible." *She's not just a pretty face. Stop that. Friends.*

"Drink before we head out?"

Barney was still sniffling about at the underside of the door. Mel took pity on her and opened the door, the little dog racing out to explore.

"It's fine, my house is fairly dog-proof."

"You'll have to give me the tour," Ruby replied. "And a glass of water would be just the ticket."

Mel filled two glasses with water and handed one to Ruby. Then she led the way Barney had gone into a large and long living room, with a dining area to the right and doors further off the same way. "So, I guess this is the living room."

It was decorated simply but tastefully, with a few beach items placed on various surfaces and a gas fire on the far wall. The big bay window showed her small back garden, which had a greenhouse and a shed. A glass door to the left led into a small conservatory, holding a wicker chair set and a small table.

They went through the door to the right and into a small hexagonal hallway that had three doors leading off it. Barney was in what could only be the spare room, a small box room with a computer, a bookcase, and a single bed standing under the small window. She sniffed under the bed and looked up at them to send them a wag and a grin.

Mel held a hand out to the other two doors. "Bathroom, and my bedroom." She looked at the floor with a shy shrug. "It's not big, but it does me well enough."

"It's lovely." Ruby reached to touch a framed black-and-white photograph of an older gentleman in a suit and tie, taking in his kind-looking features. "Your dad?"

Mel seemed to swell with pride. "That's right. At a company dinner."

"He's really handsome." Ruby took a chance, figuring it couldn't hurt to compliment. Friends did that, didn't they? "You take after your dad."

"I know. Both ginger as anything."

"I didn't mean that," Ruby said, determined to be kind and make sure Mel knew what she meant. "I meant you're both nice looking." Ruby's cheeks burned.

There was a pause while Mel smiled at Ruby. "Thanks."

Barney sniffed around their feet and trotted up to Mel's closed bedroom door, inhaling deeply at the gap underneath.

"Aha, have you found her?"

"I don't allow her on the bed at home," Ruby warned Mel.

"That's okay." Mel swung open the door and allowed the dog inside.

Barney skittered around the room, poking her nose into every little nook and cranny she could find. Then she stopped and lifted her front half, resting her paws on the edge of the mattress.

A multi-coloured cat sat up from her curled-up posture and stared at the new visitor with wide eyes.

"Ruby, meet Epione."

"She's beautiful," Ruby said, unsure about whether she should properly enter Mel's bedroom but wanting to greet the cat before Barney chased her away. Eventually deciding that Mel seemed comfortable enough, Ruby shuffled into the room and perched on the edge of the large double bed.

Yapping happily, Barney scampered to get onto the bed, but Ruby clicked her fingers and gave the dog a look. "Just wait." Barney obediently backed away and sat on her podgy behind.

Ruby shifted towards the cat, who sat watching her with those large eyes, and reached out a hand. An inch away, she stopped, hoping Epione would come towards her. White paws spread wide and a fluffy tail emerged from beneath the small cat as she stood and stretched, her backside popping up comically. Then the furry face butted against Ruby's hand, and Ruby's body flooded with warmth.

"Oh hey, hiya. Nice to meet you."

"Mrow."

Both Mel and Ruby chuckled at the response, until Ruby turned back to Mel and her dog, the latter trembling with excitement. "Would it be okay if she…"

"Of course."

"Hup, Barney." Ruby patted the bedspread.

Barney jumped onto the bed and nearly tumbled over her own feet as she came face-to-face with an affronted feline, her mouth opening and a deliberate hiss escaping. Barney sensibly stopped and elongated her neck to sniff the cat, without moving her feet any closer.

Lifting a soft paw, Epione smacked Barney around the muzzle. The fact that the dog did not squeal meant that Epione had not unsheathed her claws.

"A friendly greeting," Mel stated, still chuckling. "Good girl, Epi."

"And good girl, Barney." Ruby stood from the bed and smoothed the covers straight where they'd become wrinkled underneath her. "And now, I think *down* would be appropriate."

The dog hopped from the bed and padded back into the hallway, in search of something else to investigate. Perhaps something that wouldn't smack her on the nose.

---

They got ready and walked down the short way to the beach. Mel relished the seaweed and salty smells that hit her regularly, and always made her feel bright and alive. Sometimes she wondered whether she had fish genes somewhere along the line, although she wouldn't go so far as to swim in the Bristol Channel, which was mostly mud and rubbish these days. One could get stuck in the mud, trying to walk out far enough to actually see the sea at low tide. Biggest tide difference in Europe, and people still tried to walk out. Idiots.

The day was windy but clear. They could see for miles, right over to the small islands dotted between the seashore and Wales. They could see the lighthouse near Swansea, flickering steadily. A few tankers on the water looked like Lego constructions. Mel showed her the docks and the different towns across the water. Ruby leaned in close to follow the direction of her pointed finger.

They walked along the beach towards town, and then turned back, heading for the sand dunes and boatyard. Barney skipped in and out of the dunes, her brown muzzle poking between clumps of dry grass, making them laugh. She seemed to know what would humour them and kept doing it, until Ruby called her to heel and she bounded over for a biscuit.

Mel leant down to fuss the soft fur and bouncing ears, tracing a wrinkle or two in the dog's forehead. "You're having a good time, hmm?"

"She is." Ruby stood with her arms folded and looked out to sea, her gaze drifting over the half-sunken boats and plastic barrels that littered the landscape.

"My dad had a boat for a while," Mel said, her voice getting a little lost in the sea breeze.

Ruby beamed at her, her dark wavy hair swiping about her face. She gathered it up and stuffed it down her scarf. "That must've been nice."

"Was great. He didn't take it out on the water much, but he loved tinkering with it, and taking a flask out here to sit by it."

"What was it called?" Ruby turned towards one large blue boat, weathered by the elements, its paint flecked, the name however stark against the wood: 'Saint Maria'.

"Katy," Mel said. "After my mother."

"That's lovely."

Mel just nodded, her eyes tearing up. *Must be the wind. It's rather bracing this afternoon.*

They continued on, heading through the boatyard and towards a concrete path through some countryside. Barbed-wire fences stood on either side, and Ruby seemed comfortable to continue to allow Barney to roam where she liked. She took a plastic bag out of her shoulder bag and produced a ball.

"Want to play?" she asked the dog.

Barney wagged her tail and jumped up and down on her little feet.

Ruby threw the ball behind them, and the dog skittered off after it. Little feet scraping the concrete as she slid to a halt and caught the ball. "So, I just realised what date it is," Ruby said, her focus following a few birds flying from one tree to another.

"Yes, I did notice," Mel said, her own gaze moving to the ground by her feet.

"We're spending Valentine's Day together."

"We are."

"Any reason?" When Mel looked back up, Ruby's shoulders appeared tense, although she wasn't sure whether it was from the conversation or the chilled wind.

"Well, neither of us have a date, I presume?"

"You presume correctly."

"So, why not spend the day with a new friend?"

Ruby turned to look at her. "So this is a friend thing, not just two random people who've met and have found a few things in common?"

"Isn't that what friendship is?"

Ruby appeared to think deeply for a while, small lines appearing between her eyes. "I suppose so." She laughed slightly. "I guess I thought that you were just helping me with the garden. Making money for the Air Ambulance. That it was a... professional thing."

"I like your company," Mel said with a shrug. "I wouldn't help out with something like that if I didn't enjoy spending time with you."

"Really?" Ruby seemed shy and uncertain.

Mel stopped walking and rested her hand on Ruby's upper arm. "Listen. Despite the fact that we've identified a few differences—namely you're as opinionated at they come—I've still chosen you as a friend."

"Why?"

"Because you're willing to forgo some of those beliefs if I think they're stupid."

"You've opened my eyes to the whole paramedics-not-being-gung-ho-heroes thing." Ruby was biting her lip, as if she was trying not to smile.

"Ah good, glad we got that sorted." Mel rubbed the beige of Ruby's coat with her thumb. "I feel like you're the kind of person who doesn't make friends easily." At Ruby's look of incredulousness, Mel lifted both hands. "No, it's a compliment. You're picky."

"I am picky."

"Who would you say your best friend was?"

They turned back to walk again, and Mel made sure to walk closer to Ruby than she had before.

Barney bounded about by their feet, and Ruby grabbed onto Mel's arm as the dog clattered into Mel's knee to steady her. She seemed to go still for just a beat but then slid her hand into the crook of Mel's arm, apparently content to leave it there for the time being. *Perhaps in case her dog tries to kill me again.*

"I know it's not good to say this, but my girls."

"You're friends with Jasmine and Chloe?"

Ruby nodded. "I think they're the closest friends I have." She chuckled, shaking her head so her hair fell about her shoulders and out of her eyes. She pushed her glasses up her nose. "Is that terrible?"

"Of course not. I think people find friendships in all sorts of places."

Ruby squeezed her arm. "I don't have many female friends. I have Alexander, who supports me at work, more so than a PA ought to really. He lets me have a moan."

"Like all good friends should."

"That's right."

They turned a corner and came in sight of a large gate that led out onto the road again. "The café's just through the gate and to the right."

Ruby stooped down and whistled. Barney raced up to her and sat excitedly. After Ruby clipped her lead back on, she gave her a treat and stuffed the ball back into the plastic bag. "Dogs are allowed?"

"I would never invite Barney out for a coffee if she wasn't allowed in the café. That's just rude."

Ruby chuckled. They made their way through the gate, allowing it to swing closed behind them, before scraping their feet on the rough mat and going inside.

The café was one of Mel's favourites. She and James often frequented the establishment if she wanted a change of scenery from her conservatory. It was set into the hillside, with exposed rock jutting out into the café area. A few mothers with very small children sat chatting and drinking tea.

Once they found a table and Mel had gone to the counter to place their orders, Ruby attached Barney to the leg of her chair and rested back into her seat with a sigh. "A lovely walk."

"Bracing," Mel agreed. "Got rid of the cobwebs."

"Do you walk regularly?"

"I try to do a walk a day when I'm off. And one good cycle a week." She shifted her feet around under the table uncomfortably. "Although I'm still not allowed. Yet."

"Did you manage to get to the baths?" Ruby leant forward, took a napkin from the holder, and placed it in front of her.

"Yeah, did a few lengths last week."

"They're not too bad. So long as you don't catch it when the kids are there."

"Ah yes, you don't have much of an affinity with kids, do you?"

Ruby just grimaced and slid her fingers into her hair.

Reaching forward to touch her hand, Mel sent her a kind wink. "Don't worry. We've still got a month, and you'll have me to protect you from the scary children." She said the last two words with a fake-shaky voice.

Ruby chuckled. "Oh good."

"So, I went to get the wood the other day, and the manure is sitting waiting for Wednesday, when I'll pop it in my car and bring it up."

"Fantastic. Do I owe you for those?"

"Just a fiver for the wood. The manure, my friend was happy to get rid of."

"Great."

"When did you want to go to the garden centre to get the other stuff?"

Ruby fumbled in her pocket for her phone as their drinks arrived: one big pot of tea and two china cups. Barney shifted about on her bottom, clearly expecting a treat to come out of the pocket instead of Ruby's phone. Ruby rolled her eyes and slipped her a biscuit. "As you're being so good."

Barney lay down on her front and chomped away.

"I was thinking," Ruby continued. "Would it be okay to get everything from the internet?"

"If that's less scary for you, and more convenient." *That's a shame. I was looking forward to showing her the different plants at our local place.* Mel chose to hide her disappointment.

"Okay. I made a wish list."

*How organised.* Mel couldn't help the grin that spread onto her face. "Good idea."

After flicking through her phone, Ruby held it out and turned the screen round so that Mel could see.

Mel blinked rapidly as the words on the screen bounced a little, but not as much as they usually did. The space behind the letters wasn't as white as it could be—Ruby obviously kept the screen on a dim setting. It helped. She didn't want to miss anything, her stomach fluttering with nerves and the hope that Ruby wouldn't notice as she lingered over the list. She pulled a look onto her face that she hoped would suggest she was considering the options, rather than struggling. "Yep, yep, all good. You'll need canes though," Mel said as she got to the end. "And tomato feed. Good thinking getting some small trowels; I wouldn't have thought about that."

"Then the kids can dig or do whatever jobs you give them." Ruby caught Mel's gaze and cleared her throat at her raised eyebrow. "*We*. We give them."

"Love the colours. Nothing like a bit of rainbow-themed fun to pass a Wednesday afternoon."

Ruby poured their tea from the huge pot, holding the strainer between thumb and forefinger. *Loose tea; how terribly decadent.* She and James usually only had coffee when they frequented the café.

Mel turned to study the cake display but turned swiftly back around when she felt Ruby's gaze on her.

Ruby smiled. "Did you want cake?"

"I'm good with tea, actually."

"So, the seeds are okay?"

"They're a good brand," Mel replied, going back to the list on Ruby's phone. "And the compost you've chosen is perfect. Absolutely the one I would have chosen." She gave Ruby a thumbs up.

Ruby visibly blushed, and her eyes were bright behind her glasses.

"So, I reckon, the bed closest to the greenhouse—we put flowers in that one. I see you found some marigolds and loads of different sunflowers. Good thinking." She handed the phone back to Ruby, who scrolled through and nodded at the amendments Mel had made. "Then the one behind it—we'll plant the potatoes one side, and the onions the other. If we have room we can pop some salad in there too, but I have a feeling the potatoes will take up most of the room.

Then the other one, at the back, we can save for when it's warmer and plant with tomatoes and peppers."

"Will it be too cold, putting them outside?" The blatant worry in Ruby's voice for her future baby seedlings was endearing.

"We'll have to see what the summer temperature's like," Mel replied. "If it stays above fifteen, we should be fine. We can always put cloches over them."

"Cloches?"

"Little…" Mel held up her hand in a spider-like shape to indicate the see-through bell-shaped covers for plants. "Plastic things to keep the sunlight in but the cold out."

"All right."

"If the plants are small enough we can use coke bottles."

Ruby tapped away at her phone and then set it on the table with a flourish. "Bought. I've ordered it to arrive at uni in a couple of weeks."

"Fabulous."

They sipped at their tea. The murmuring of other customers was gentle and soothing, especially after their blustery, cold walk earlier. Mel felt her whole body sinking into the plastic chair and stretched her legs under the table, wiggling her foot around on her ankle. It was still a bit stiff, but it was getting there. Eight weeks in a cast had caused her ankle to seize up on occasion, but a short stretch and roll was all it took to loosen it.

She looked across at the woman that sat a few feet from her. She seemed calm as well. Even Barney was curled up at her feet, the hour walking and playing apparently enough for the small dog.

Ruby tucked her hair behind one ear and caught Mel's gaze. There was something in those eyes, a knowing look that indicated Ruby was aware she was being looked at. Mel didn't mind so much; she hoped Ruby knew she was something she enjoyed looking at.

Considering Ruby's earlier comment about Mel being attractive, Mel contemplated whether to return the favour. *I suppose it's only fair.*

She settled on: "Your hair looks lovely today." But immediately blanched and put a hand to her hot cheek.

Ruby chuckled and averted her gaze, her fingertip playing with the delicate handle of her teacup. "Thank you."

"You're welcome." *Is that clear enough? Do I need to say anything else to let her know that I think she's pretty?* "Uh…" Mel scratched the back of her neck. "…and your glasses really suit you."

"Smooth," Ruby said, pulling forth a chuckle from Mel. "I get the gist."

"Okay." Mel hung her head, but her heart soured. *Message received.* She stared into her tea for a while, hoping Ruby thought her inability to talk was endearing, rather than an element of her suspected stupidity.

# Chapter 12

The items arrived in good time and Mel and Ruby spent a sunny but fresh afternoon organising them all into the shed and greenhouse. It seemed to Ruby as if the clean and empty spaces had been taken over by a hundred-thousand pots—all of varying size, and huge bags of compost. The seeds were contained within a clipped plastic box to keep them dry, and Mel had set up several hooks for the children's gardening gloves and trowels.

Everything was ready. Ruby spent the occasional free period during the week alone, looking over her neatly organised allotment. It really had started to feel like hers; something that she had created.

Mel was part of that too and had started to become part of other things in Ruby's life as well. Their aquarium visit was drawing closer, and it wasn't simply the new rays that were making Ruby's stomach flutter and causing her face to break into a grin every time she thought about it.

On the first day of the gardening group, Ruby sat on the patio area bouncing her foot and tapping her fingertips on her coffee mug. When Mel poked her head out of the paramedic block door, Ruby felt her stuttering heart relax a bit. "Hiya," she called, a cleansing breath filling her lungs and calming her further.

"Hey. All ready?"

Ruby nodded and swept her gaze one last time over the small garden patch. When she looked back at Mel, she was settling herself into the plastic chair opposite.

"You're nervous."

"Thanks for pointing that out."

Mel lifted a hand and laid it carefully on Ruby's shoulder. Her thumb rubbed soothing circles onto her jacket. "It'll be fine. I'm here."

Ruby felt a shudder go through her, but once she locked her gaze with Mel's, her shoulders softened. "Thank you." She covered Mel's hand.

"Drink up. Kids aren't too careful when they're digging. I expect the risk of a piece of compost *accidentally* landing in your coffee will go up once the kids arrive."

Ruby finished her coffee. *It's not raining; everything is ready; Mel is here. Stop being a wimp.*

"And today is all to do with learning about plants. Very messy, but nothing they can really get wrong."

"Yep." Ruby exhaled with pursed lips.

"Kids like to get messy."

"Yeah, I just hope their teacher doesn't mind them getting covered in goodness-knows-what."

Mel laughed. "They're here to garden. If a teacher isn't intelligent enough to know they're going to get at least a bit dirty..." Mel left the sentence unfinished with a wave of her hand.

"Anyway," Ruby said, deciding to focus on something else for a while: a distraction from her nerves. "How are things? You've stopped limping, I see."

"Yep." Mel rubbed her leg. "It's not too bad. Still twinges sometimes."

"That's good. How's your dad? I've not actually seen you all week."

"True. And he's okay. Played some lovely tunes for the other residents while I was visiting the other day." Mel's face appeared touched by the sunshine of the memory. "Sometimes he does this thing where he messes up, then pretends it was deliberate. Like a comedy sketch."

Ruby chuckled. "Sounds a good giggle."

"Yeah, he's got a great sense of humour. He was a big fan of Morecambe and Wise. I remember sitting in with him on a Saturday night; he'd have a glass of bitter, my mum a sherry, and dad would pour a bit of his beer into my lemonade. It was mostly foam, but it made me feel like a grown up while we shared a bag of peanuts and watched Eric and Ernie ham it up."

"My dad loved the skit they did with Angela Rippon."

Mel laughed. "It was her legs, right?"

Ruby grinned. "Can't fault him, can you?"

"Not a bit."

They were quiet when the chuckles died down, until the sound of a large vehicle reversing in the car park made Ruby turn her head. Her pulse quickened again, and she sat up straight. She lifted her shaking hand towards Mel before she could stop herself.

Mel grasped her fingers with a reassuring expression before standing. "Come on, let's go meet them."

Around thirty children had arrived, all of them with a flicker of energy remaining from lunchtime play. A sea of little faces, all differently coloured and shaped, met Ruby and Mel as they strode—Mel purposefully, in contrast to her own reluctant strides—through the entrance. Ruby forced a wide smile onto her face, trying to mirror Mel's bouncy enthusiasm.

Mel leant back and allowed Ruby to introduce them, her arms folded loosely, her stance relaxed. Ruby took strength and comfort from Mel's confidence. Even without a touch from her, she felt warm and grounded.

The teacher, a Mrs Denzie, wore a beige coat and sported a designer handbag and a pinched expression, which Ruby associated with sucking lemons. She walked with an attitude that exuded boredom and confidence in equal measure.

Ruby strode up to the woman, who seemed around their age, and offered her a hand. "Hiya. I'm Ms Clark. Ruby. I'm not sure what the protocol is about what the children call me. I'm happy with Ruby, if you think it appropriate?"

Mrs Denzie shook her hand and perhaps squeezed a little too hard. She was obviously as enamoured by the prospect of gardening as Ruby had been at first. However, Ruby was now feeling quite excited at the prospect of growing things, teaching the kids, and—shockingly—having fun.

"Whatever you like," Mrs Denzie replied, indicating it was up to Ruby what she allowed the children to call her.

"Ruby it is, then."

"And I'm Mel Jackson." Mel held out her own hand, and as she did so, her sleeve rode up, displaying the three rubber charity bands she always wore. Ruby had asked her about them previously, and Mel had explained that one was for bullying, one for dementia, and one was a pride bracelet she'd purchased from the last parade she'd been to.

One of Mrs Denzie's eyebrows rose, and Ruby tracked her gaze down to the rainbow bangle on Mel's wrist. Discomfort tugged at Ruby's insides. Was Mrs Denzie homophobic? Did she even know what a rainbow bangle meant? Mel appeared oblivious.

They led the children through the grounds and into the allotment area. A few straggling university students were gathered on benches, but Ruby tried to ignore them. She recognised a few and hoped they'd keep their mouths closed and let her get on with the daunting job of organising the group.

"Welcome, everyone." Ruby's chest tightened as every pair of eyes stared at her. "I hope your journey was okay."

A pause while most of the children looked at her in confusion.

Ruby swallowed. "So, our aim here is to make some money for the Air Ambulance."

"What's that?" a dark-skinned boy asked.

Mel stepped forward. "Sometimes, when someone really hurts themselves and needs to be taken to a big hospital really quickly, it's better to take them in a helicopter." She grinned directly at the lad who had asked the question. "And the helicopter is run by a charity called the Air Ambulance Charity. They rely on donations from the public."

"So, like, in proper emergencies. When someone's been shot, or they've had their leg cut off?"

Most of the kids grimaced. Ruby tried to remain stoic but caught the sparkle of amusement in Mel's eyes.

"That's right. So, we're going to make some money at the end of the year to help them out. Sound good?"

Murmurs of agreement floated across the garden. Ruby relaxed—just a bit.

"Right, today we're going to work boys against girls," Ruby explained, the previously agreed-upon plan with Mel giving her confidence. "Boys on this side." She held her left hand out. "Girls on this side." Her right hand stuck out, and she waited for the jostling and fidgeting to die down as they sorted themselves out. "Excellent." She rubbed her hands together, a ripple of excitement running through her. "Now, you're all going to grab some gloves, and a trowel, and I want you to see how many earth worms you can find."

Most of the children appeared excited by the prospect, but one girl, blonde and pretty with pink wellies, stepped up to Ruby. "Don't they bite?" she asked, her nose wrinkled as she crossed her arms.

"Nope. They don't have teeth. And they only eat earth."

"That's why they're called earth worms, ninny," the dark-skinned boy told her.

Blondie rolled her eyes and huffed in a very adolescent way, despite her being five years away from being a teenager.

"Less of the name calling, lad," Ruby replied kindly. "What's your name?"

"Michael," he replied grinning, obviously pleased he wasn't being told off by the adult for his rudeness. "That's Chelsea."

"We could do with name badges, what d'you think, Ruby?" Mel was touching her chin in an over-exaggerated thoughtful way.

Ruby remembered Mel's suggestion that she act as if everything was exciting. "That's a great idea, Mel."

"Including Mrs Denzie?" Michael asked carefully and a little worriedly.

"Of course." Ruby looked around the group. "And, as there are more girls than boys, maybe she can help the lads out?"

The boys all cheered, which made Ruby laugh with relief, although Mrs Denzie seemed less than thrilled with the idea of wearing a name badge... or maybe it was the thought of collecting earth worms. Ruby sniggered—inwardly.

Ruby asked Mel to go to her office and grab some labels, and on her return, they all made their own name badges and stuck them to their coats. Ruby was awed by the array of names. *What a mixture. I'd never have seen such a collection when I was at school. Everyone was called David or Ann; Ruby was about the most unique name there was.*

Thirty trowels and sixty gloves were handed out. Ruby was pleased to see some of the boys taking the more 'girly' gloves, and some of the girls taking some gloves with fewer pink flowers on them. *I wish my childhood had been so free of gender stereotypes.* She thought back to her mother, who had insisted she wore pretty dresses, played with dolls, and the little wooden kitchen her grandfather had fashioned for her.

Mrs Denzie approached a boy with 'Frank' on his badge. "Perhaps a blue pair?" Lines appeared either side of her nose.

Ruby smiled. "You can have whatever gloves you like," she reassured him.

Frank considered his flowery gloves, his eyebrows furrowed. "My mum has some like these. I like these." His hopeful expression faltered as he looked at Mrs Denzie.

"Try the blue ones." Her tone was soft, but the look in her eyes made Ruby think of a rhinoceros about to charge.

Frank looked from Ruby to Mrs Denzie, confusion coming off him in waves. "I…"

"Remember what I said last week? When you grazed your knee?"

Pink tinged his chubby cheeks. "That I should be a man." He looked at his wellies.

"That's right." Mrs Denzie clasped her hands. "And would flowery gloves make you look like a man?"

He toed the ground, let out a huge sigh, and then shook his head.

"Okay, then."

Frank took the blue gloves she offered and slunk away.

Mrs Denzie looked very pleased with herself. The pinching around her lips had subsided.

*Spoke too soon. It seems as if some people still think gender roles are non-negotiable.*

The boys started work on the patch in front of the greenhouse, and the girls began in the one next to it. They knelt side by side on the grassy paths bisecting the earthy rectangles and chatted as they searched for earth worms, everyone now apparently happy that worms did not bite.

Michael held up a particularly large worm, and everyone cheered his worm-catching prowess. Mel led the applause, and Michael beamed at her, obviously pleased as punch that he was being rewarded.

As the afternoon went on, Ruby watched Mel interact with the children. She was so complimentary and so relaxed, and Ruby shivered with delight at the look of pleasure on Mel's face. Her eyes shone with affection and excitement each time a child found a worm. It didn't seem fake or forced, either. Mel genuinely appeared to be having a fabulous time.

When Mel looked up at her and caught her eye, a smear of mud on her cheek, Ruby could do nothing but smile back at her. She resisted the urge to go over and rub the mud from her face; that would be inappropriate. The kids were here to learn and have fun, not watch her flirt with her co-facilitator. *My friend. No need to flirt, even when they're not here.*

She'd been busy getting the garden ready for the kids and hadn't had time to check the university policies. She was still unsure about teacher-student relationships and the rules surrounding them. She didn't want to do anything that would cause a problem for them, or, goodness forbid, get her fired. Mel didn't deserve the drama, especially as she was being so kind as to help her with the group.

*Friends is good. I shouldn't complain.* After another glance over at Mel, she settled back into the group, kneeling beside Michael, who had found another huge worm and was wiggling it about in Frank's face.

Frank was laughing but very obviously uncomfortably at either the attention from the assertive Michael, or the fact that there was a squirming, dirty worm a centimetre from his nose. Ruby tapped

Michael's hand and kept her eyes gentle while sending him a look she hoped would resolve the situation.

Michael grinned and dropped his hand, nodding placidly at Ruby. Ruby took a chance and gave him a thumbs up. Both boys grinned and continued with their worm-hunting pursuits. *They're not so scary after all. And not one of them has a snotty nose.*

Mrs Denzie had donned a pair of her own gardening gloves; a Cath Kidson pair, if Ruby wasn't mistaken. An expensive, designer brand that most people refused to use for fear of dirtying them. She wore smart wellies, also of an expensive brand, and picked at the earth as if *it* might bite her, let alone the worms. She didn't even touch the trowel one of the boys offered to share with her. Her face remained drawn, pinched… citric, sculpted.

Once all the worms had been found, at least according to the children, Ruby stood up and winced as her knees cracked. "You've all done so well, guys. Give each other a pat on the back."

This, inevitably, turned out to be a terrible idea. Every child, still wearing mud-sodden gloves, and not caring about the dirt, slapped each other's backs and shoulders as the celebration turned into a mini-slapping war. Squeals of laughter from the girl's side only emphasised the issue. Mrs Denzie's mouth nearly disappeared into a small point in the middle of her face.

Ruby ignored her while trying to hide her amusement. "Okay, let's settle down so we can go on to our next task." She gave them time to turn back to her and begin paying attention again. "Thank you. Now, I'm going to split you up into four teams. They'll all be named after a fruit or vegetable, something we're going to grow in the garden."

A tremor of excitement went through the group at the mention of their planned activities, and Ruby was surprised.

"I'm just going to have a word with your teacher, so if you could do me a favour and make sure the earth is flat on the places you've been working, that'd be great."

The kids all bent down again and started pattering their trowels into the soil in front of them.

Ruby held a hand out and led Mrs Denzie over to one side, away from ear shot of the kids. Mel joined them. "Now, I just wanted to make sure that if I put the kids into groups there won't be any disagreements."

"What on earth do you mean?" Mrs Denzie asked, her tone disgusted.

Ruby blinked, unused to other adults treating her in such a way. *Especially another teacher—where's the professionalism? What is her problem?* "Um... so do all the kids get on? There've been no big squabbles recently?"

"We plan on mixing them up a bit," Mel interjected. "Make sure they learn to communicate with those who aren't their friends." She put a hand against Ruby's shoulder blades and rubbed.

A shiver ran through Ruby at the touch, and she couldn't help but smile affectionately at her friend. Mel returned the smile.

"I'm sure *my* class will behave impeccably, whatever groups you put them in."

"Are you sure?" Ruby asked.

"Completely."

"Good." Ruby stepped away and felt the loss of Mel's hand on her back. She tried to ignore it. *She's just being supportive. No need to go all drooling teenager over her.* Mel still had the smear of mud on her face. *Oh blimey. Okay, focus on the task at hand.*

Ruby gave each child the name of either tomato, pepper, potato, or onion. Then she asked them to stand in the groups they had been given. She made sure there was a good mix of gender, race, and confidence in each group, just as she and Mel had discussed in previous weeks. "The name of your group is the name of the thing you will be growing. How does that sound?"

All the kids cheered, and their enthusiasm affected her deeply. She couldn't help cheering with them. *What is going on with me? Why am I enjoying this so much?*

"Potatoes and Onions, you get to have a little break for a minute while Tomatoes and Peppers will be setting up pots ready for next week. I hope you have your pot-filling skills at the ready?"

## The Words Shimmer

As per their pre-agreed plan, Mel took the Peppers and Ruby took the Tomatoes. The Potato and Onion groups sat on the grass across the area, and Mrs Denzie handed out the squash and biscuits that Ruby had provided for them. Each child filled two pots full of compost, which made thirty pots all together. Michael—a tomato—intently pressed down his compost, then attempted to juggle with the pots. Mel instructed him to clear up the mess through tears of laughter at his forlorn expression. *He's one to keep an eye on, but not in a negative way.* Mel watched him with interest as he sensibly swept the compost back into the pots with the blade of his hand.

Chelsea—a pepper—concentrated so hard on filling her pots that she ended up with the neatest two out of the whole class. Mel shook her hand seriously and rained praise on the blonde girl. Obviously unused to such achievement, Chelsea's grin appeared permanently fixed on her face for the rest of the afternoon.

Each child carried their pots into the greenhouse and labelled them with their name. Then the groups swapped over, and Tomato and Pepper groups sat on the grass, enjoying a drink and a snack.

"Who knows where potatoes come from?" Ruby asked. Mel marvelled at how her brown hair took on golden tones in the sun.

A small girl, whose badge said Lauren, wiggled as she raised her hand. "Asda."

Everyone chuckled, and Mel wasn't sure whether Lauren was joking or serious.

"That's right. But what about before that? Where do they grow?"

Frank put up one chubby hand. "In the ground."

"Good, Frank. Yes, they do. And does anyone know which bit of the potato plant we eat?" A sea of confused faces made Ruby smile. "We actually eat the root."

"Isn't that the bottom bit?" a girl with black sleek hair and a severely cut fringe piped up. Her name badge read: *Becca*.

"It is the bottom bit, clever girl." Ruby winced, perhaps at the phrase she'd used, but then seemed to realise these were not young adults they were teaching. It was okay to use the term "good girl" or "good boy" when praising them. "The root of a plant lives beneath the soil and pulls up water and nutrients for the plant to feed it. Who knows what else plants need to make energy?"

A chorus of "Sunlight!" rang through the garden.

"Very good. You guys really know your stuff."

Mel stepped forwards. "So, what about onions? Where do they grow?"

"In a tree?" Frank asked.

"Good try, but not quite." Mel nodded kindly at him.

Frank deflated in disappointment, but she made a point of continuing to smile at him and he relented, looking back at her with shy eyes.

"They grow underground too, like the potatoes. Their roots dangle from the bottom, like a little beard."

The group giggled, and Mel waited until they calmed to continue.

"The leaves grow out of the top of the onion. Has anyone got daffodils in their garden at home?"

Becca piped up. "We have loads. Mum always puts about a… a hundred in every year."

"And what do they grow from, Becca?"

"From bulbs. She gets them from the garden centre."

Mel turned back to the group. "The bulbs that daffodils grow from are very similar to onions. But please don't eat daffodil bulbs; they don't taste very nice."

"Neither do onions," Becca said as she screwed up her face. A titter ran through the group.

"So, we're going to plant the onions and potatoes in this bed just here." Mel indicated the bed the girls had been searching through for earthworms. "And we'll do that next week. But first, we need to add some nutrients to the soil. Who's up for that?"

A consensus of cheers ran through the group. Mel and Ruby exchanged a grin.

Mel stepped back, and Ruby explained how to take a handful of feed and scatter it over the bed. The children each took a handful and, with a whole host of different techniques and dramatic flares, deposited it onto the soil. Then they took their little trowels and dug in the feed.

"Make sure it's all mixed in, like you would when you make a cake."

After their jobs were done, the kids hung up their gloves and trowels and went to the outside tap to wash their hands. Mel ran her hands under the tap too and watched the bubbles from the handwash they were required to use—infection-control regulations—disappear down the drain.

Before she could push her sleeves back down, Chelsea came up to her and fingered the rubber bands around her wrist. The kids were clean and gathered all around her, biscuits in their little hands—a reward for their hard work. "What's this, Miss?" Chelsea asked.

"You don't have to call me 'Miss', I'm not a teacher. My name's Mel." Mel tapped the name badge that was half hanging off her coat and looking a little worse for wear.

"Okay. Mel. What's that?"

"It's a charity band."

Chelsea's little fingers were poking at the rainbow band. "What does it mean?"

Mel smiled at her before taking it off and holding it out so she could look at it more closely. "It's a Gay Pride band. It shows my support for Gay Pride."

Chelsea's face coloured, and she looked over at Mrs Denzie, who appeared to be listening, her mouth pinched into a small hole again. Chelsea snapped her mouth closed and looked at her feet.

"It's okay if you want to ask questions," Mel encouraged. *These kids need to feel comfortable with me, with every bit of me.*

Mel heard Ruby gathering a few discarded pots into the greenhouse behind her. Then footsteps as she approached the group.

"So... are you gay, then?" Chelsea asked, one finger in her mouth as she chewed on the side of it.

"I am, yes," Mel stated, but forced her expression to remain casual and pleasant.

"That's cool," Michael said, which caused the rest of the group to laugh, hesitantly.

"Why is it cool?" Mel asked, intrigued.

Ruby shifted about on the concrete, looking over at the path towards the university door. *Is she uncomfortable with this? Does she think I'm going to out her?*

"My uncle's gay. And his flat's well wicked." Michael grinned and displayed a gap in his front teeth where he was waiting for one to grow. "His boyfriend's well cool too. He's an Olympic runner."

"Is he?" Mel asked, chuckling.

"No, he isn't," another boy said. "He works in a bank."

"Yeah well," Michael countered, his brow furrowed in defence. "He might be… in a few months. Uncle Gary says he's well on the way."

"He does sound cool," Mel said. "But it just sounds like he's cool because of who he is, rather than because he's gay. What d'you think?"

"Yeah, I suppose so." Michael seemed happier with this explanation.

"Does anyone else have any more questions?" Mel asked.

Mrs Denzie bustled over and elbowed her way past her children, who parted the way for her, their expressions uncomfortable again. "I think it's time to go. The bus will be waiting."

Mel inwardly rolled her eyes. "It's been such a nice day, guys," she said, pushing a happy expression onto her face despite her annoyance at the teacher's interruption.

"What a lot we've got done." Ruby seemed to have gathered herself and was smiling again.

Mel lifted a hand to squeeze her shoulder but dropped it when Ruby stepped away, out of reach.

The kids all gathered their stuff together and waited by the picnic benches. Mrs Denzie strode over to Mel and Ruby, who had begun tidying the big bags of compost into the shed. She lowered her head and her voice, so that the children couldn't hear her words. "The children are here to learn about plants and growing vegetables. Not about the gay lifestyle. They're far too young for that sort of thing. If you could keep your relationship out of this situation, that would be grand." Her tone was bitter.

Mel stepped back and blinked. "Oh. Well, I don't think we did anything—"

"I think the way you were... touching. And... everything. My class does not need to see that." Mrs Denzie's mouth completely disappeared, until she opened it again to speak. "And inviting the children to ask questions about you... about your sexuality. That is absolutely unacceptable."

Ruby stood next to Mel, seemingly struck dumb by Mrs Denzie's tirade.

"If kids ask me about myself, especially if they ask whether I'm gay, I'm not going to lie. Kids are curious, and the more we're honest and open with them, the less they'll grow up worried about their own sexuality." Mel wanted to reach out and touch Ruby, to let her know it was okay, and that she'd had this discussion before. *I've had this discussion a few times, actually. There are a lot of kids in my neighbourhood, and they don't shy away from talking to me.* "Surely we're on the same page here?" *I can't imagine anyone who wouldn't want a loving world that isn't full of bigots and hateful people.*

"We shall have to agree to disagree," Mrs Denzie replied. "But I do not wish to see you mauling one another in front of the children again, do you hear me?"

Mel sighed. "Fine. Not that it's any of your business, Mrs Denzie, but we're just friends. Ruby isn't my girlfriend. Just a friend." She looked to Ruby for clarification.

"That's right," seemed to be all Ruby could manage.

"I saw you," Mrs Denzie said, her eyes narrowing further. "You were touching her."

"I touch my friends from time to time. It's a way of offering support and comfort. Surely you have friends and touch them from time to time?"

"Hm." She continued to scrutinise Mel until she was apparently satisfied, if not ecstatic, with the conclusion of the issue. "Then perhaps you'd be so kind as to keep your opinions and rhetoric to yourself in the future to avoid confusion. Children are impressionable, and I have a responsibility for them and their morality." With that, she spun on her heel and led the class out of the garden area and into the university building.

Mel was staring after her, her mouth open in shock. It wasn't Mel's first encounter with homophobia, nor would it be the last. But it never failed to shock her that someone who was supposed to be educated, who was in charge of helping to shape the minds of the future, could display such short-sighted bigotry. Never. She turned towards Ruby, ready to make sure she was okay, and then bitch and moan about the old bag. But Ruby wasn't looking at her.

She was breathing quickly and grasping her head in her hands. Muttering to herself, she went into the shed and closed the door behind her.

Left alone in the garden, Mel stood awkwardly and decided to allow Ruby some space. She assumed Ruby was feeling vulnerable and needed time to process. Noting the similarities between the way Ruby and her own father used the shed—when she was a child, he would disappear into it when things got a bit much—Mel cleared away the remaining compost bags and took a brush to sweep the grass free from discarded debris.

Once the area was clean and there was nothing more she could occupy herself with, Mel stepped up to the shed and knocked on the door. When no answer emerged, she knocked again. "Ruby, let me in?"

A soft and resigned voice filtered through the wood: "Okay."

Mel pulled the door open and clumped her boots onto the wooden base as she closed the door behind her.

Ruby leant against the shelf by the small window, the light from outside reflecting off her glasses. Tears had gathered in her eyes behind them but hadn't yet fallen.

Stepping up carefully to her, Mel reached out to place a hand on her shoulder. "Hey, don't be upset."

"Why did you have to go and come out to a load of Year 4s? Couldn't you have kept your blooming mouth shut?" Ruby's voice was thin and hitched with sobs.

Mel bit her lip and shook her head. "No. I don't do that unless I'm at work." She sighed. "Actually, even if I'm at work, I talk openly about it, so long as it's not going to cause more trouble than it's worth."

"Why?" Ruby sounded as if she'd never heard anything so terrible.

"I realised I was gay at a time when it was considered dirty and dangerous. The eighties weren't exactly kind to gay people, in general. I'm sure you remember."

"I do," Ruby said, snuffling. She moved a step closer on the wooden floor and touched Mel's elbow.

"I had friends that hid. And so did I for a while. But once it became more acceptable, and Section Twenty-Eight was repealed in 2003, I made a promise to myself to never hide who I am. From anyone."

Ruby just nodded, using her free hand to wipe her eyes underneath her glasses.

"It's never gone wrong. I always explain myself openly if people have an issue with it, and I've never had any serious problems. People tend to be pretty understanding about it."

"What if they're not though? And you get assaulted or something?"

"Happy to take that risk, believe it or not." Mel took a chance and shifted her feet so she could slide her arm around Ruby's shoulders.

Ruby rested her forehead against Mel's neck, and Mel pulled her in for a warm hug with both arms. Ruby's hands came to settle against Mel's back.

"If people choose to react like that to my gay-ness..." Mel paused at Ruby's snort into her coat. "Then that's their problem."

Snuffling, Ruby pulled back and wiped at her eyes again. "I'm sorry. Blimey, look at me. I don't cry, usually, I promise."

"It's okay," Mel said gently, stroking the back of her fingers over Ruby's cheek once before dropping her hand. "I suppose it must be difficult to deal with if you're not used to being out."

"I'm just a very private person." Ruby turned to look out of the window, her sobs finished and her face relaxing. "I do worry about what she said though—Mrs Denzie—about it being inappropriate."

"She was seeing things that weren't there."

"Was she?"

"Wasn't she?"

"I suppose it's not exactly something we've properly talked about."

"Apart from the fact that we both admitted we find each other attractive." Mel grinned, and when Ruby turned back to her, she winked. She was pleased at the smile she got in return.

"True." Ruby seemed to gather herself. "She said it was inappropriate."

"Do you believe that?"

"It's not really what I believe that's important." Ruby looked at her wellies and scuffed one on the scratchy floor. "I need to look into it."

"Look into what?"

"The whole... teacher-student relationship... The policy."

"There's a policy about whether I'm allowed to find you attractive?" Mel tried to make the mood light, but something stone-like was settling into her stomach. *Does she really think that being in a romantic relationship in front of the kids is inappropriate?*

"I need to check." Ruby nodded once, and then glanced up at Mel. "Give me a few days to figure it out?"

"Of course." Mel blinked. She tried to work out from Ruby's expression what she meant, but couldn't. *I suppose she knows what she's talking about. I'm sure she'll tell me once she knows where we stand.*

"Thank you." Ruby rubbed Mel's arm, and Mel looked down at her hand, the short and pretty nails, and the silver ring that rested on her middle finger.

"It's fine."

"I think I'm ready to go outside now." Ruby's blush was visible even in the dim light of the shed.

"Oh, I don't know, I rather like it in here." Mel looked around at the collection of tools and various bags of things they were keeping in the shed.

Ruby smacked her lightly on the arm. "This really is inappropriate. Utilising university property to engage in light flirtation."

Mel raised her hands in the air. "Who said I was flirting?"

Ruby just smiled at her and pushed the shed door open. Sunlight streamed in, and Mel followed her out of the wooden construction, chuckling.

# Chapter 13

Tapping away at her computer, Ruby groaned out loud. She had found the policy she had been looking for and had read it. And re-read it. Phrases like *educational development and wellbeing, professional integrity,* and *inequality of power* screamed out at her from the screen. She rubbed her palms against her trouser legs hurriedly and sat ramrod straight. *It's wrong. It doesn't feel wrong, but it says it here in black and white.*

The consensus appeared to be that relationships between students and staff were inappropriate, as Ruby had first suspected. She skimmed the remainder of the policy, her heart thudding and her head aching, as if she had been kicked. *I'm a teacher; she's a student. Our relationship needs to be purely professional.*

Tears stung her eyes, surprising her. She wiped at them and shook her head slowly as the words on the screen blurred. She closed the window and leant her head on her hand, her fingers gripping the hair at her temple as it hung down and formed a curtain around her face. She used it to hide from the world... just for a heartbeat or two. She had a class in ten minutes anyway.

Footsteps into her office alerted her to Alexander's presence. She heard him stand still somewhere, probably unsure what to do when confronted with a distraught superior, so she pushed her hair back and offered him a small nod of acknowledgement. She took off her glasses and wiped her eyes again, then spent a few seconds cleaning her lenses before pushing them back onto her nose. Sighing, she pulled a more cheerful expression onto her face.

"Afternoon," she said, patting down her hair and tucking it behind her ears.

"Afternoon, Ruby," he replied in his straightforward way.

Regarding him from across the room, Ruby took in his kind face, pale skin, and blue eyes. He was, as usual, wearing a business suit to work, and she wondered curiously what he wore at home. Somehow, she couldn't imagine him in jeans or jogging bottoms. *Perhaps he just takes off his jacket and rolls up his sleeves.*

"I have a question for you," Ruby said, reaching over her desk to turn off her computer screen.

"Professional or personal?" He always made sure he knew the context of a conversation before he engaged in responding. She admired that—he always wanted to be so prepared.

"A bit of both, actually." Her foot tapped the footrest she used under her desk, and she forced her knee to stop bouncing. "Have you ever known anyone to engage in a personal relationship with a student?" She paused, then realised her mistake at his confused look. "A member of staff, I mean."

"A member of staff and a student?" he repeated. "Yes. Two couples spring to mind."

"Do they?" She knew that he knew this was a prompt for him to continue.

"One five years ago, and one about… eight." He touched his chin and moved towards his own desk.

"What happened?"

"No names, of course."

She nodded.

"One was a female member of staff, from the pastoral services, I believe, who met privately for a drink with a male student. He was going to her because he was being bullied. It appears as though they met a few times, for drinks, or coffee, in very much a personal capacity. Someone saw them together and reported it to the dean."

"What happened?"

"She was fired. He was transferred, I think." His eyebrows turned downwards, little lines appearing between them. "The other instance was a little longer ago. I believe it was a similar situation; however, the genders were reversed."

Lead gathered inside Ruby. She blinked and looked down at her knees. Scratching methodically at her trouser leg, she pulled her bottom lip into her mouth.

"Is there a reason why you are asking?"

Ruby looked back up at him and then leant tiredly against the back of her chair, closing her eyes.

He shuffled towards her, and his hand smoothed against her shoulder. Unused to him, or anyone, touching her in so intimate a manner, her eyes popped open.

The concern in his eyes was plain, and it took away some of the lead in her belly. "Mel and I... I was researching into... Because my girls *helpfully* reminded me that she's a student and I'm a teacher. Like it's some kind of blue movie or..." She huffed and turned her head to press her cheek against the back of his hand.

He removed it. "I don't understand the concept of blue movies. However, if you're dating a student, I'm afraid it's against university policy."

"As I feared." She groaned and then shrugged. "I suppose even being friends with a student is inappropriate."

"Not strictly. The university understands that it is not a police state, and that it cannot dictate who you meet socially." A smile tugged the sides of his mouth. "Just who you sleep with."

"Oh. So friends is fine?"

"I believe so. But you really should read the policy."

Ruby nodded once and pushed herself out from under her desk. "I have a class."

"Third-year anatomy, I know."

"You are good to me," Ruby sighed, sending him a soft look.

He returned to his desk, straightened his tie, and gave her a one-handed wave.

---

The aquarium was almost completely empty. One or two young mothers with small children hung around any particularly colourful or energetic tanks, gazes mostly fixed on their phones as their children pressed their little noses up against the glass, anxious to see as many fish as possible; or perhaps to give themselves a permanent squint from the curved surface of the glass.

The smeared tanks made Ruby wrinkle her nose; Mel simply chuckled. Ruby's continued reluctance to go anywhere near a child remained, despite their first, mostly successful, gardening group. Mel watched her face crinkle as another small, snotty child wiped its face all over a starfish tank, and she pressed her hand to her mouth to catch the laugh that bubbled up.

"You're not going to catch anything," Mel said, her hand moving to the small of Ruby's back—right where she remembered Ruby's hand had strayed when she had helped her on her very first day. "Look. All clean." Mel rubbed the glass with the sleeve of her hoodie, and Ruby's face crumpled even more.

"Disgusting. Who knows how many germs these kids have deposited on the tanks? You know…" she leant sideways towards Mel and dropped her voice to a hiss, "… I believe this is how Ebola started."

"Could be," Mel said mock-seriously.

Ruby seemed to notice Mel's hand at her back and smiled before stepping away.

Mel blinked, and her heart fell. *Am I reading this wrong? She hasn't stopped finding me attractive, surely?* Then she remembered she was supposed to be giving Ruby time to… do something. Find something out? She never had really got to the bottom of that. She still didn't understand.

But she pushed the thoughts away. They were here as friends, and that was okay. It wasn't exactly the most romantic of venues anyway—an aquarium made of mostly hardboard and filled with huge tanks containing various sea creatures. Having said that, it was well lit, and the water made the light flicker back and forth over the walls, giving the whole place an ethereal feel.

The light played over Ruby's hair as well, and her pretty skin. Mel thought she looked a bit like a mermaid, with her long wavy dark hair, her curvy hips, and interest in the creatures.

An energy took Ruby over as they rounded the corner, and she balled her fists, trotting further into the huge room they had just entered. The walls curled up from waist height into a domed ceiling made of glass, and various larger sea monsters flew above their heads like large dragons in some fantasy film. The room was circular, with an entrance and an exit at opposite sides. Soft, smooth music played over the speakers, and the room itself was not lit. The only light came from the massive tank above their heads.

Blue, green, and white lights danced across the floor as the sharks, rays, and larger fish swam about above them. Cushioned stools created a large block in the middle of the room—the size of a king-sized bed.

A mother entered with her children, but one of them started to cry at the big scary fish, so they moved on. Mel could see no one behind them, so she lowered her backside onto the edge of the stool platform and then lay backwards, her feet on the floor.

After a few moments of what Mel assumed were consideration, she felt Ruby settle beside her. One arm stuck straight up into the air, her finger pointing upwards. "The sixgill stingray. That's the one I was telling you about."

A long-nosed ray, around the size of those Mel had seen before in aquariums, skittered across the surface of the tank and then dived down. It had a short tail and pink wings and looked more spaceship-like than its grey cousins.

"Tell me about the sixgill stingray," Mel requested, watching the ray flutter its wings and speed through the water, dodging sharks.

"It's only been found recently—well, classified at any rate. They thought there were a few different species of sixgill until they realised that individual differences made them look different when actually they're the same." Ruby dropped her hand, and her fingers touched Mel's.

Mel trailed one fingertip against Ruby's before Ruby pulled away. Pulling her hands onto her belly, Mel laced her fingers together and continued to watch the ray dancing around.

"Its nose is full of a gel material, and if you take it out of the water, or catch it, its nose shrinks."

"Sort of like a backwards Pinocchio."

A chuckle vibrated through their makeshift bed. "A bit, yes. And as you've probably guessed, they have six pairs of gills rather than five."

Ruby stopped talking as the ray spun upside down and glided close to them, its small eyes visible through the glass. Mel wondered whether it could see them and was checking them out, these strange animals that were lying on their backs and scrutinising the ray so devotedly.

"If you look closely... Oh hello, gorgeous."

Mel turned her head to the side on the stools to look at the woman next to her, but apparently Ruby was addressing the ray, whom she was clearly very enamoured with. Instead of feeling disappointed, Mel chose to watch the fascination on Ruby's face. She felt tingles shoot through her when Ruby beamed at the ray, giving it the same expression most people would give a new-born baby.

"Sorry. He's just so beautiful."

Mel chuckled and shifted her shoulders into the hard surface beneath her. "I do see the appeal. What am I looking closely at?"

"Oh. His tail." Ruby's finger pointed again. "See, at the tip, it has a leaf-shaped bit? That's his caudal fin. Isn't it lovely?"

"Very." Mel wasn't sure if she was talking about the ray or her own experience of being taught about it. She continued to watch Ruby's face as she watched the fish. *She almost looks blissed out, like she could fall asleep.* Warmth flooded her. *And she is so beautiful. I could look at her for hours.*

Shaking herself and sitting up with a grunt, Mel stretched her arms forward, chuckling at the cracks of both shoulder joints. She turned to watch Ruby for a minute or so, then stood and strolled slowly around the tank, giving the remaining fish her attention.

An information board mounted on a plinth stood at one end. Mel eyed it warily. She walked up to it, dragging her feet a bit. *I can at least find out if anything has a name.* She peered at the board, but the words jumped around even more in the flickering light from the water above them. She backed away and stuffed her hands into her hoodie pockets, turning her gaze back towards the tank.

She was relieved when Ruby stood, swinging her arms and pushing up her shoulders, the widest and most sparkly expression on her face. Mel returned the smile and followed Ruby out of the tank and into another room.

A few rooms later, they found one with a central tank containing piranha. Mel approached it with caution and sent Ruby a piercing look when she laughed at her.

"They're harmless, really. Unless you're dead or actively bleeding."

"Are they scavengers, then?" Mel asked, peering into the large tank at the dangerous-looking fish staring back at her.

"Pretty much. That film, it wasn't true to life."

"They look lazy." The fish swam around with barely a hint of motivation.

The other tanks in the room were full of equally lazy but exceptionally beautiful creatures, including bright red starfish, blue crustaceans, and delicate seahorses, one of which Mel was convinced had babies in its belly.

"I do wish my ex had carried at least one of the girls, just so it was fair."

Mel chuckled and considered Ruby, with her shorter stature, and hips currently hugged by a pair of dark blue jeans. "Were you huge with either of them?"

"Jasmine. Ugh." Ruby wiped her hands down her face before rolling her eyes. "I was a whale. Absolutely humungous."

Mel studied her before forcing her gaze from Ruby's body to rest on the floor by her feet. "I can imagine you pregnant."

"Oh great, thanks for that."

"No," Mel said immediately, holding out a hand. "No. That's not what I meant I just..." She looked around at anything but the woman giving her such a flustered stare. "I think it's beautiful."

"Really?"

When Mel looked back up at her, Ruby was shooting her an intrigued look. "Don't ask me why," Mel laughed, her hand to her cheek. "I just think it's... terribly marvellous."

Ruby pressed her lips together and then grinned at her. "Where on earth were you when I was pregnant, hmm? To boost my self-image."

"Probably working as a teaching assistant somewhere."

"Ah," Ruby said, her lips parting and her teeth showing. "I knew you had experience."

It was Mel's turn to blush. "Only a year or two. I didn't much like having to book holidays when the kids were off."

"Makes sense. Did you enjoy the work though?"

"Very much." Mel's gaze fell on another cluster of stools under a medium-sized tank full of seahorses. She moved to it and sat, patting the stool next to her. Ruby joined her. From that location, they could see most of the room and take in all the bright colours and flickering lights.

"Shame you gave it up; I bet you were wonderful at it."

"Well," Mel said, scissoring her fingers together and wishing she could do the same with Ruby, "I wanted to work in healthcare."

"Have you always been a paramedic?"

"I've only been qualified seven years. I was an ECA before that."

"An emergency care assistant? You must have seen some awful things in both roles." Ruby's voice was gentle, and her thigh was warm against Mel's. Mel wanted to put her arm around her, but Ruby's body language and subtle behaviour so far during their visit to the aquarium had indicated she didn't want that. The feeling rose up briefly in Mel's body—something between affection and lust—but she pushed it away.

"Some wonderful things too. New babies tend to make an appearance whenever I'm on shift, and I've seen a few heroic saves by members of the public. A teenager once dived into the river after his nan and saved her life when she fell from the bike path."

"Oh blimey. Were they both okay?"

"After we got them warmed up, yes. She had a gash on her face from something in the river, but otherwise, cold, wet, and relieved."

"Amazing." Ruby looked up at Mel through shuttered eyes, and Mel noticed for the first time how dark and long her eyelashes were. "Have you ever done anything like that?"

"Not... not really."

"So you're not gung-ho and macho?" Ruby seemed almost disappointed.

Mel lifted an eyebrow in suspicion. "I thought you didn't like that?" *Is she flirting with me?*

"Not usually. But the thought of you—"

A child squealed as he entered the room they were occupying, and his mother followed, with an equally noisy toddler in a pushchair.

Mel snorted and stood quickly, and Ruby seemed amused as well. They allowed the little family to enjoy the room and headed towards the café, which was, thankfully, deserted.

The day was rainy and dismal, and the usual influx of children wanting ice creams was missing; they were probably cuddled up in their car seats, or already at home having a nap in their warm beds. Mel took the seat opposite Ruby as she laid the tray on the table between them, pushing a china cup on a saucer and a pot of tea towards her.

Mel took a sip from her coffee before resting her elbows on the table and considering the woman across from her. "So, you've always been a nurse?"

"Yes, since I was twenty-two. Obviously with short hiatuses to have and look after the brats at home."

"Were your parents in healthcare?"

"No, my parents were both teachers. Dad taught maths, and Mum taught art."

"Siblings?"

"I have a sister, but we don't really speak. She lives up in Huddersfield near my mother."

"Dad?"

"Died when I was thirty-five. Bowel cancer."

"Sorry." Mel slid her hand across the table but stopped just short of touching Ruby's fingers.

"That's okay. He went quickly and with little effort really. He had a good care package. I made sure of that."

"Does your mum still work?"

"No, she's retired. Just after Dad died." Ruby poured and stirred her tea. The tinkling of her spoon against the china sounded comforting. "How's work?"

"Yeah. Okay." Sadness trickled into her at the memory of a patient from the previous day. "We attended a woman in the final stages of cancer yesterday."

"Oh." Ruby's voice was gentle, and it made Mel look up.

"She had no one. All her kids were overseas; husband had died a few years ago. She was coping okay, with carers in and that, but she still looked so lonely in that little flat."

"Wouldn't she have been better in a care home?"

Mel shrugged, tears starting to burn her eyes. "She had an infection but she was doing okay. Just dying."

"That must've been very sad to see."

Ruby covered her hand and her soft brown gaze held Mel's gently. Mel found sympathy, and affection, but no pity. She was glad of that. She didn't need pity from anyone, let alone Ruby.

As quickly as she'd touched her, Ruby pulled away. Mel felt the loss of the warmth of her skin like an icy wind. The hairs on the back of her hand stood up, despite the heat from her coffee mug. She pressed her lips together and looked down into its depths again.

"Antibiotics for the infection?" Ruby asked.

"Yes. Had to get an out-of-hours appointment with a GP. We don't prescribe antibiotics as paramedics. She should be feeling better soon."

"Good. It's a shame you don't get to follow-up on patients, isn't it? And you're right: if someone doesn't need a care home… Not all of them are lovely."

"I know," Mel replied, trying to rid herself of sadness. "The number of homes I've been to with my job—"

"Oh, of course you would have."

"I've been in some dives, I'll tell you. Luckily the one Dad's in is lovely. They have an activity co-ordinator that organises things for them to do every day. Dad's in charge of musical entertainment."

"Does he have a preference for the type of music he plays?" Ruby asked.

Mel's smile grew. "This week he's not felt up to playing much. But last week he was having a crack at some music-hall songs."

"Knees Up Mother Brown?" Ruby asked, a chuckle in her voice.

"Things like that."

"Fabulous. I'd love to hear him play."

Visions of Mel arriving to visit her dad with Ruby in tow, of introducing them as friends, of George eyeing them with that knowing look, swam in front of her like the ray they had watched earlier. He would know Mel was attracted to Ruby. She stared hard into her coffee and swirled it around with her spoon. A few bubbles formed and then popped on the surface.

When she looked up again, Ruby was looking at her wristwatch. "It's nearly four-thirty. We should head off if we're going to miss the rush-hour traffic."

## Chapter 14

At the second gardening group, Ruby taught the children how to sow seeds and plant baby potatoes and onion sets.

"This is the best, I think!" Frank held up a potato the size of a tennis ball. His gaze then fell to another, further away. "Oh! No!" His second choice was bigger.

"Okay." Ruby pointed into the trench they had created. "Pop it in then, and tuck it in like a baby."

Frank giggled and, after searching the pile just to check there wasn't a better one, placed the potato into the hole. The way he gently smoothed the soil over the top made Ruby want to hug him. His handwriting wasn't the best, but the tag was readable when he slid it into the ground next to his potato.

On the other side of the allotment, Becca was dusting her onion with her eyebrows furrowed. When it was void of all muck, and under Mel's watchful eye, she screwed it into the bed and tucked it in as well.

Occasional giggling and soft teasing filled the garden. Potato and Onion groups finished planting their vegetables and went to sit on the benches for drinks and snacks. Mrs Denzie insisted they all use a hand wipes and then inspected each small pair of hands for any sign of dirt. The look Mrs Denzie shot Ruby while she was doing this was disgusted, as if Ruby should have insisted they keep their hands clean while digging around in a bed of dirt.

Seeds were sown by Tomato and Pepper groups inside the greenhouse, and the kids went inside in small groups to do so.

Michael rubbed his hands together. "I'm going to sow one pot of Sungold, and one pot of Gardener's Delight."

"You can do that if you like." Ruby patted his shoulder, then regretted it as she glanced out of the greenhouse, towards where Mrs Denzie was sitting.

Compost floated onto the floor from Michael's hands.

Mrs Denzie poked her head in just as Mel was sliding past Ruby towards Michael. Her gaze lingered on the inch of space between them, and then on Mel's hand where it rested on Ruby's arm. "We've spoken about this."

Ruby shrank away from Mel's hand.

"There really isn't that much room in here, Mrs Denzie," Mel said lightly. "I can't keep away from Ruby if I need to help someone, can I?"

Mrs Denzie's mouth twisted, and her nostrils flared. "Such a confined space. Could you not have ordered a larger greenhouse?"

"You think we bought this especially for the group?" Mel snorted.

"Did you not?"

"God no. It's been here… How long, Ruby?"

"I've been here a few years, and it was already here then." Ruby's cheeks burned, and she tried to focus on Chelsea and the way she was tenderly smoothing the compost over her own seeds.

"A bigger greenhouse would have been more suitable."

"Why does Mel need to keep away from Ruby?" Michael asked. "Does she have a cold?"

Mel chuckled.

"No." Mrs Denzie folded her arms. "We've had a discussion about it, and it's not for your ears."

Michael appeared affronted as he went back to his tomatoes. "She should be at home with a hot totty if she's got a cold." He looked brighter. "That's what my gran says."

Ruby stifled a snigger at his incorrect pronunciation of "toddy" while Mrs Denzie continued to stand just outside the door. It felt as if her gaze blazed through the glass and followed their every move.

"Let me help you," Chelsea said to a boy called Charlie. "Do you need help?"

Charlie nodded.

"Okay. Ruby said you have to make a little hole." She took his hand and gently poked his finger into his pot. "And then you put the seed in. Go on, you can do it."

Warmth flooded through Ruby as she watched Chelsea continue to help a couple more of the shyer children. Chelsea passed the small watering can around and grinned encouragingly when one of the kids watered their pot without the seed floating to the top.

As uncomfortable and unsure as Ruby had felt at the beginning of last week's group, this week she was feeling a lot more confident. Her heart wasn't racing, and her palms were dry. She could concentrate on remembering what Mel had already taught her, and on sharing that knowledge with the group of young minds. Except she couldn't. Instead, she had to focus on making sure her behaviour wasn't inappropriate for the children. She was constantly aware that her every movement, every word was being scrutinised by Mrs Denzie. And that she—they—were being judged as unfit to speak to the impressionable kids.

Every time she looked at Mel, she felt simultaneously supported and worried. The twisting in her gut remained, amplified by the occasional concerned look from Mel every time Ruby moved out of her touch or personal space.

And every critical look Mrs Denzie threw their way felt like it left a mark on Ruby's skin; a tattoo in rainbow colours for the world to see.

Because of the amount of extra pots Chelsea had been poking in order to help her classmates to sow their seeds, her hands were caked in compost. Mrs Denzie's critical gaze slid over her, taking in the added soil down her front. "Children with dirty hands don't have biscuits."

Chelsea inspected her fingers with dismay, then shuffled over to the outside tap to re-wash them. An air of desperation surrounded her, and the frustrated way she was scrubbing at her hands made water splash all around her wellies.

When she came back to the benches, Mrs Denzie lifted an eyebrow. Her expression clearly stated she wasn't quite satisfied, but she nodded and didn't argue when Chelsea sat with a biscuit and some squash, swinging her legs and chatting with her friends.

After the group had drunk all the squash and finished off the biscuits, they left. Ruby rinsed her hands under the outside tap and half-dried them on the sodden tea towel the kids had used. She rubbed the back of her neck with chilly fingers, stepping away when Mel moved behind her to use the washing facilities.

"They're great, aren't they?" Mel said, her gaze intent on her own hands.

"They are. I know I said I didn't like kids, but they're growing on me."

A small chuckle from Mel before she turned the tap off and took the tea towel from Ruby. "Oh," she said, suddenly remembering something. "I'll be right back." Mel raced off, towards the car park, and Ruby stood dumbly staring at the tea towel she'd just been thrown.

A good few minutes later, Ruby was wondering whether Mel would be returning. She glanced at her watch, then huffed, looking around her. The kids had left the garden tidy, for which she was grateful.

Mel did return, with a long-potted plant under one arm and some pieces of wood in the other hand. As she set the plant onto the ground, Ruby realised the wood was a folded-down trellis, and that there was a hammer and a packet of nails sticking out of Mel's back pocket. "You wanted a clematis?" Mel held her hand towards the plant invitingly.

Ruby stooped down and lifted the plant label, so she could read. "Wildfire?" The picture on the label was of a flower with purple and red petals.

Her lips pulling upwards, Mel stooped down close to her and nodded. "I figured it was fitting. You're a bit feisty, so..." She shrugged, pink blossoming on her cheeks.

Ruby carefully fingered the tiny leaves on the plant. Small curly tendrils were already winding their way up the small supports sticking out of the pot.

"You like it?" Mel rubbed her chin and cast Ruby an unsure glance.

"I do, thank you."

"Thought it was a bit different from the usual purple ones you can get."

"And, apparently, I'm a wildfire." Ruby's lips were pursed, but Mel seemed to understand that she was pleased.

"You are." Mel stood and waggled the trellis so that it unfolded into a criss-crossed wall of about four feet long. "I'm okay to nail this onto the shed?"

Ruby nodded.

Mel produced two short pieces of wood. "We have to make sure the trellis is a couple of centimetres away from the shed wall, otherwise the vines won't be able to creep up it."

"Oh. Okay."

"Could you give me a hand?"

They worked together, Ruby holding the pieces of wood in place while Mel hammered nails to secure them to the wooden wall. They'd chosen the sunniest side, Ruby noticed, and she decided that the fact that she *had* noticed meant she was learning. *Gardening is easier than I thought. It's all logic.*

They attached the trellis into place with wooden pieces at each end. Mel carried the clematis plant into the greenhouse and placed it into the blue ceramic pot Ruby had found while they were cleaning the area. Mel held the plant still in the middle of the pot, and Ruby gathered handfuls of compost to tuck around it.

The activity meant they had to be close to each other, and Ruby found her face right next to Mel's on more than one occasion. As well as the sweet smell of the compost, wafts of Mel's perfume washed over her too. *The kids are gone. It doesn't matter if we're close now.* Green eyes watched her carefully as their gazes locked for a breath. Ruby's hands were full of compost, and she nearly dropped it. "Sorry."

"No, it's okay. I'm sorry. I'm a bit close, I know."

"Nearly done," Ruby said with a forced breeziness.

Mel's gaze was calm and understanding. The minute the plant was sturdy, she stepped away, brushing her hands together. "You said you wanted some space."

Ruby nodded and pressed the compost around the plant to hold it safely in the pot. "I know. I just have some…" She sighed and closed her eyes for a heartbeat. "Things are a little bit full on at the moment. I just need a little bit more time, and then…" She gazed up at Mel, taking in the way her red hair shone in the sunshine. Her eyes seemed as green as the leaves on her new clematis, possibly even greener than the grass outside the greenhouse.

"It's okay," Mel said with a nod. "Whatever you have to do." She nudged Ruby with her elbow, however, which made Ruby smile. "I hope you're going to explain at some point why I'm having to keep my distance though. It's all a bit confusing for me, I must admit."

"I will. Once I know what's what."

"Okay."

Ruby rearranged some of the small seed pots, pushing them closer together and more into line with one another. She could feel Mel's gaze on her as she did so and cocked an eyebrow once she had finished. "What?"

"You ever been diagnosed with OCD?" There was humour in Mel's voice.

"No. I just like things neat." Ruby turned around and leant back against the shelf, her hands curling around the edge.

Mel stood a little to the side, her arms folded. The humour shone from her eyes as well. "Oh, you're one of *those* people."

"One of what people?" Ruby folded her arms too, pouting to cover a grin.

"Those neat people who has to have their pen…" Mel indicated with a pinched forefinger and thumb, "…perpendicular to their notebook. And their mouse perpendicular to their computer keyboard."

It was true, but Ruby didn't want to admit it. "I don't." Conscious that her northern accent was emphasised when she was indignant, she rephrased. "I do not. I am perfectly happy with things being… un-neat."

"Dis-tidy?" Mel teased.

Ruby took a chance and reached to poke Mel in the side.

Mel retracted and grinned. "Please don't make it harder for me."

"Harder for you?" Ruby's hand reached out again, and Mel moved away properly, towards the door of the greenhouse.

"To keep my distance…" She snorted and put up both hands. "You're really very attractive, you know."

"So you've said." Ruby quietened and was relieved to see Mel's shoulders relax. "So are you. Okay." She put her up hands too. "I'll refrain from the flirting until… I've sorted out what I need to sort."

"Deal."

"Now, is offering you a coffee in my warm office too much for you, or…?"

"I think I can handle that." Mel sauntered out of the greenhouse with the clematis in both hands, and Ruby followed, a grin plastered to her face.

# Chapter 15

RUBY'S FIRST-YEAR ANATOMY CLASS SEEMED to be settling down. It had been a few weeks since she'd had any kind of disruption from Francesca. *That part of my life seems to have sorted itself out. If only I could say the same for my love life.* She hadn't found any more information and was reluctant to bring it up with anyone more senior than Alexander, as she didn't want to cause herself any embarrassment. *At least while we're keeping away from one another, that blooming school teacher can't complain.*

The lesson went as expected, until fifteen minutes before the end of class. Francesca was sitting alone, with her hair over her face as she bent over her textbook. Ruby's plan was to have them all take part in a fun activity to remember the twelve pairs of cranial nerves, something many people had written rhymes for before. Although it wasn't compulsory for the students to learn these nerves, at least not in their first year, she enjoyed the activity of creating funny poems and ditties to help her students remember things.

"So, the cranial nerves are: olfactory, optic, oculomotor, trochlear, trigeminal, abducens, facial, vestibulocochlear, glossopharyngeal, vagus, accessory, and hypoglossal. If you take the first letter from each, you can make a phrase that might help you remember them." She looked around the class at a sea of interested faces, and one not-so-interested curtain of hair. "Shall we all have a go? I'll give you five minutes."

Everyone murmured between themselves and started scribbling. Ruby smirked, but her face fell as she saw Francesca, head still down, not engaging with anyone else, let alone in the activity. Ruby moved around the tables to lean against the empty one in front of the young woman.

After a few minutes of silence, Francesca looked up. She rolled her eyes and leaned back, her knuckles white in front of her on the desk. "What do you want?" she asked, her voice barely louder than a whisper.

"Well, I do believe this is my lesson, and you're taking it." Ruby squinted at Francesca and furrowed her eyebrows. "Sometimes we're, unfortunately, going to have to interact."

"Yeah, whatever." Francesca leant over her book again, but Ruby could see she wasn't taking in anything that was written inside.

"Look, I know you don't like me. But this is a fun exercise, and it might help you to remember the cranial nerves."

Francesca's head shot up again, her hair flicking backwards with the force of the movement. "It's stupid."

"It's not stupid, if you just—"

"No, it really is."

"Would you like some help?" Ruby leaned closer to check the book lay open in front of her and noticed that she wasn't even on the correct page. "Chuck us the book and I'll find the right page for you."

"No." Francesca scraped her chair back and pushed the book away at the same time. Then she stood and snapped the book closed. "Just... stop interfering."

"I'm trying to help you. It's my job."

"Go help someone else." The large dark eyes glaring at her were wet.

Ruby's heart ached for the girl, and for her own seeming inability to make things better. *What on earth is going on with her?* "Is something happening at home I should be aware of?" She made sure she spoke quietly enough, that no one but Francesca could hear.

"What? Like what?"

"Is home life okay? Are you eating enough? Is someone in your family poorly?" Ruby had taught kids with sick family members before and it always impacted on their studies. "Is... is someone being nasty to you?"

"No! Of course not." A tear fell in a winding trail down Francesca's cheek. She swiped hastily at it and shook her head. "Literally, stop bugging me. You're in my face all the bloody time." Her voice was catching, and the sobs were starting.

Ruby held out a hand to her, but Francesca smacked it away. Ruby cradled her stinging hand and watched, shocked, as Francesca stormed out of the classroom, leaving her book and pencil case behind.

It appeared everyone had observed the outburst, even if no one really knew the content of it. Ruby was thankful for this. She thought briefly about following Francesca, and perhaps trying to console her, but decided against it. *I've already made her cry.* Her stomach hurt at that thought, and she pressed a hand to it to try to ease it. Then she moved as calmly as she could to the head of the classroom to continue the last ten minutes of the lesson.

---

After another interesting but slightly mind-boggling lecture about wrist injuries, Mel hauled her backpack onto one shoulder and made her way towards Ruby's office for lunch. It had gone well. Her Dictaphone had not run out of memory midway through, and she'd understood all the things she'd been shown and most of the things she'd been told. They'd looked at each other's wrist joints and felt the different bone structures, identifying ligaments, tendons and muscles. She felt good.

A dark-haired girl of about eighteen rushed past her, head lowered. She could see tears in the girl's eyes. Stopping in the corridor, Mel bit her lip, wondering whether she should follow her and see what the problem was. *It's probably just someone who's been dumped. Poor kid. I'm sure she has friends to support her though.*

Knocking on Ruby's office door, she stepped back and waited. No one came to answer it, so she leant against the wall next to it, one knee bent and her fingers playing with the strap of her bag. *I hurried to get here straight after we finished. She's probably still finishing her lecture.* She thought amusedly that she'd like to attend one of Ruby's lectures, just to see what it was like being spoken to in such academic terms by someone so beautiful. *I'd never be able to concentrate.* She chuckled to herself and spied Ruby making her way down the hallway.

"Hey," she said, putting one hand up in greeting.

A flicker of happiness graced Ruby's features, but it didn't hit her eyes.

Mel frowned and followed Ruby into her office, taking a seat at the other end of the sofa and placing her lunch on the coffee table. She crossed her legs and studied the forlorn face beside her. "What's happened?" Her hands itched to touch Ruby, but she forced herself to sit back.

Ruby let out a shaky sigh and shook her head slowly. Then she turned to face Mel on the sofa, leaning on one hip. She made no move to take her lunch out of her bag or make a drink from the small drinks-making station which Mel knew her personal assistant always kept stocked up for her.

"Come on," Mel coaxed, her hand shifting towards her along the back of the sofa but not getting close enough to touch her. Ruby's gaze followed her fingers as they waved at her—a cute gesture, she hoped. Something to make Ruby smile.

Ruby didn't smile. Her throat worked as she swallowed, and her eyes blinked until they shone with tears.

Again, Mel fought the urge to move close and touch her. *It's not what she wants.* "Talk to me," she whispered, her heart rate escalating. *Has someone hurt her?*

"It's my student. Francesca."

"The girl with the problems?"

Ruby nodded.

"What did she do?" Mel set her jaw and watched as Ruby rubbed the back of her knuckles, which seemed far too red for her taste. "Did she hurt you?"

"No." Ruby shook her head but then furrowed her eyebrows.

"You don't look convinced of that fact," Mel replied, anger building inside her. She pushed it down. *We're not heroes, remember? We're not gung-ho or confrontational.* She laid both hands on her knees and leant closer. "You can tell me." Tilting her head to one side, she forced a concerned but calm expression onto her face.

"I made her cry."

"Francesca?" Mel's slow and soft voice appeared to be soothing Ruby, which in turn calmed Mel's racing pulse.

"Yeah."

"Start from the beginning."

Ruby balled a fist and then wiggled her fingers as if to relax herself. "We were doing the cranial nerves. Have you studied them?"

Mel felt a chuckle rising inside her. "Um… Old Ogling Octopi Try to Assess Family Vaginas, Glorious Vases, and Hippos."

Laughter bubbled forth from Ruby's belly, and Mel was thrilled. Tears spilled over her eyelids too, however, and Mel could no longer sit still.

She shifted towards her and put an arm around her shoulders.

"Family vaginas?" Ruby half-cried, half-laughed into her shoulder as she leant against her. Tears blotted Mel's jumper, but she didn't care.

"Hey, it helped me remember them."

"You see, that's what I was trying to do." Ruby lifted her head and stared desperately into Mel's eyes. She did not move away from her arm, so Mel left it in place. "Mnemonics for remembering, like you just said."

Mel rubbed Ruby's opposite shoulder with her thumb, making little circles in a hopefully soothing way. She stayed silent while Ruby described the events of the last twenty minutes.

"And then she just ran out crying. I don't know what to do."

"You asked her if there was anything going on at home?"

"Yes. She seemed appalled by the idea."

Mel slid her arm away and sat back. She sucked her bottom lip and looked across the room, out of the windows, at the trees swaying in the light wind. Rubbing at her chin, she inhaled deeply before turning back to Ruby, whose tears had, thankfully, stopped.

"I have a theory," Mel stated, her gaze flicking to the door and back again.

"You do?" A spark of hope entered Ruby's expression. "Well, let's have it, Professor."

Mel snorted gently, but the cheer fled a moment later from her face. "Let's just check a few things."

Ruby nodded quickly, sat up straight, and folded her hands in her lap.

*She looks so excited that I might have a solution. I hope I'm not wrong.* "So, this girl, Francesca? She tends to kick off when you ask her to participate in group activities?"

"Not just group ones. Even something as simple as reading out loud."

"Okay." Mel nodded. "And you've not seen any evidence that she's stressed or depressed or…?"

"I wouldn't say that," Ruby replied. "Actually, I think she's really depressed, but I can't figure out why."

*Better bite the bullet and just tell her. You know you're right— don't worry about what she thinks.* But Mel couldn't help it. What if Ruby looked at her differently after she knew the truth?

"I think she might be dyslexic." The words sprang out of her mouth in a rush, and Mel wondered whether they had been too garbled for Ruby to understand.

"Dyslexic?" Ruby put her elbow on the arm of the sofa and threaded her fingers into her hair at the back of her head.

"You… know what it is?"

"Of course I do. I've just never met anyone who hasn't been diagnosed by the time they're… at least ten. Certainly before they reach me."

"Really?" Mel didn't care that her voice was disapproving. *Doesn't she realise that some people slip through the cracks?*

"I've obviously taught students that have had it. But they all get diagnosed way before they reach university level. Mostly at school or…" Mel's expression must have displayed the shock she felt, because Ruby's voice trailed into silence.

"I never got diagnosed at school." Mel's voice was quiet but clear, each word enunciated with intent and thick with challenge.

Ruby stared at her, her brown eyes wider than Mel had even seen them.

"It wasn't picked up until I started uni seven years ago. No one knew I was struggling. My previous jobs were a pain in the arse because I was expected to do things that I couldn't do without extra time in which to do them. That's why I wasn't a teaching assistant for more than a couple of years. I was trying to help the kids and I couldn't even do some of the things myself."

"Oh."

"I was in a special needs class at school. But my mum just thought I was slow. Dad was kind, gave me extra help at home when he could, but he was so busy. And then a bunch of the mature students on my course at uni when I first started said I should get tested. Luckily I wasn't working at the time, so I got the test for free."

"Right."

"Not wanting to read out loud, struggling with reading in general, getting frustrated enough that you act up in lessons. I remember feeling like I wanted to do that when I first started my course. I was forty years old, so I obviously didn't do it, but I did feel like an outsider, like I was thick. Like there was something wrong with me. I recognise some of the behaviours you've talked about."

Ruby sat, her lips parted, her gaze trained somewhere across the room. Then realisation flourished across her features, and Mel finally found she was able to loosen her hands from where they had been clenched on the edge of the sofa.

"Why didn't I think of that?" Ruby whispered, her gaze finally flicking up to Mel's. "With Francesca?"

"It's not something that's picked up every single time. Her behaviour just rang a bell with me, but it's not like she said to you, 'I can't read this because the words jump about.'"

"Is that what it's like for you?" Ruby's hand started shifting across the back of the sofa, but she pulled it back into her lap with an embarrassed laugh.

Mel returned the laugh with a level of understanding. *At least I'm not the only one struggling with no physical contact here.* "If I don't wear my specs, yes."

"You have glasses?" Ruby tapped the side of her own black-framed ones.

"They're not as aesthetically pleasing as yours. They don't really suit me."

"I want to see."

Mel chuckled and rolled her eyes before delving into a small pocket in the side of her rucksack and pulling out her case. She popped it open and held her glasses up for Ruby to see.

The lenses in her glasses were bright yellow, and Mel knew that had she revealed them without Ruby knowing why she wore them, Ruby would have been confused.

Reaching forward, Ruby touched a fingertip to the frames. "Come on, Professor, pop them on."

Mel laughed again and slid them into place.

"So you can read better with them on?"

"The words don't dance about quite as much," Mel said. "If the background on a page is white, it makes my head hurt." She plucked the glasses from her nose and stowed them back into her bag. "I'm sorry that I didn't tell you sooner."

Ruby shook her head and shrugged. "It's fine." She beamed at Mel and took her hand in both of her own. "I'm going to assume it was a big thing for you to tell me."

Mel bit her lip and looked cautiously back at her. "Is it okay? I mean…" She swallowed and felt her gut coiling into a stressful mess. "You don't think any… any less of me, do you?"

"Of course not!" Ruby appeared almost disgusted at the notion and rubbed her palm against the back of Mel's fingers, which made Mel relax. "So is it just words jumping about that you have trouble with or…?"

"Sometimes I get letters mixed up: B and D; O and C. Sometimes I read words wrong because the letters look mixed up. And I prefer to use a laptop than write by hand. Certain fonts are more difficult for me to read than others." She grinned. "They did a study."

"On fonts? What came out top?"

"Helvetica, or Arial, I think."

Ruby nodded. "If I ever write you a letter, I'll try to remember." The image of Ruby writing Mel a love letter, and of her specifically choosing a font that Mel could read, made Mel's body temperature rise. Her hand, still cosy between Ruby's, tingled. "I can't believe no one thought to test you at school though." Ruby seemed upset about that.

"It wasn't exactly a well-known condition when I went to school."

"Of course. Oh, I remember."

"Which is why you need to get this Francesca to study support as soon as possible. It must be awful for her, trying to do a degree when she's struggling so much to read."

Ruby deflated somewhat. "I don't know how I'm going to broach the subject, even. She doesn't trust me in any sense of the word." She hung her head.

"Try. She needs your help."

Ruby nodded and sighed deeply.

Their hands were still joined, both of Ruby's around Mel's one. Mel gazed down at their hands, noting the difference in colour: the orange freckles on her own skin were so unlike the dark moles that dusted Ruby's. Mel's hands were slightly bigger too, her fingers longer and her nails shorter.

Ruby noticed Mel's attention where they touched and carefully dropped her hold. She wrapped her arms around herself and smiled, all traces of her crying gone. Her gaze settled on Mel for a beat, and then flicked down to her bag. "Oh, we'd better have some lunch, otherwise my stomach will be growling while I'm elbow-deep in fertiliser."

"Ah yes," Mel teased. "The seedlings will be getting fed and we won't have been."

"A tragedy."

"Exactly."

# Chapter 16

Ruby pondered all she had learned during the afternoon's garden group. Having proved herself to be a calm and helpful teacher, Chelsea was in charge of helping the others sow sunflower seeds.

"I hope you're all making sure your seeds are the right way up, and watered well," Ruby said as she watched over Chelsea's ministrations. "We'll be having a competition."

"I think whoever has the most yellow sunflower should get the top prize," Michael said. Everyone laughed.

Mrs Denzie's mouth had been stuck at lemon-tasting level since Mel had poked her fingers into Ruby's trouser pocket to grab a pencil.

"What about the tallest?"

A cheer went up.

"And we'll work in teams," Mel continued. "Whichever team grows the tallest one will get a prize."

"I like that idea better," Michael agreed.

Mel sent him a wink.

Ruby watched the kids sow seeds and label them individually. She liked the variety name of the sunflower they were using for the competition: Titan. It sounded strong and sturdy and reminded her of the university building: tall and indestructible.

Maybe it reminded her a little tiny bit of Mel as well. Mel was tall, and she'd been through a lot, Ruby reckoned. Going through forty years of not being able to read, and not being given a reason other than 'special needs', must have been rough for her. She seemed so intelligent, so articulate. Ruby would never have guessed she had dyslexia.

Mel's hand on Ruby's arm made her start. Her gaze flicked from Mrs Denzie, who was eyeing them disapprovingly, and then back to Mel. "Can we not?" Ruby hissed.

Mel glanced over to Mrs Denzie and rolled her eyes. "Sorry."

"You don't look it."

Mel put her hands up. "Oh no, I am sorry. Just not for touching your arm." She frowned at Mrs Denzie. "This is stupid. I'm not doing anything."

After stomping over in her designer wellies, Mrs Denzie stood in front of them, expression determined. "I'm going to have to do something about this."

"Please," Ruby replied, her gaze flicking desperately around the allotment. "There's no need to. We're not doing anything." She stepped away.

Mel folded her arms and rolled her head back.

"I've asked you—politely, I might add—and you continue to…"

"We're not." Ruby took another step backwards.

"This is getting a bit silly now." Mel sighed and gestured towards the children. "They don't care. No one is suddenly becoming gay because we're touching in a way that friends do. Stop making a big thing about it."

"You have no idea what is going on in those children's heads. You have no idea how disturbed they are by your antics." Mrs Denzie was spitting the words out as if they were on fire.

"We'll stop. We won't touch." Panic rolled inside Ruby. "Will we?" She didn't care that the look she sent Mel was pleading.

Mel blinked in confusion, then sighed and shook her head.

Relief flooded Ruby's belly. True to her word, Mel remained at a distance during the rest of the session.

---

That evening, after dinner with her daughters during which they had chattered about their days while Ruby remained thoughtfully eating and staring into space, she went online and searched for the term. She read that people with dyslexia don't learn any more slowly than people without, apart from in the area of reading. She learned that there was a version relating to numbers—dyscalculia—a condition which included weak mental arithmetic skills, difficulty remembering or understanding basic calculations, and an aversion to maths.

Mel didn't seem to have dyscalculia, but Ruby forced herself to remember that it was probably not something Mel shouted about. She certainly hadn't with her dyslexia. She cast her mind back over their various outings together. She'd never once seen Mel read, not properly. This surprised her. They'd been to a restaurant together, so she assumed Mel had read the menu. She did remember that Mel had ordered a plain cheese and tomato pizza; perhaps Mel hadn't wanted to spend so much time over reading the menu. Perhaps she had felt worried that Ruby would cotton on to her difficulties.

That made Ruby feel bad. She wished Mel had told her earlier—then she could have worn her glasses and perhaps chosen something more interesting.

The aquarium had been a lovely day out. There had been information points in front of every tank, but she couldn't remember Mel ever going up to one to read it. Mel had seemed content to watch the fish and to listen to Ruby drone on about them.

Her stomach hurt, and she rubbed her midriff. Chloe, ever the sensitive of her two daughters, glanced over from where she was seated, her legs thrown over the side of the armchair. The television was showing some reality show that the girls had wanted to watch. Chloe slid off the armchair and moved towards her mother. "All right?"

"Yes, lovely. I'm fine."

Chloe's eyes flicked to Ruby's belly. "You got your period or..."

"No, no. I'm good."

Chloe twisted her lips. "Want a cuddle?"

"That would be lovely," Ruby almost-whined, holding an arm open when Chloe settled next to her.

Chloe smelled of clean deodorant and hair dye. She'd coloured some of her hair purple, which Ruby had been dismayed by—those beautiful blonde locks that she'd brushed every day until Chloe was fifteen, tainted by indigo streaks. *It'll wash out.* She pressed her nose into Chloe's hair and squeezed her.

"Bad day at work?"

"The morning was a bit crap," Ruby admitted, sighing deeply.

Jasmine looked over from her armchair, her untainted blonde hair straightened within an inch of its life. *Neither of my girls are happy with their wavy hair. What is that about?* "What happened?" Jasmine asked.

"I have a student that's struggling." Ruby sighed affectionately at the admission. Her student was struggling, not kicking off or causing trouble, or being rude to her just for the sake of making her life hell. She felt bad that she hadn't known what the issue was, and about the way she had reacted, but she was happy that the next time she saw the girl, she could talk to her about it properly and offer a solution.

"That sucks," Jasmine said before turning back to the television.

"Is she okay?" Chloe asked, her big green eyes blinking up at her.

"I'm hoping she will be. Once I get her sorted with some help."

Chloe squeezed her back and nodded against her shoulder, moving her attention back to the television. "Good." She patted her mother's knee. "You're a good teacher, Mum."

"Thank you, lovely."

---

Ruby's phone rang on Saturday morning, and she raced to get it. No one ever phoned her; somehow, she knew it would be Mel. As expected, Mel's name was plastered across her phone screen.

"Hiya, Mel."

"Hey. How's your weekend going?"

Ruby flopped back onto the sofa and beamed, allowing a pleased hum to escape. "Okay. Bit boring today. Mostly housework. Walk the dog." She glanced over at Barney, who had decided to roll onto her back in her dog bed with her feet in the air, her tongue hanging out. "Who is currently upside down and exposing herself. I think she's waiting for a fella."

Mel chuckled. "Little hussy."

"That she is." Ruby moved the phone to her other ear so she could lift the cup of coffee she'd just made to her lips. "Please tell me you called me to invite me out."

"I did."

"Brilliant. What did you have in mind?"

"Well, as it's a nice day, and I've not had any lunch yet, I was hoping…"

Ruby withheld a smile and waited.

"Perhaps you'd maybe like to go for a picnic?"

"Sounds lovely. Where?"

"Is there a nice park near you? We came to mine last time."

Ruby remembered their dog walk and the café visit. The memory was a happy one. "There's Queen's Park, just down the road from me."

"I'll do the picnic. Sandwiches okay?"

"Not tuna, but yes anything else."

"You don't like tuna? And there was me thinking you were a fish-loving person."

"I like other fish. Just not tuna. Pregnancy incident when I was carrying Jasmine. Serious aversion since. Lots of vomiting involved."

"Okay, okay, I won't make tuna sandwiches."

"Thank you."

"See you at about one-ish?"

"Meet you by the swings."

"All right."

Ruby ended the call, beaming from ear to ear. She hopped into her kitchen, scouring cupboards for some sweet things she could provide. She found cans of soft drink and packed a variety so Mel could choose what she liked. She also discovered some cupcakes that were bordering on out of date. She checked them top and bottom for any signs of green, furry growths, decided they were fine, and added them to her stash. The whole lot went into a large bag.

The park was in walking distance from her house. Ruby pulled on her trainers and strolled out into the sunshine. The girls were out, so she scrawled a note and made sure she had her phone: that way if they could reach her if they needed her. The sunshine made her squint, but Ruby turned her face into it, sighing as the warm rays caressed her face. She'd grabbed a floaty scarf but had forgone her beige jacket in favour of a purple mackintosh, just in case of showers. *Must be prepared.*

When she turned through the archway of the park, she immediately spotted Mel's car in the car park; the woman herself was leaning against the gate. Ruby lifted a hand in greeting, and Mel crossed the distance between them to pull her into a hug.

Mel smelled like flowers and her hair was sleek and loose, and shone with golden streaks in the sunshine. She was wearing a leather jacket, jeans, a black-and-white chequered blouse, and her customary walking boots. A cool box hung from its handle over her arm, a picnic blanket tucked atop it.

"Hello," Mel said as they broke apart.

"Lovely to see you." Ruby's gaze scanned the park. "Where did you want to sit?"

"I already found the perfect spot." She led her to a small grassy clearing, with a gnarly oak tree a few feet away. At Ruby's nod, Mel spread the blanket out on the grass and sat down.

Ruby sat opposite her, so close their knees nearly touched. She chose to stay so close and eagerly wiggled her fingers at the cool box Mel had brought. "What did you bring?"

"What did *you* bring?" Mel asked, eyeing Ruby's bag.

A group of children dashed past them, and Mel's gaze followed them before returning to Ruby's bag.

"Just some goodies." Ruby obliged, opening the bag and laying out various cans onto the blanket. "Help yourself."

"Thanks."

When Ruby pulled the plastic box from her bag and unclipped the top, Mel's eyes became wide. "Oh, cake."

"Cake, indeed."

Mel scuffed her palms together and grinned.

"But you don't get cake until you've finished your greens."

"I'm afraid the sandwiches are cheese and pickle. No green in them at all."

"You won't get cake, then," Ruby said mock-seriously.

Mel shrugged. "Shame." She unloaded the sandwiches and put them on a plastic plate. "The pickle has vegetables in it. And fruit."

"Apples?"

"Yep."

"They'll do. You can have cake."

Mel laughed and placed the plate between them. She opened a packet of crisps and nestled it into the blanket so it wouldn't fall over. "Honestly, help yourself." She popped open a can of ginger beer with a fizz and sipped. "Oh, that's fantastic."

Ruby opened a can of fizzy orange and sipped at the sweet drink, allowing the bubbles to play over her tongue. There was something fresh about being outside with a cold drink, especially when the weather was fine, even if it was a bit chilly. She relished her scarf and set her can of drink aside to tuck into the sandwiches.

They were neat, well-filled, and cut into triangles. The care Mel had taken to make them made Ruby feel like she was glowing inside. The leaves from the oak tree caused the sunlight to dapple around them, and the regular screams and thumps from the play area were muffled as they drifted by. Birds sang above, twittering out their enjoyment of the day. Ruby wondered whether there were baby birds in the tree and the parents were singing their joy at having raised a family. She hoped so. It was a nice thought.

"I did some research…" Ruby said after a few minutes of silence, other than the munching of sandwiches and crisps. When she looked up, she realised Mel had a crisp crumb on her chin, but Ruby just smiled to herself. "…into dyslexia." She spoke quietly but nonchalantly, hoping that she would express how Mel's admission hadn't changed things between them.

"Did you?" Mel appeared amused, but the look in her eyes was tender, as if she was pleased that Ruby was interested in that small part of her.

"Yeah." Ruby sucked some pickle off her thumb and reached for a crisp. She popped it in her mouth and crunched before wiping the sides of her mouth with her fingers. "I feel a bit more informed generally about the condition now."

"You feel better about talking to… Francesca?"

"Hopefully. I hope I can actually talk to her. That she doesn't just close down and fly off the handle."

"All you can do is try."

Ruby sipped her drink, then nodded and patted Mel's hand. "Thanks for your help. I'd never have realised without you."

Mel continued to gaze at her, her eyes shining. "Unfortunately, I can't resist helping a pretty lady. It's just in my nature." She was being chivalrous, but Ruby could see the sincerity behind it.

"I bet you say that to all the girls," Ruby said, lowering her gaze.

Mel's fingers touched Ruby's, and Mel shook her head when Ruby looked back up. "I don't."

A pang of guilt mixed with frustration gathered inside Ruby. She rubbed the back of her neck and looked down at where Mel's fingers touched her. "We have a problem, and, try as I might, I haven't yet found a solution."

Obviously sensing that Ruby was going to tell her the reason for them not touching one another or getting close, Mel sat back, her fingers leaving Ruby's. Her gaze was steady and gentle.

"The problem is..." Ruby sighed. She tapped her forefinger on her half-empty can of drink. "I'm a teacher, and you're a student."

"Right." Mel nodded, indicating she understood so far.

"The university has a policy against students and members of staff... having relationships."

Realisation dawned on Mel's pale features. She squinted in the sunlight and bit her lip.

"So, friendship is frowned upon, but allowed, and r-romantic relationships... definitely not allowed."

"Wait, let me get this straight." They both rolled their eyes at Mel's choice of words. "So, because you're a member of staff, and I'm a student, we're not allowed to have a relationship?"

"That's right." Ruby shrugged and wrapped her arms around herself, resting her can on her elbow.

"But aren't those rules to protect the vulnerable party, usually the student, from being treated unfairly, or given extra privileges?"

"Exactly."

"But you don't directly teach me. I'm not going to be doing any of your classes."

"True."

A smile began to form on Mel's face. "So, it's not a teacher-student relationship. You're not responsible for any of my learning." Her joy grew. "It would be like an English tutor dating a music student."

Ruby wrinkled her nose. "It's still inappropriate."

"Why?" Mel's question wasn't critical, and it wasn't charged with derision.

"Because I could still be seen as giving you special treatment."

"When?"

Ruby stopped. She pushed her eyebrows down and opened her mouth to answer, but no answer came. *I was so sure about this. Where has my argument gone?* "I'm not sure."

"Would you have to mark any of my logs? Or my portfolio at the end of the course?"

"I don't think so."

Mel flicked her eyebrows up once and clasped her hands on her raised knees. She pressed her lips together and trailed her gaze down to the empty packet of crisps between them. She grasped the packet, producing a crackling noise as she scrunched it up, and then she pushed the bag into the cool box.

"So it… It's okay? For me to date you?" Ruby blinked hard.

"I'm, what, five years older than you? It's not like you'd be dating an eighteen-year-old."

Ruby wrinkled her nose again, but a laugh bubbled up inside her. She let it out, and out with it came the frustration, the fear, and the guilt from the last few weeks. It was okay. Of course it was okay. How could she have thought otherwise?

"I think we should tell your head of department though," Mel said. Then she stopped and her cheeks pinked. "Oh. I mean. If you still do want to…"

"Date you? Of course I do." Ruby was giggling like a teenager, sitting on a picnic blanket in the middle of a park. She placed her can down on the blanket before shuffling closer to Mel and then sitting back on her heels. "I really want to," she said, a bit more soberly.

Mel looked at her, and a slow smile spread over her face. The sunlight caught a few pale streaks in her hair, and Ruby wondered whether they were grey or simply sun-bleached. They'd spent every Wednesday afternoon together, outside, for the last two months. They'd enjoyed one another's company and chatted about their lives. Ruby already felt closer to Mel than she'd felt with anyone in a very long time.

Mel hadn't moved, not even when Ruby had knelt in front of her. Their knees were touching on the blanket. Slowly lifting one hand, Ruby decided to throw caution to the wind and tucked a piece of fly-away hair behind Mel's ear. Her fingers lingered against the skin of her neck, and Mel visibly shivered when Ruby trailed them downwards, stopping at the collar of Mel's jacket. She fingered the soft leather, rubbing it between thumb and finger, before sinking her fingers into Mel's soft hair just behind her ear.

Seemingly waking from a long slumber, Mel's hand rose to touch Ruby's cheek to take her neck and pull her in. Their lips touched, and Ruby felt a swooping sensation make her head spin. Mel's lips were so silky she had to close her eyes.

Hunger that wasn't related to food rolled within Ruby as the taste of pickle and ginger touched her tongue. Her nose filled with the scent of flowers as they kissed, and without the usual compost, Mel smelt fresh and clean. Finally—*finally*—they were actually here—kissing. The instinct to shift closer, to sit in Mel's lap or push her down onto the picnic blanket, nearly consumed Ruby, but her kiss-addled brain remembered where they were.

The pull and tug between wanting Mel and not wanting to do anything that would get her into trouble was distant, as if it had happened years ago—decades maybe. There was just the two of them, soft lips against soft lips; the birds twittering overhead as if they agreed. They felt close, as if their pulses were synced, or their blood had mingled. The thought made Ruby want to giggle, but the press of Mel's lips against her own stilled the humour inside her. She wanted to kiss Mel forever.

Mel made a small noise in her throat, as if she were sinking into a warm bath. Luxuriously, Ruby made the noise back, hoping it would flutter away into silence on the breeze. The noise was for Mel and nobody else. It connected them.

When the kiss broke, Ruby sat back, keeping one hand in Mel's hair and the other around her waist, where it had drifted.

Mel's lips parted, and she showed her teeth when she smiled. "Oh." She laughed. "Am I allowed to say 'Wow'?"

"Not if I say it first," Ruby replied, her voice sounding very far away. "Wow!"

Mel looked around them but seemed to want to stay touching Ruby. "So is this our first date?"

"I think our first date was that play you took me to."

"Ah. Yes." Mel cleared her throat and brushed her thumbs over the sides of Ruby's neck.

Ruby stretched her neck to one side and lowered her lashes, goose bumps rising along her shoulders and arms. *I love how she touches me. I love it already.*

"Hardly fair to call it our first date though."

"Why?" Ruby opened her eyes properly again and pouted, making Mel's happiness surge.

"I never got a goodnight kiss."

"Is that a prerequisite for a first date?"

"If there's going to be a second one, yes."

"Oh." Ruby leaned forwards again and brushed her lips to Mel's.

Mel gathered her around the waist and pulled her closer, their fronts touching now. Conscious of their location, and of the kids all around them, they kept the kiss light and moderately chaste.

When Mel's tongue touched her bottom lip, Ruby broke the kiss and pulled back. They were both breathing deeply. Someone wolf-whistled behind them, although Ruby was unsure whether it was just a kid playing or that someone had actually noticed them. She blushed anyway.

Touching a finger to her lips, she slid to sit next to Mel, slipping her hand, palm up, underneath Mel's. "So, I guess we're… dating?"

"Going out. Seeing each other. Whatever you want to call it." Mel pressed her lips against Ruby's cheek. "I would very much like to do all those things, if that's okay?"

"I think it is."

They looked around at the mess they'd made with lunch, and Ruby realised they hadn't eaten pudding.

"You definitely deserve cake, now," Ruby teased, handing Mel one.

"Because I ate my greens?" Mel was grinning proudly.

"Because you kiss like an angel." Ruby was aware she didn't usually say such bold things. She wasn't the sort of person who wore her heart on her sleeve. But she trusted Mel, and Mel obviously trusted her. The grin that spread over Mel's face at her words made it clear she'd said the right thing.

# Chapter 17

April blossomed into fantastic sunshine and the occasional wonderful shower that glazed everything with glistening droplets of water. The pier, stretching out in front of them, glittered with an array of colours, and the people walking up and down all seemed very happy.

*Everything seems wonderful. I wonder why.* Mel rolled her eyes at her own thoughts. She knew why. She was finally allowed to do all the things she wanted to do when Ruby was around. Stand close to her, stroke her cheek, and hold her hand.

Of course, they had refrained from any personal displays of affection while they were surrounded by eight- and nine-year olds, and especially when Mrs Denzie was looking their way. Mel couldn't help the occasional fleeting look, or taking in the way Ruby's T-shirt rode up ever so slightly when she bent over a seedling.

She sipped from her coffee and leant back to stretch as much of her body out as she could in the cab of the ambulance truck she was currently occupying. She was in the driver's seat, and James was sprawled over the passenger's seat, a knowing grin on his face.

Smacking him with a limp hand, Mel grinned back and let out a deep sigh. "I'm sure you were like this when you started going out with Jade," she said.

"Yes, and I distinctly remember you taking the mickey the whole time."

"True." Mel stared out the windscreen, watching a few pre-school-aged children running about on the beach. They had a good view when they parked up on the seafront in the centre of town. It was a great place to do "stand-by" when they were waiting for a job, or having a coffee, watching the world go by. Mel sipped semi-hurriedly, knowing that their radio would buzz and they'd be forced to leave at any moment.

"So let me have my fun." When Mel turned to him, he was studying her closely. "You really like her."

"I do." Her cheeks felt hot.

"You've never been like this about a girl before." He nodded, submissively. "Sorry. *Woman*."

"Not since… Rach, I suppose."

He shook his head in an adamant way. "She's nothing like Rach, is she? She's not thrown you out the minute you told her you were dyslexic. Or treated you like a kid who can't do anything for themselves."

Her throat tightening, Mel tried to push away the memory. "So far, she's treated me just fine. Nothing like Rach. Ugh." She grimaced at the topic of conversation and at the dregs of coffee as they scratched the back of her mouth. She couldn't hide her fear from her crewmate. "But it's early days."

"You think she could change her mind?"

"Rach did. She seemed perfectly fine with it until… until it was an inconvenience."

"Ah. The café incident." Although James's tone was humorous, the look he gave her was sympathetic. "Has Ruby tried to order food for you?"

"She's not had the chance." Mel sighed. "Still time though."

"And she actually *liked* your specs?"

Chuckles bubbled up inside Mel. "She said she did."

"Well, that's good, surely? Rach wasn't so complimentary, from what I remember you saying. Didn't you say she made a face whenever you had to wear them?"

Mel shrugged and then nodded.

"Stop worrying. Like I've said a hundred times, Rach was a bitch. Who treats someone like that?"

Mel imagined her emotions flying over the beach and getting caught up in a wave. "Not Ruby." She opened a flapjack she'd bought and bit into it. The sweet, buttery taste helped her to relax.

"Must be love," he replied, shrinking back when her hand flew out to smack him again. "Hey. Workplace assault."

"Oh, shut up, you plonker."

He laughed. "Eat your flapjack, woman." That earned him a third slap.

# Chapter 18

UNFORTUNATELY, RUBY STILL HADN'T MANAGED to catch Francesca to talk to her about her reading. Every single time a lesson had ended, she'd scooted off without so much as a good-bye, and Ruby had been left half-relieved and half-frustrated.

Mel knew this from the fact that Ruby hadn't spoken about the subject, and one day, as May rolled in with warm sunshine and blossoming flowers, she gave her a stern look over a coffee at her bungalow.

Without having to talk about it, Ruby knew what the look meant. She needed to talk to Francesca and sort out the problem. She was scared of a meltdown and half-hoped the problem would go away by itself. But if Francesca failed everything because she hadn't had the correct support that came with a firm diagnosis, or if she simply dropped out one day, Ruby knew how devastated she'd be about it. And it tugged at her heart, as if the thought pulled the organ away from its moorings leaving it damaged, and separate, and useless.

So one day, a Wednesday morning, right before a lecture on tendons and ligaments, Ruby set her jaw, squared her shoulders, and prepared herself for whatever was to come.

Pulling Francesca aside the minute she walked into the theatre, Ruby led her over to the computer she used to give her lectures, out of earshot of the other students. "Francesca."

"Yes, Ruby." *I see we've dropped the 'Miss' name. That's promising.*

"I need to speak with you about something."

Francesca looked at the floor. Gone was the rude and witty girl Ruby was so used to. In her place stood a destitute student, with no spark radiating from her and a mouth that looked like it had been tugged into a frown for weeks. Dark circles underscored her eyes, and all the fight had left her.

*I've never seen anyone so depressed. I have got to say something now.*

"I've noticed, over the last few months, that you've been struggling."

Francesca shrugged.

"And I think I have a solution, or at least a path to a solution. Would you mind if we discussed it after the lecture?"

"Whatever." No rudeness coloured Francesca's words, just hopelessness and sadness.

Ruby nodded and laid a hand on Francesca's arm. "Okay. I'll see you in a bit."

During the lecture, Ruby began to notice things. She spoke a lot and brought up a huge amount of words on the projector, with nothing in the way of showing rather than explaining. Her mind half on the things she was teaching, she wondered whether she really *should* change the way her classes were delivered. *More videos, maybe. And a lot more pictures. And my seminars need to be more hands-on. Less wordy. It would be more interesting, even for those people who don't struggle to read.*

Her gaze kept flicking to Francesca, who sat with her notebook, her eyes dark and downward-cast, a pen held tightly between her fingers. She wrote nothing. She didn't look up once, at least not when Ruby was looking at her. She sat away from her fellow classmates, did not interact, and didn't engage in the lesson in any way. Ruby felt like crying.

As the lecture ended, Francesca stepped up to Ruby and nodded, her bottom lip between her teeth. "What did you want?"

"I have a theory." Ruby watched everyone else leave before she continued. "I think you're struggling to read."

Francesca blinked up at her with wide eyes, finally making eye contact.

"I don't know if you've always struggled, always battled your way through without much of a care for books, but I suspect you worked incredibly hard to get into university. Am I wrong?"

"Everyone worked hard. It's a hard course to get onto."

*At least she isn't denying it.* "I know. But am I wrong about you struggling to read?"

"Are you calling me thick?" A match had lit in Francesca's eyes.

Ruby took a small step backwards. "Not at all. I think you're a very intelligent woman."

"You are though. Because who can't read when they're eighteen?"

"Some people struggle."

"Yeah. Thick people. People who fucked around at school and college, if they even bloody went to college."

"No. That's not true."

Menace burned brightly in Francesca's eyes. "There is nothing wrong with me. I'm not thick and I don't struggle." Tears tumbled down her cheeks as she spoke, and Ruby reached out a hand to her, instinctually.

"I didn't—"

"Who can't bloody read?" Francesca shouted, her face turning beetroot. "I *can* bloody read, *Miss*." So the distasteful name was back. "There's absolutely nothing wrong with me. It's your lectures that are shit."

Ruby felt tears pooling in her own eyes, and a lump formed in her throat the size of a county. "I'm—"

"They're so boring, and because of that they go in one side and come out the other." Francesca smacked the side of her own head with force. Then she knocked Ruby's hovering hand away, the contact ringing like a snap through the auditorium. "I want to learn." Her voice was pleading, but the anger in her expression was still evident. "And I can't fucking do it."

At that, she raced from the theatre, the door banging sharply behind her.

*I'm such a failure.* Ruby sunk to the floor, her hands covering her face. Her whole body shook with sobs, right there on the theatre floor, and she wished that the world would swallow her up. *I'm the reason she can't learn. And she won't let me help her. I'm such a failure.*

---

Mel was just coming out of a very interesting lecture about the anatomy of the foot when she nearly skidded headlong into the dark-haired girl she'd walked past a few weeks ago. The girl looked upset again, and somehow Mel knew right away who the girl was, and why she was in such a state.

She grabbed the girl by the arm and forced her to stop. "Wait. Francesca?"

Dark eyes set into tear-streaked skin looked up at her. Francesca let out a strained sob and tried to pull her arm away.

"It's okay. My name's Mel." She rubbed her hand up and down Francesca's arm where she'd grabbed her, to sooth the muscle and encourage her to stay.

Francesca seemed to sag where she stood. She nodded, as if to give permission for Mel to continue. She looked exhausted and pitiful.

Mel forced a gentle expression onto her face and looked around her. Narrowing her eyes in thought, she guided Francesca down the corridor and towards Ruby's office. The door was unlocked, and Alexander was at his desk. When he saw them, he immediately stood up and went to the kettle to fill it.

"How do you take your tea?" he asked, eyeing Francesca with a tentative questioning look.

Mel tried to send him her thanks through a look.

He nodded towards her as acknowledgement, his smart suit and tie a navy blue today, which brought out the deep blue of his eyes.

"One… one sugar," Francesca managed, looking around her as if she had never been in the office before. *Maybe she hasn't.*

Mel sat them both down on the little sofa and leant her elbows on her knees. "I'm friends with…" Clearing her throat she shook her head. "Ruby's my friend. She's been really concerned about you."

"I know." Francesca wiped her face with her sleeve, so Mel handed the box of tissues from the coffee table to her. Francesca's face pulled into a tiny smile that didn't linger.

"She told me everything that's happened over the last few months."

Francesca nodded and blew her nose.

"She told me you've been a pain in the bum in lectures, and seminars. That you're more interested in causing havoc than learning. Is that true?"

Snuffling, Francesca shook her head.

"I didn't think so. And she doesn't really think so either."

Francesca looked up sharply, her eyebrows raised. "She doesn't?"

"Of course she doesn't. This is uni. People don't do uni unless they want to. It's not the law, you know."

Francesca's lips curled upwards, and she nodded again.

"What happened just now?" Mel kept her voice very quiet and spoke slowly. *Please don't rush off. Please don't run away.*

Alexander set two cups of tea by them and went back to his desk, his face disappearing behind his monitor.

"She...she wanted to talk to me. To say she'd seen me struggling." Sipping at her tea, Francesca closed her eyes and sighed. "I need to say I'm sorry. I was really horrible to her."

"You weren't, were you?" Mel caught her gaze and cocked an eyebrow.

Another smile threatened to appear. "I told her it was her fault that I couldn't learn. That her lectures were boring."

"Oh dear. Yes, that is pretty horrible." Francesca's face creased again, so Mel put a hand on her shoulder briefly. "Listen, we can sort it out, I promise you."

"No, we can't. I'm a hopeless case."

"That's what I thought seven years ago, when I tried to do uni and I really struggled."

Francesca looked up at her curiously, and then looked Mel up and down. "But you're, like, really old."

"Thanks."

"That's not what I... I didn't mean that."

Mel grinned. "I'm forty-seven, and when I was forty, I got tested for dyslexia."

Blinking, Francesca stared into her tea. Then she looked up at Mel again. "Dyslexia?"

"That's right."

"When you were forty?"

"Glad to hear you're listening."

Francesca glared at her in jest.

Mel was overwhelmingly pleased to see her responding to a gentle tease and not running away. "I started my paramedic science course at uni, and discovered that reading books and writing essays was really difficult for me. And I looked back and remembered I'd always found it difficult. That things were always difficult for me at school, and since becoming an adult, I'd just found ways around them. I even left my job as a teaching assistant when I couldn't keep up with the kids."

"Did you like it?"

"I loved it, very much."

"That's sad."

"I didn't know I had an actual, diagnosable problem. I didn't know there were things I could do to help myself; tried and tested things. And I didn't know I could get support from work for it. So I just did things where I wouldn't really need to read or write." Mel spoke a bit more about her career: about being an ECA and struggling with the paperwork.

Then she told Francesca about starting university, about how her peers had encouraged her to get tested, and how things had looked up from then on.

"I was in special needs at school, but I was a kid at a time when dyslexia wasn't a thing; so no one knew what it was." She picked up her tea, sipped from it, and allowed the warmth to calm her soul. "The words jump around when I read sometimes. Does that happen to you?"

Francesca stared at her, her mouth open and her teacup forgotten in her hands. She tilted her head one way, then the other, wetness gathering in her eyes again.

Mel continued. "And sometimes they get scrambled, and I have to look at each letter on its own, whereas everyone else seems to be just reading words quickly and as whole things."

"Oh my God," Francesca whispered, a tear running down her cheek in a haphazard pattern.

The door to the office opened and a forlorn-looking Ruby shuffled through, her briefcase hanging from her shoulder like a dead weight. She blinked when she took in the sight before her, and her gaze flicked from Mel to Francesca.

"Ruby," Mel said, grinning at her, sending her unspoken reassurance.

Francesca looked up, and a blush swept across her features. "Oh."

Ruby's mascara had run, but it looked like she'd wiped it clean. She looked terribly upset, and Mel stood to go to her briefly, to smooth a hand over her shoulder.

"We're just having a chat," Mel explained.

Ruby perched instead on the edge of the coffee table. Mel stood a little way away, giving them some space.

There were a few moments of silence, and Ruby seemed to be waiting for Francesca to start. Mel tried not to fidget. *I've started the ball rolling. Whatever happened in the lesson needs to be put aside. I hope they can sort it out together.*

"I'm sorry," Francesca said, her voice breaking with true sincerity. "I didn't mean what I said." She shrugged miserably. "Your lectures are okay."

"I think I need to change them."

Mel looked up and blinked. Francesca did as well.

"They're too wordy, I think," Ruby continued. "I need more visual stuff, maybe some videos. And I need to get some models for our seminars, so we can handle body parts and see where they fit together. Rather than me explaining how they do, without any point of reference." She swallowed and clasped her hands together. "I'm sorry."

"What for?"

"For not being able to talk to you. For not saying the right things. For not being able to teach in a way you understood."

"I think I'm dyslexic." Francesca blinked harshly, and a brightness flourished in her whole being. "I think I might be dyslexic."

"Why do you think that?" Ruby asked, and Mel was glad she hadn't been privy to their conversation. She could come at it from a clear perspective, without knowing what they had spoken about just seconds before.

"Mel says *she* is." Francesca's gaze floated over to Mel. "She says the words move about when she reads. And the letters get mixed up. That happens to me all the time."

"It does?"

Francesca nodded.

"Okay. Would you like some advice?"

"Yes, please." She sounded like a small child, and it was wonderful to see a gleam of hope shimmering in Francesca's eyes, amongst the gathered tears.

"I think we should get you tested. We'll go to student services, together if you like, and we'll get you booked in for a proper assessment."

"And then we'll know?"

"And then we'll know."

Francesca nodded and drank the rest of her tea before laying the cup carefully on the coffee table. She fiddled with her fingers, staring at them in contemplation. Then she lifted her head to look at her teacher. "Okay."

"Okay?"

"Yes. Let's do it. Things can't get any worse than they are now." Her lips twisted, and she blushed again. "I'm sorry I was a bitch."

"Ah, that's okay. I'm sorry I've not been the best teacher."

Smiling finally, Francesca stood from the sofa. As they passed by to go out of the door, Ruby gave Mel a wide, watery look and mouthed "Thank you".

Mel mouthed back "You're welcome", and the door snicked closed behind them.

Flopping onto the sofa, Mel drank deeply from her teacup and then exhaled.

Alexander bent his head to look around his computer screen. "Aren't you going with them?"

"No. I think it's something Ruby needs to support her with now." She put a hand to her lips, smothering a snigger. "I'd totally forgotten you were there, mate. Quiet little thing, aren't you?" She thought of James, how loud and playful he was. In comparison, Alexander had always seemed stoic, straight-laced, and cold. His sensitivity when they had come in, however—making them a drink each and silently allowing them to talk—had changed her mind.

"I find it pays to be quiet. You learn a lot."

"This is true." She settled back into the comfortable sofa and sighed again. "What a day."

"I didn't know you were dyslexic." He seemed interested but not judgemental.

"I tend to leave my banner and business cards at home."

He snorted, an uncharacteristic noise coming from the neat and tidy man across from her. "I suppose there's a lot underneath everyone that we don't know."

"I suppose there is."

# Chapter 19

Late May had brought warm sunshine and dew that hung on each blade of grass every morning, making the garden glisten. The seedlings had popped through a few weeks ago and were now growing strongly. Sixteen peppers, fourteen tomatoes, and thirty small flower seedlings created a blanket of green featheriness across the shelves of the greenhouse. Ruby loved it; the different colours and textures. She loved watching the kids' eyes brighten as they saw the fruits—literally—of their labours each time they arrived.

"I read this awesome book," Michael said as soon as they had settled into their groups. "Gran gave it to me. It's all about the ground and how you have to rotationalate the vegetables you grow."

"Rotate, Michael," Mel corrected, kindly. "And that's right, you do have to. Different plants need different nutrients from the soil."

"So one year you could grow peas… and the next, you could grow brassicas." Michael frowned. "But I don't know what a brassica is."

"Does anyone else know?" Mel asked the group.

Frank raised his hand. "Cabbage?" He looked unsure.

Ruby beamed. "That's right. And things like broccoli and cauliflower."

Half the class wrinkled their noses, and one child made a gagging noise. This was followed by a muffled set of giggling.

Mel looked flabbergasted. "Don't tell me you don't like cauliflower!"

Another titter.

"But they're the best thing since forever!"

The whole class laughed. The echoing of various children gagging and retching made Ruby shake her head in amused disbelief.

"And tomatoes have suckers. They're little branches that are bad." Michael wiggled one finger in explanation.

"And you have to take them off, don't you?" Mel replied.

Michael nodded.

Ruby was pleased she had at least one budding gardener from their little group. *If I've influenced one child out of thirty, I can live with that.*

Mel moved over the other side of the garden to help the Potato and Onion groups check the soil was clear of debris. Her expression was bright and her gestures animated. The kids all appeared to be hanging on to her every word.

Ruby combed a hand through her hair and focussed back on Michael, who was continuing to express his newfound knowledge of tomato plants. "You should pinch out the top leaves once you have three lots of tomato flowers."

"You're teaching me things that I don't even know," Ruby said, pulling her gardening gloves on, ready to work. "You'll have me out of a job."

Michael giggled and clasped his hands behind his back. "You carry on," he said in an overly posh voice, and everyone laughed.

"You don't know everything, do you, young man?" Mrs Denzie had her arms folded over her designer jacket.

Michael's expression changed to one of defiance. "I read a book, Mrs Denzie. It was about gardening. I'm just talking about it."

"You're disrespecting your teacher. Well…" She looked Ruby up and down. "Whatever you want to call her."

"I'm enjoying listening to Michael," Ruby explained, attempting to keep her tone level. It wouldn't do to create a drama in front of the kids. "It's okay with me if he wants to tell us what he's learned."

"It's not okay with me." Mrs Denzie's mouth had tightened into a small hole. "The children need to realise that we are here to teach *them*, not the other way around."

"Well, I don't mind if we learn from each other. I don't know everything." Ruby gave Michael a wink, which made him grin a bit shyly.

A vein popped at Mrs Denzie's temple. She chucked her head in one direction, indicating for Michael to step to the side with her. He followed, his feet dragging.

Their voices were muffled, but Ruby could hear their conversation. She knelt with Chelsea, who had found a pretty stone in the bed, and tilted her head so she could listen.

"You are really starting to try my patience," Mrs Denzie said.

"I just want to be helpful." Michael sounded forlorn, but there was strength in his voice. He sounded used to Mrs Denzie's criticism of him.

"It would be a shame, wouldn't it, if your lovely Ruby found out about the little incident before Christmas?"

A pregnant pause followed. Ruby turned her head to look. Michael was shifting about and fidgeting with his fingers. "I don't…" He looked up with wide eyes. "Please don't say anything about that."

"Embarrassed? By a little vomiting?"

"It… it went all over the desk."

"It wasn't your fault, was it?"

He shrugged. "I was poorly."

"You were. But think of how Ruby might react if she knew that you'd done that."

More uncomfortable twitching from Michael. Eventually, he sighed, his sad gaze lifting towards Ruby.

"I don't think you want that, do you, Michael?"

Ruby went back to her inspection of Chelsea's stone. *Poor Michael. And why on earth is his teacher talking to him in such a way?* Ruby wondered whether Mrs Denzie had had previous issues with Michael—whether he had misbehaved before and needed to be reminded of the way things were. She was unsure whether she agreed with Mrs Denzie or not. *Maybe this is the only way she can keep him in line? She knows these children better than I do.*

"No." The singular word held so much misery that Ruby had a great urge to go cuddle him.

"Good boy."

He returned to the Tomato group, and it was as if he became invisible, merging with the rest of the children and their plants.

*I hope I don't annoy her. Heaven knows she's good at getting people to do what she wants them to do.*

Mel sidled up to Ruby, and Ruby felt the brush of her fingers against her back before they were gone. "Sorry," Mel whispered close to her ear. "Sometimes I forget."

"So do I," Ruby replied in kind, turning her head a little to blink up at Mel. Her gaze flicked down to Mel's lips, but she pressed her own lips together and stepped backwards. Growling deep in her throat, she stuffed her hands into her pockets in a very Mel-like gesture. *My goodness, we're becoming twins.* She took her hands back out and folded her arms.

There was laughter in Mel's eyes as she obviously recognised Ruby's behaviour. Ruby wanted to shove her playfully or admonish her, but she was grinning too widely. *Focus.* Ruby took Tomato group into the greenhouse while Mel took Potato and Onion groups to their vegetable patch. She watched out of the glass panels and saw Mel lifting each potato leaf to check for insects. Turning her attention back to her own collection of curious faces, she showed them how to check that their plants had four leaves, and if they did, to bring them outside.

A line of children, each carrying their own two plants, followed her out of the greenhouse, which was starting to heat up in the day and make the collar of her T-shirt damp. The Peppers sat on the picnic benches with drinks and snacks, occasionally chatting, and occasionally watching the other groups with interest.

"Michael, have you read about how to repot tomato plants?" Ruby squinted in the sun at him.

He looked uncomfortable. But then he nodded, and she allowed him to dig the first little hole in the soil they'd prepared last week, making sure there were no stones or rubbish in it. Turning his first pot upside down, he splayed his little fingers around the plant to cradle it safely and then shook the whole thing. The plant dropped into his hand, and there was a mini applause from the group. She noticed the fire from his eyes had gone, but a smile tugged his lips as he took in everyone else's joy.

Ruby watched him gently turn the plant back the right way up. He slid it into the perfectly sized hole and gathered the soil around it, pressing it in like a cake in a tin.

She clapped herself, warmth filling every part of her body, and glanced over at Mel.

Mel caught her eye across the garden and nodded, her arms smeared with mud up to the elbow, as usual.

"Fantastic, Michael. Well done." Stepping behind the little line of kids, she helped each of those who needed it, and when they were done there was a row of spindly tomato plants along the edge of the vegetable patch.

Next, she put Michael and his friends to work with some canes and twine, creating a long cage to support the tomatoes. *He's a born leader. He'd be a great teacher.* She watched him affectionately as he grinned at her. She allowed the group to work together and come up with something fairly stable without her interference. *I can always check it once they're gone, to make sure it doesn't bend in the wind.*

The Peppers were beginning to fidget a bit, so Ruby instructed them to check their plants in the greenhouse. She went in with them, and they were all delighted to see tiny roots sticking out from the bottoms of their pots. "Time to give them bigger homes, what do you think?"

They agreed and set about choosing new pots and placing the plants into them.

Tomato group had finished their construction, and Ruby watched through the glass as Michael led them to affix it into the ground either side of the tomato plants. "Good job, guys. I'll be out in a minute. Go grab a drink."

Chelsea pulled her pepper plant from its container so roughly that the stalk broke. She held it as if hoping Ruby could glue it back together, and her bottom lip quivered.

"Oh darling, it's okay. That's why everyone has two, you see?"

Chelsea nodded, sniffling a little, and Ruby showed her how to properly and carefully take her one remaining pepper out of its pot and introduce it to its new one. The bottom lip retracted, and Chelsea looked a lot happier once she'd received praise for the care she had taken, as well as a pointed acknowledgement that she no longer wanted to wear gloves.

"I can feel things better," she explained. "I want to feel the mud on my hands, because it makes me feel closer to the plants."

Ruby nearly cried at the depth of emotion Chelsea was expressing. Who knew the girl had a deep side?

The pepper plants stayed in the greenhouse. "It's still a bit cold for them," Ruby explained. She pointed to the thermometer inside the greenhouse. "Twenty is perfect for them, but it's only ten outside overnight. They wouldn't like that."

"But they'll go outside when it's warmer?" Chelsea asked, clearly unhappy about her plant's inability to grow to its full potential.

"Yes. Once it's warmer, we can pop them in with the tomatoes."

Exiting the sticky greenhouse, Ruby and the Pepper group wandered over to Potato and Onion groups, intrigued about what they were spending their time doing. Mel had them all on their knees, looking under the large leaves of the potato plants, checking for anything that might eat them. Frank laughed loudly when he pulled out a fat slug, holding it between a chubby thumb and forefinger and waggling it about in Becca's face.

Becca's expression was nothing short of disgusted, which made it all the more amusing. The whole class was giggling and squealing.

"Right, then," Mel said after she and Ruby exchanged a glance. "The group that finds the biggest slug gets to water their plants first."

An insignificant prize in Ruby's opinion, but it seemed to get the kids invested. Tomato and Pepper groups sank to their knees too and began to search their own patch.

Mrs Denzie sat, one leg crossed over the other, her nose slightly wrinkled at the children's activity. Ruby arched her eyebrow as the teacher huffed, rolled her eyes, and uncrossed her legs, re-crossing them the other way. *Thank goodness her class hasn't seemed to notice her disinterest.* Ruby hoped they never would, and that their enthusiasm would continue until the end of their time with her.

Deciding to ignore the critical looks being thrown in the general direction of thirty pairs of mucky hands, Ruby walked around the bed and stepped up to Mel. "Good idea," she said, her voice low.

Mel nodded and reached up to touch her cheek.

Ruby's eyes went wide as Mel's thumb brushed her skin, but when the thumb came away with a smear of brown on it, she felt her cheeks reddening. "Oh."

"I mean, it was adorable," Mel said, quiet enough so the kids couldn't hear. "But not very professional."

"Thank you."

"All part of the service." Stepping away again, Mel gave her a shy look.

Nothing would have pleased Ruby more than to have the opportunity to envelope Mel in her arms and press their lips together. Despite having only kissed once at the park, she missed the feeling and wanted to experience it again. But they were surrounded by thirty curious small people, most of them unwilling to refrain from asking questions. *Mel wouldn't mind that. She'd be quite happy to talk about our relationship with these kids. Should I be more like Mel?*

Ruby had never really discussed her sexuality with anyone apart from her own daughters and her mother. The former conversation had been difficult; the girls had been younger, but old enough to understand what 'gay' meant. They'd heard the word used at school and had wondered why it was usually used in such a negative capacity. Ruby remembered having to explain to them that it shouldn't be used in this way, but that her girls shouldn't feel they had to stand up for her sexuality if they didn't want people to know about it.

*Mel wouldn't have said that if she'd had kids.* Ruby gazed at the beautiful woman with the shining strawberry-blonde hair and saw the spark in her, her joy for life, and her strength of character. *She'd have told her own children, if she had them, to always stand up for what they believe in.*

It made her insides ache. Mel was so wonderfully strong. She felt bad though, that she'd never been like that. She stood up for other people, where appropriate, of course, but she'd never had to stand up for herself. It wasn't as if she had hidden her sexuality; her forays into the world of lesbianism hadn't been brief or varied, but she'd never shouted about it. A bit of hand-holding down a street was all she had exposed to the world.

She could imagine Mel at Pride festivals, and not just because Mel had outright told the kids she'd attended the last one. She could see her tall frame, strong arms raised in joy at the drums and floats and dancers in the parade. She could see those green eyes full of life, surrounded by rainbow face paint, or her head adorned with a headband pronouncing *Gay Is Okay*, or some other phrase of love. She could imagine a whistle in her mouth, her hands joining with those of others as they walked together, a mass of love and trust and respect, through the roads of the city.

She could imagine her jumping about inside a tent, glow sticks held up in the air, her body brushing against other sweaty bodies as the music thumped around them.

The image was delicious and exciting.

After a few heartbeats, Ruby realised she had been staring. She snapped her gaze down to her boots and felt a blush creeping into her cheeks. She wasn't sure if she'd been caught by anyone and didn't particularly care to find out.

When she looked back up, Mel was pronouncing one of the children from Potato group the winner. The kid held up her slug, the body of it fatter than a sausage, and she went to place it into the fountain for the fish to have for dinner. Mel came over to Ruby and squeezed her shoulder briefly.

Mrs Denzie strode over to them as the kids were washing their hands and stamping their wellies on the concrete to shake off the mud. Her arms were folded, and her face was stony. Ruby immediately tensed and took a step backwards.

"Hi, great class today. What fun the kids had," Mel said, apparently unaware of the aggression coming off Mrs Denzie in waves.

"It's absolutely disgusting," Mrs Denzie said. "You two... carrying on like it's okay. We've had words before. I made my feelings about your... relationship very clear. And you carry on like it's... normal."

"Whatever you think, it's really none of your business," Mel said, keeping her voice level and reasonably soft.

"It absolutely *is* my business when you're subjecting my class to... They're innocent and impressionable and I do not wish for them to be... For them to think this is..." Clearly struggling to get her words out, Mrs Denzie's hands were shaking; her jaw was clenched, and her mouth a tiny lemon-sucking hole.

Mel sighed deeply and put her fingers to her forehead. When she dropped her hand, her expression was frustrated. "You sound like a caveman." She shook her head, obviously bewildered, and held her arms open. "We barely touch one another; we never say anything to one another, or to any of the children, that would be deemed inappropriate. The kids are having fun, they're learning, they're growing things they will be able to eat when harvest time arrives. I don't see what the problem is."

Some of the children had looked up, and Michael, followed by Becca and a few of the others, crept closer.

Ruby started to feel like a spare part. She chewed on her lip before taking a deep breath. "If you have a problem with the way we're running the group, can I suggest you speak with my superior?"

"Oh, I'm sure he's a proper lefty!" Mrs Denzie replied, her head tilted to the side and her gaze hard.

"What's a lefty?" Michael asked, the children now close enough to hear everything.

"It's someone who believes that all walks of life should be allowed. Including murderers and..." Mrs Denzie clearly had a whole list of "lowlifes" she intended on naming but had decided that the list was too extensive for little ears.

"No, that's not what a lefty is," Ruby said, speaking directly to Michael rather than give his teacher any attention. "It's someone who is open to new ideas, who thinks all people should be treated equally." Ruby felt her own hands shaking so folded her arms, tucking her fingers under her elbows. "Black people, gay people, disabled people, people with learning difficulties..." She realised what she had said and looked over at Mel, her gut clenching.

The smile on Mel's face made everything fall away: her fears, her nerves, and her worry. *Is that approval I can see in those green eyes?*

"What's the problem with that?" Michael asked, folding his arms too. Some of his classmates followed suit, copying his stance.

"The *problem* is," Mrs Denzie began, "that you are far too young to learn about things like that." She hissed the last three words, as if they were some kind of swear phrase.

"Like what?" Michael seemed appalled. "I can talk about being black if I want to." It wasn't a question, and Mrs Denzie seemed surprised and frustrated in equal measures.

"Of course you... That's not what I meant."

"What did you mean?" Frank asked, as if he had suddenly discovered an assertiveness he never knew he had.

"These two... women. They are obviously in a... a *lesbian* relationship." Her nose crinkled, and Ruby had the overwhelming urge to laugh. *She really has come from a cave.* "And they should not be... exposing that to young minds."

"Are you girlfriends?" Chelsea asked, her words plain and without criticism.

Ruby looked at Mel, who nodded to her, an encouraging gesture. "Yes. We are girlfriends," Ruby said.

Chelsea's face split into a wide grin. "That's really nice."

Michael whooped and clapped. A few of the other kids did too.

Becca eyed them both, her gaze more suspicious. "But are you gay though?"

Mel nodded kindly at the girl. "I'm gay. I told you that a while ago."

Becca nodded and then turned to Ruby. One eyebrow crept towards her severe fringe.

"I'm gay too." The admission left Ruby's shoulders floppy and loose. A bubble of relief rose up inside her, and she felt like laughing again. She didn't care that she'd come out to the kids, and she didn't care what they thought, not really. She did care that Mel's approving look had intensified and that the light shining from her eyes was all for Ruby.

"Awesome." Michael nodded and looked between the two of them. "But you're not going to snog in front of us." Again, the statement, accompanied by several fake-retching noises from the class, was not a question.

"That'd be weird, wouldn't it?" Mel said, and they all laughed. When they had quietened, Mel looked around the group. "We're here to teach you to grow things and make sure you have a nice time. That's all."

Ruby stood silently, wondering what Mrs Denzie was going to say. If she'd been sitting, she'd have been on the edge of her seat.

Mel's smile widened. "Look, you seem like a cool bunch, right?"

Cheers erupted briefly.

"So, do you have a problem with me being gay?"

A chorus of "No!" rang through the garden.

"And do you have a problem with Ruby being gay?"

An echoing "No".

"And you don't have an issue with us being together?"

A pause of contemplation stretched between them all. It gave Mrs Denzie the perfect opportunity to interject. "See? They're so uncomfortable with it. You've brought something up that they're simply too young to understand."

"We're not too young," Becca said.

"I've had three girlfriends," Michael said. "I understand what love is."

"I've told you before about your habit of voicing your opinions, Michael. Any more of this nonsense and I'll be explaining to Ruby and Mel exactly what happened before Christmas."

Michael shrank away, but the look in his eyes was defiant. Ruby nearly laughed again.

"You've had *three girlfriends*?" Mel asked in amazement, and Michael nodded proudly. "Quite an achievement. I hope you treated them all well."

Michael folded his arms. "Of course I did." Three of the girls, including Chelsea, nodded their agreement.

Mrs Denzie spluttered. "It's hardly the same. Your little relationships are nothing like you'll experience when you're an adult, Michael."

Michael stared at her. "That's not fair. I told you, I know what love is." He turned to Mel. "Are you in love with Ruby?"

Ruby nearly fell over. Her insides twisted uncomfortably.

Mel considered him. "What do you think?"

"I think you are." Michael nodded once and then looked around at his classmates. "Who thinks Mrs Denzie's being a ninny, and being nasty to Ruby and Mel because they're gay?"

"Now, come on," Ruby said gently. "That's a very rude thing to say." *However much I agree with him.*

"Sorry," Michael said, deflating a bit. His lips twisted in thought. "Who thinks Mrs Denzie should be nice to Ruby and Mel, and not be nasty to them because they're gay?"

A unanimous murmur of agreement flooded through the group.

"That's settled, then." Michael looked overwhelmingly pleased with himself.

Mrs Denzie looked anything but. Steam was practically coming out of her ears, and her face had taken on a beetroot quality. She stamped her foot—actually stamped it, her fashionably Wellington boot making an imprint in the edge of the grass. "I'm sorry, I disagree. I'm going to have to go to the dean." She narrowed her eyes. "I'm sure he will be incredibly interested to know that I saw you... doing inappropriate things... in the greenhouse when we arrived." She glared at Michael. "I'm sure you will back up my story."

He stared in horror, his fingers sliding sweatily in and out of each other. Then he looked down at the ground. He hadn't agreed, but definitely hadn't said he wouldn't.

"Inappropriate things? What on earth are you talking about?" Mel asked.

And then it hit Ruby. Being caught in a compromising position with Mel, in full view of the children and the rest of the university, would end her career for sure. The volcano in Mrs Denzie's eyes was tempered by triumph when she locked her gaze with Ruby's and realised she was onto a winner. She wouldn't hold back any illicit details of what she had apparently seen. No way. The glee transforming her face made that abundantly clear. And that would be it for Ruby. Her reputation would be left in shreds. And her job... the job she needed to pay the bills, feed her daughters... Well, she could kiss that good-bye.

"People like you should not be allowed to work with children, and by the time I'm through, you'll never work with them again." She turned on her heel and left the garden area, the door into the main building thumping behind her.

Everyone stared at one another. Mel patted Michael's shoulder as his face dropped. He clearly felt responsible for their teacher going off in a rage. His gaze was locked on the door, until Mel's hand started a back-and-forth rub and he seemed to jolt out of his reverie.

"Thank you for standing up for us," Mel murmured to him, and he looked a bit brighter at that, exchanging glances with his group of friends.

"I didn't." A tear trickled down his face. Then he looked up and caught Ruby's gaze. "Um… I don't want her to tell you what happened last year."

"That's okay," Mel continued to rub his shoulder. "It's private?"

Michael nodded.

"I'll stick my fingers in my ears."

That appeared to ease his worries, and his cheerfulness returned.

Time stretched, and the kids became restless. "Has she just left us?" Becca's sensible voice carried across the group.

A swirling began in Ruby's insides. She felt like she was going to vomit.

"I'll go check." Mel gave them all a thumbs up, as if to let them know she was okay, before jogging out of the garden and into the university building.

Ruby shifted her feet from one side to the other but couldn't meet each child's gaze when they looked at her.

Frank shuffled over to her and hesitantly put his hand on her elbow. He was shorter than his classmates, and pudgier too, but the look in his eye made her wonder whether he had a sensitive father. "It's all right, Ruby," he said, smiling up at her.

She tried to smile back and felt everything melting just a bit at the caring look in his eyes. She placed her hand atop his, and they all waited for Mel to return.

Mel came back, a few minutes later. "Looks like she went to the dean, but now she's gone. Called a taxi apparently and left campus."

Ruby stared at her feet. She allowed Mel to organise the children and was faintly aware of her phoning the school to let them know what had happened.

*What am I going to do? If I lose my job, that'll be it: the house, my daughters all set to go to university. I won't have the money to send either of them. My lovely car, the dinners out we have, the nice things we have to eat. Even Jasmine's blooming pasta.*

*And the repercussions for Mel will be no better. I'm sure she'll be booted off her course after being seen engaging in inappropriate activity in a public place. Maybe the university will contact her employer too. They'd have to. Her course was linked to her job. Oh God, what a mess!*

It was warm in the garden, but shivers brushed along her shoulders. She clasped her hands together and yanked a smile onto her face when Mel approached.

"Hey. All right?"

"I'm good." Ruby felt anything but, but she didn't want Mel to know.

A note of uncertainty flickered across Mel's gaze. "Okay." There was an awkward pause. "They're sending another teacher to take the kids home."

"Good."

"So, that's sorted."

Ruby shook herself inwardly. "Yes. Sorry. Thank you for doing that."

Mel softened. "That's okay. We're a team."

Ruby shivered again.

# Chapter 20

"Oh my God, Mum, so what happened?"

"Unfortunately, we had to phone the school."

"Why? Couldn't you just take the kids back to their school on the bus? It was already there, right?"

Ruby shook her head. "Not as simple as that when it comes to the care and responsibility of school kids. Especially primary-school kids. While we both have police checks and such, neither of us is insured to take thirty children on a school bus. Besides, how would we have got back to campus?"

"One of you could have followed the bus in a car to pick the other up. I can't believe she just left," Chloe said, easily keeping up with her mother as they walked along the path that outlined the park, Barney trotting at their heels. Chloe's long corduroys brushed the concrete and Ruby rolled her eyes at them.

"Yeah, we were pretty shocked too."

"What did the school say?" Chloe bent down to let the dog off the lead and held her hand out for the ball stowed safely in Ruby's handbag.

Ruby handed it to her daughter. "I'm not sure what they'll do about the teacher. They sent a replacement in a taxi to accompany the kids."

Chloe's expression scrunched, and she blinked a few times, then threw the ball for Barney, who scampered after it. "So, this woman went to the dean?"

"Yes." Tension coiled inside Ruby.

"What's she going to do?"

"I've been called in. For a formal meeting."

Chloe stared at Ruby. "Blimey. That's a bit harsh."

"It's going to be a disaster."

"You think?"

Ruby nodded. "My job might be on the line."

Those trailing trouser bottoms nearly caused Chloe to trip. "What?"

"Yep."

Barney ran up to them and dropped the ball at Chloe's feet, her tail hitting the sides of her bottom one after the other.

Ruby watched Barney race up to another dog instead of chasing the ball that Chloe had thrown for her. Bum-sniffing commenced before Barney arrived back in front of them, an expectant look on her face.

"I don't have it. You lost it. Go find it." Chloe's voice was commanding but kind.

Barney sped away, her nose to the ground. She sneezed a couple of times.

"You really think you might get fired?"

Ruby shrugged and blinked back tears. "The teacher threatened to... She's going to tell the dean..." She gazed down at her daughter, and the overwhelming need to keep her safe at all costs consumed her. *I'm supposed to be setting a good example to my children. What kind of mother puts her romantic life before her professional integrity?*

"Brian offered me more shifts at the shop," Chloe said nonchalantly.

Ruby's heart swelled. "They really think you're a good employee, don't they?"

"I mean, like..." Chloe chewed the side of a finger until her mother tapped her hand, a chastisement. "I could work more, help with the mortgage. If you have trouble."

"But, darling, you're at college full-time. You already work a day and a half at the weekend."

Chloe shrugged. "Yeah."

"You're not giving college up. Your A levels are important."

She shrugged once more. "I know. But if you need me to… I will. I could drop two, and do the other two next year, or the year after."

Nausea rolled inside her. "No. Your studies are more important than…" Ruby swallowed. "Don't worry. I'll sort it."

Chloe stared back at her, and something settled in her eyes, something understanding. She came up on her toes and slipped her arms around her mother's neck, resting against her front. "You always know what to do, Mum. So you shouldn't worry either."

Ruby gripped Chloe and inhaled her hair-dye-tinged scent. She needed to make some changes. She needed protect her job and her family. The tension in her shoulders clicked up a notch, but she pulled away with renewed determination. "I'll sort it."

---

*My legs hurt.* Mel flopped back onto her sofa with a groan. Epione slunk past, purring, her tail high. The purring intensified as Mel rubbed her ears. "Hey, matey. Bet you're hungry?"

"Mrow."

Everything ached as Mel pulled herself to her feet and went into the kitchen in search of a drink for herself and something to quench Epione's hunger. A couple of cat treats later, the fluffy feline was settling down back in the living room, her eyes closing in a cat-smile.

Mel flopped down with her glass of water, the ice clinking against the sides. She drank languidly, then placed the glass on her coffee table. A few minutes of silence and tranquillity, after the drama of the day.

*I wonder if Mrs Denzie will get fired. There's really no talking to some people.*

Her phone rang, breaking the comfortable moment, but Mel wasn't too fazed. Ruby's name flashed on the screen.

"Hey." She pressed the phone to her ear, trying to sound gentle. She'd got the feeling that Ruby hadn't been all that pleased with Mrs Denzie's reaction.

"Hiya. Listen."

Mel's mouth went dry, and she was suddenly on high alert. "You all right?"

"I'm fine." Clipped and stark words.

"Because, I know today was difficult."

"Yes. It was."

Mel swallowed. She rubbed her slick palm against her trousers.

"Listen. I want to stop what we're doing."

A lead weight knocked inside her "But everything's growing really well, and I reckon we're going to make loads of money."

"No." Ruby huffed, as if in frustration. "Not the gardening group."

"What, then?" Mel blinked. "Wait. You want to break up with me?"

"I don't want to, but it's the right thing to do."

"Why?" Mel searched the room for some kind of explanation. *Did I do something wrong?*

"Because... it's inappropriate. I can't have my private life and my personal life mixing like this."

Standing from the sofa, Mel started to pace. "What are you talking about? We went through this; it's not inappropriate. You're not my lecturer, and I'm not your student."

"It's wrong. I'm at work and you're... you're all over me. Students see me and God knows what they think." Something caught in Ruby's voice, as if it was suddenly difficult for her to talk. *Is she crying?*

"I'm not all over you." Mel stopped walking and looked out of the window at her greenhouse. She wracked her brains to try to remember a time she'd touched Ruby inappropriately while in the garden at university. "Come on, tell the truth." *Is it my inability to read?* Her chest hurt, suddenly.

"I am." A pause. "I don't like my private life bandied about like it's common knowledge. Especially where I work. I'm sorry."

"You're not sorry." The words were growled through gritted teeth. "You're small-minded and opinionated."

"I know. I'm sorry for that too."

"Stop saying that." Tears collected in Mel's eyes and she rubbed them away. "If you were sorry, you wouldn't have strung me along." She exhaled sharply and wrapped an arm around her middle. "You really weren't okay with it, were you?"

"It's too much for me. I can't do this."

And the phone went dead.

Mel thumped her palm against the window ledge. It stung all up her arm, but she didn't care. She dropped her phone onto the sofa, then flopped down next to it. Turning her face into the soft cushions, she cried.

*I knew it. She's changed her mind about my condition. She thinks I'm broken, abnormal… stupid.*

Images of Ruby in the sunshine by the shed, her hair shining with golden streaks and her eyes dancing, made Mel cry all the more.

---

Mel hated the smell of the care home. Too much disinfectant, and flowers in every corner. Maybe she just associated the smell with the place where she knew her father was going to die. The thoughts rushed her whenever she entered the foyer, but she always pushed them back. Today was not a good day.

She said hello to the various carers and nurses that worked at the home before peeking around the door-frame into the living area. Several old people sat in high-backed chairs, the television showing some programme about making over someone's home. It was reasonably mindless, but at least it wasn't Jeremy Kyle. One home she'd visited with her brothers had been showing that when she'd walked in. She'd walked out seven minutes later, with the decision that no one she loved would ever go there.

She caught sight of her father through the glass door in the sun room—a bright and warm room with light-coloured furniture and views out into the garden. He was asleep, his gnarled hands resting on either chair arm.

A sense of calm settled over her at the expression on his face. The lines that usually tainted his features were almost non-existent. Perhaps he was dreaming about happy times with her mother. A cup of tea, still steaming away, sat next to him.

She sat in the chair at his elbow. "Hi, Dad."

He stirred but didn't wake. She listened to the sounds of the home for a while: the occasional grunt from a fellow occupant, the tinkling of the water feature in the garden that carried through the open window. Then she sighed and rested properly back into the large armchair.

"I didn't tell you. I met a woman." She checked he was still asleep and found him snoring softly now. "She's called Ruby. She's amazing." A lump formed in her throat, and she swallowed. "You'd like her, actually. She's strong and determined and funny." She placed her hand over her father's and squeezed. "But she broke up with me. So I'm feeling a bit..." She looked around. No one seemed to be listening, and all the carers were clumped together in the staff room drinking tea. "A bit heartbroken, I suppose."

She remembered being younger, when her dad was fully functional, in mind and body. Going home from her little flat and falling into his waiting arms after Rach had ended their relationship. They'd sat together on the overstuffed sofa, his big arms around her. He'd even stroked her hair and had sung silly songs to her, to make her feel better. He'd done that when she was a child.

"So I'm sad. Because she ended it because I'm stupid and thick and can't read properly." She brushed away a tear and sat up a little straighter. "Anyway, you're being a right sleepy-head this morning. What's that about, hm?" She squeezed his hand and patted it.

He wriggled in his seat and squinted as he opened his eyes. She sent him a hopeful look. He stared at her with a hint of confusion.

"Hey, Dad."

"Who are you?"

The tightness in her throat swelled into a burning. "I'm... I'm Mel. I'm your daughter."

He squinted some more at her. "I don't have a daughter. Where's my Katy?"

The carpet beneath her trainers was new. She bit her lip and forced away the shudder that threatened to pass over her. "Mum's not here." *I need to stick with the care plan. No use telling him she's dead. Just play along.* "She's out at the moment. What do you need her for?"

"Mum?" His eyes were hazy. "My mother lives in Liverpool. Katy lives with me. Where's Katy?" His voice was rising.

"Dad, it's okay." She attempted to calm him with a gentle hand on his arm. He batted her away.

"I'm late for dinner. Why am I sitting here? Who made this tea for me?"

"Mum… I mean, Katy did. It's okay." Mel sat back in the chair. *I want my dad. I want my dad.*

He stared down at the cup, and eventually the lines on his face receded. He sighed. "Oh. Yes, that's right."

Her throat loosened a bit, but more tears threatened to fall. She took a couple of deep breaths. *So much for Dad telling me it's all okay. He's not going to do that much anymore.*

It was as if the whole traumatic event hadn't happened. Once he had finished his cup of tea, he stood shakily and moved to the electric organ on the other side of the sun room. She helped him turn it on, turned the volume right down, and pulled the sliding door closed so they wouldn't disturb the other residents. Then she settled back in her chair, flopped her head to the side, and listened while his feet and fingers danced over the keys and pedals; an old show tune she recognised but couldn't name.

# Chapter 21

THE CORRIDOR WAS SILENT AS Ruby waited outside the dean's office. She pulled her hand through her hair a few times, her fingers snagging on the occasional knot. Her shirt was too constrictive, and she longed to open the top button but refrained. It was too hot in the corridor, the walls too close. She felt trapped, cornered; like an animal on the way to slaughter.

When Sonya opened the door, Ruby felt lightheaded and put a hand against the wall to steady herself.

*I have a plan. Things will be okay.* Pushing out her chin, she met Sonya's gaze with her own. "Afternoon."

"Come in." Sonya moved away, and Ruby entered the office. Sonya held a hand out to the chair opposite her desk and sat in the larger, more luxurious, chair behind it. "Now, this business with Mrs Denzie."

"It's all sorted." Ruby clasped her hands and made sure she was sitting up straight. She hoped Sonya couldn't see the sweat patches under her arms.

"It most definitely is not. I'm incredibly concerned."

Ruby looked into her lap. She fingered the ring on her middle finger.

"That our local primary school employs someone who treats *my staff* with such disrespect. I'm appalled, Ruby, truly appalled." She placed a hand across the desk. "And I'm very sorry you had to deal with that."

Sudden realisation made Ruby look up. "Eh?"

"We run a very inclusive establishment here, as you well know. Our diversity policy is top notch." The look in Sonya's eyes was gentle, even apologetic. "She came in here to complain about you having a relationship with one of our ECP students: Mel? She's helping you with the Air Ambulance fundraiser, isn't she?"

Ruby nodded.

"First of all, it's incredibly kind that someone who works full-time, and is completing a taxing Masters Level course, should give up their Wednesday afternoons to help out the university. I must write to her to say thank you."

Ruby gripped the chair arm. Everything went still apart from the surging of her blood which seemed to rush through her vessels.

"And I've called the primary school. They were very much unaware of Mrs Denzie's views, and that she was openly expressing them to her students. I'm sure you'll agree when I tell you that she has been sent on a diversity-awareness course. I insisted. I also insisted they replace her at the gardening group." Sonya sat back and folded her hands.

"So…wait. You've not called me in to tell me off for having an affair with a student?"

"An affair? Oh Ruby, you are awfully old fashioned." Sonya chuckled. "No. You don't teach her directly, so I don't see a problem. Like I said, we don't have an issue with anyone's sexual preference at this university. It just isn't policy."

"Oh."

"And that ludicrous story she tried to add on to her complaint when she saw I wasn't giving her any credence"—she waved her hand and shook her head—"about you and the paramedic doing whatever in the greenhouse? Please. I know you better than that for one thing, and it was so obvious she was making it up as she went along right there and then. Then telling me an eight-year-old would back her up." Another chuckle. "You absolutely should have said something before. Sounds like she's been giving you trouble from the word go."

"Yes. She has."

"Anyway, I just wanted you to know that we support you. You're doing a great job, from what I've seen on my little amblings in that garden. I think we should make it a yearly occurrence, don't you? Also, this first-year student, who I hear you have put up for a dyslexia assessment. Good work, Ruby. I'm not sure I'd have noticed that." Sonya's laugh boomed around the office. "One of the other students told me about that prank she pulled with your projector. Well done for keeping your cool. Something else I would not have managed."

Something bubbled up in Ruby's throat, so she pressed her fingers against her mouth, willing the feeling to disappear. *I was so convinced she was going to fire me. What did I know?*

With a wave of her hand, Sonya dismissed her. "Go on, out with you. You have a seminar to run in five."

Ruby stopped by her office to collect her belongings. She sank into her desk chair and eyed the leather sofa, the place she'd spent so many wonderful lunches with Mel, chatting about everything and anything. She put her face in her hands.

*What have I done?*

# Chapter 22

Mel had been curled up on her sofa with the television turned to a smooth music channel. Lyrics describing how the heart felt when it was overflowing with love had been drifting over the room for hours. Her head rested on a cushion, and the scratchy blanket she used to keep her feet warm during a winter evening was pulled haphazardly around her shoulders.

Mel heard the knock but couldn't muster the strength to get up for several seconds. She flopped back onto the cushion when the door squeaked open and James emerged. He held up a bulging shopping bag.

"Supplies." He tilted his head, and his face dropped from its usual teasing expression. "Aw, mate."

Mel didn't have the energy to respond, so she burrowed further into the cushion.

Epione, recognising a potential extra human care-giver, who might fill her food bowl, wound herself around James's legs.

"All right, Epi. Hm. Mum doesn't seem to have been taking care of herself, let alone you." He took the bag into the kitchen, and she heard him clanking about in her cupboards before the familiar noise of food clattering into the cat's metal bowl reached her ears. "There you go." She listened with some comfort as James filled and boiled the kettle. "Tea or coffee?" he shouted.

She snuffled and turned onto her back. Her voice cracked. "Coffee. Two sugars."

"Cor, Epi, it must be bad. *Two* sugars, hmm?"

Mel scrubbed her face with her hands.

Two cups of coffee appeared as James returned to the living room. He placed them on the table before nudging her feet with his hip. "Come on, you. Sit up."

"No." She put her hands back over her eyes.

"Yes." His voice was stern. She wasn't sure if he was joking or not. "Up, woman. Or we're going to have to do some manual handling."

At that, she sat up. She didn't feel like being hauled around like one of their patients. She pushed her hair out of her eyes. It was coming loose from the ponytail she'd put it in… Three days ago?

The coffee on her table steamed invitingly. She took a sip and allowed it to burn her mouth a bit. Anything to distract her from the raw feeling that was making it difficult for her to eat.

"Have you eaten?" James asked, as if he could read her thoughts.

Mel shrugged.

"Right. Drink your coffee, then food."

Mel wrinkled her nose but obliged, allowing the warmth of the mug to tickle her face.

"I brought silly movies, popcorn, and chocolate."

Tears gathered in her eyes, and her bottom lip shook. "Mate."

"Oh, shush." He put his coffee down hastily and wrapped his arms around her. "Less of the blubbering, yeah?" He was teasing, but the affection in his voice made her cry harder. He just rocked her for a while, the roughness of his beard scratchy against her forehead.

Once she'd got her emotions under control, she pulled back and wiped her face with her sleeve. She glanced down at herself and blushed as she realised that she wasn't even wearing underwear. Just pyjamas and a hoody. *Hair unbrushed and in nightclothes for three days—not hugely professional.*

Not that James seemed to care. He patted her knee and rubbed her arm vigorously. "Right. Now the crying is done, maybe you should tell me what happened?"

"She broke up with me."

"Yep, I got that from the series of depressed texts."

She looked down at her coffee. The dark brown of it reminded her of Ruby's hair. She pushed the cup across the coffee table and refused to look at it. "She said she couldn't be with me anymore, and that it was too much, having her personal and private lives mixing. She's at work and..." Mel closed her mouth and looked down at her hands.

"Aw, mate. I'm sorry. So what, she wasn't happy with you being a student or...?"

"She didn't say it out loud, but it was clear it was to do with my learning difficulty. She tried to make me believe it was to do with her privacy, but let's just say she was less than convincing on that part. She obviously thinks I'm not worth the hassle." Mel ground her teeth.

"Yes, you are."

"Nope." The memory of the way Ruby had caressed the back of her neck when they had kissed, and the way she'd looked so deeply into Mel's eyes, caused fresh tears to spring forth. The image of Ruby's eyes was replaced with Rach's, then with a whole stream of women Mel had dated. She'd kept those relationships short, not wanting to get in too deep and let them find out she couldn't read well. They all seemed like one person now, all leaving her or making her leave. She'd thought Ruby wasn't like that.

"Why these new tears?" James shifted closer.

"I don't know." Mel swiped at her face. "I suppose I wish things had gone differently."

"With Ruby?"

"With all of them maybe. But Ruby, yes." She let out a long sigh. "Good riddance to her. She's just like all the others."

James's brow wrinkled. "Really? You didn't seem to think that last week."

"Yeah, well, last week she didn't know I couldn't read."

He appeared to ignore her over-exaggeration. "But... you said she was fine with that. Didn't you?"

"She was lying."

"How do you know?"

"Because people don't keep being a gay a secret anymore. There's no need."

"I know things have changed," James said slowly. "But it can't be easy being in a respectable job and being out."

"I manage it just fine." Mel's jaw ached, and she had to consciously unclench to ease it.

"I know. But you're very confident. You always have been. Practically the first thing you said to me when we started our first shift together was 'Hey, dude, I'm a big ol' les.'"

She glared at him. "You're... Surely you're not taking her side?"

"I'm just saying... maybe she wasn't lying about why she wanted to break up."

She blinked rapidly and shook her head.

"It's such a shame," James continued. "You looked so happy when you spoke about her. Like she really *was* different. Like she was the one, or whatever."

"So what?" The tears that had been threatening for a while spilled onto her cheeks. James's image shimmered. "It's not like she's going to change her mind. That's not what she's like." She was shouting at him, but she didn't care. *Why is he reminding me how happy I was? He's not helping.*

"What about when you're finished with your Masters?" James placed a hand on Mel's. "Why not wait for her? Isn't she worth it?"

"I don't... I don't know." She put her hands over her ears, willing the conversation to end just there rather than for him to make her more upset. But when she opened her eyes again and removed her hands, he was still watching her, a gentle look in his eyes.

"Have hope, yeah? I just want you to be happy."

She laughed through her tears and sniffed hugely. "You're a good mate."

He shoved at her shoulder but then rubbed it warmly. "You can always rely on me. Now"—he reached for the bag and pulled out a massive packet of popcorn—"you start working on this and I'll pick us out a film, yeah?"

# Chapter 23

*What have I done?*

Ruby rubbed at her temple. Only a few days ago, she had been certain she was doing the right thing; now she was torn. She'd broken up with Mel on the assumption that the dean was going to fire her. She'd been ready to deny their relationship. She'd even rehearsed her speech so Sonya would believe her. *She never even gave me a chance to talk.*

She'd spent the entire night trying to figure out what to do. Questions swirled around like wasps in her brain, battering against the inside of her skull. Was she so concerned with her private life being private that having a relationship that had a connection to work was completely out of the question? Did it matter if the whole world knew she was with a woman—with Mel?

She thought back to the gardening group, back to the kids she had grown to enjoy spending time with. Their accepting faces when Mel had told them she was gay. The way they'd been curious and happy for them both when they'd said they were girlfriends.

*Well, we're not girlfriends anymore. I saw to that.*

Her whole body felt heavy and sluggish. Lack of sleep had pulled her alongside her emotions, and every time she thought of Mel, her throat tightened. She'd had to phone in sick to work; someone else was teaching her classes. She'd never done that before. Never. She'd spent the morning sitting on her sofa staring at her phone, hoping that Mel would ring. Then she'd given in to the urge to text her. She wasn't sure her words meant anything. *She probably hates me, but I have got to try.*

Seven texts and no reply later, Barney trotted over and sat, hopefully eyeing the half-empty packet of digestive biscuits resting in Ruby's lap. Ruby scowled at the dog, who reacted immediately by lowering her head. Ruby reached out a hand. "I'm sorry, Barn." She sighed deeply. Barney closed her eyes as Ruby scratched her ear, then she patted the sofa next to her.

Wagging her tail, Barney hopped onto the sofa, and a large breath escaped her as she moulded herself against Ruby's thigh. Barney's cheek was warm. Ruby rested against the back of the sofa and closed her eyes.

Tears ran occasionally down and into Ruby's hair. She kept her eyes closed but stroked Barney's head rhythmically. It was comforting, having a warm body next to her, even if it wasn't human.

Her phone bleeped. Ruby grabbed it, but her heart fell as she realised it was Chloe, asking if she needed anything. She'd told her daughters she had flu-like symptoms—an excuse not to speak the truth to them just yet.

Deciding to take a leap of faith, she straightened and replied to Chloe, then tapped Mel's name to call her.

It rang for ages before going to voicemail.

Ruby tried to steady her voice. "Mel? It's Ruby. I know I've said I'm sorry, but really, I am. I've been a complete pillock. Please can we talk? Would you just answer your phone, or phone me back? Please?"

She hung up. Her chest burned as she considered what she had lost. Then she smacked her hand against the sofa, startling Barney enough that she rolled off onto the floor.

Did Mel mean more to Ruby than her long-preferred privacy? Her life had been so orderly and so formulated until now. Did it need to be?

Wiping her eyes, Ruby stood and strode through the house to get dressed, wash her face, and do whatever it took to fix what she had broken.

Mel's first nightshift back was busy, and the sun was high in the sky as she and James returned to base. She leant her forehead against the cool passenger window as James swung the truck into the ambulance station and felt the peace settle inside her as the end of their shift hovered in sight.

A blue Mini Cooper stood in the car park. Mel squinted at it.

"Isn't that Ruby's car?" James asked.

Without commenting, Mel waited until James had put the truck into park before jumping out. She went over to the car and peered inside. "Can't be. Why would she be here?"

"Because you've neglected to answer any of her texts or phone calls?"

She swiped at him with her jacket and then tiptoed in through the station building. On entering the staff room, she found the day staff accumulating on the small sofas. Mel got the impression they were waiting for someone.

"She's here," one of the ECAs shouted.

Mel wondered whose birthday it was.

Then she took in the room properly. A large banner stretched the entire width of the ceiling, covering the message board and most of the staff lockers. It draped half way down to the floor and in big red letters proclaimed: *I (Ruby) love Mel Jackson.*

She stared at the banner, running her fingers through her ponytail. Then, when she realised the number of gazes on her, her cheeks burned.

James stepped into the room and peered at the banner. Then he looked behind Mel, his eyes widening. "Oh. Hi."

"I'm going... going to assume you're James."

Mel whirled around to find Ruby holding out her hand. Under Mel's stare, Ruby shrank back a bit, her gaze lowered to the floor.

Her colleagues all seemed fascinated, with beaming smiles and less-than-subtle nudges to one another. To James's credit, he shook Ruby's hand, then turned to the rest of them. "Come on, guys. Out."

As everyone filed out to check their vehicles and medications for their shifts, Mel glared at him. "Did you know she was going to be here?"

His arms opened. "I didn't. Really." He patted her shoulder and left the room as well.

The banner pulled her attention with its large red letters. Mel shook her head and turned back to Ruby. "What on earth are you doing here?"

"I needed to see you."

"Here?" Mel huffed and looked out of the door, the redness in her cheeks flaring anew. "I have a professional reputation to uphold, you know. How dare you come into my place of work and embarrass me in front of my colleagues." She folded her arms. "Imagine if I had done that to you."

"I wanted to explain. I've been thinking…" Ruby's shoulders drooped. "I shouldn't have done what I did."

"String me along like a puppy? Yeah. You really shouldn't have." Mel sighed and stared at the floor.

"No." Ruby stepped closer. "Broken up with you."

"I'm glad you did."

"Don't say that." When Mel looked up again, she found Ruby's eyes glistening with tears. "I was… I was scared."

"Well, if you're too scared to get over the fact that I'm thick, I'm really glad you broke up with me."

Ruby furrowed her eyebrows. "What?"

"Dyslexia. Damaged goods, and all that. No need to explain; I've been through it all before."

"Dyslexia… What?" Ruby shook her head emphatically. "No, no. That's not what this was about."

"You reckon?"

"Absolutely."

Mel shook her head, not believing a word Ruby was offering her.

"It really wasn't."

A hand lifted near Mel's shoulder, but Mel stepped back so that Ruby couldn't touch her.

"It was about my own blooming insecurities. My own fear that if I don't have privacy, I'll… My life will be over. Or something."

Her arms still folded, Mel settled her gaze on Ruby. A spark of something hopeful ignited inside her. *Is she different from Rach?*

*Ruby did research dyslexia. No other woman has ever done that. And she was so understanding with that student, once we'd got to the bottom of her problem. And she liked my glasses. Maybe James is right, and she is telling the truth.* "Okay, I'm listening. Explain."

Ruby placed her hands together and looked down at the floor before she spoke. "I've always had this thing where I have to keep my professional and personal lives separate. Shortly after Mrs Denzie went to the dean, I got a call saying the dean wanted to speak to me. The simple truth is that I panicked. I couldn't handle the thought that I'd lose my job, and someone accusing me of engaging in sexual behaviour in public would certainly have done that. I have my daughters to look after, the mortgage to pay, bills. Blooming heck, Mel, I can't afford to lose my job, simply from a practical standpoint. If I did, how would I feed my girls?"

"Or Barney."

Ruby smiled softly. "Or Barney, of course."

"You said that was the practical part. I can understand that fear. But that doesn't explain the other part. The privacy part and your life being over."

"No, it doesn't." She shrugged. "I'm forty-two years old and to all intents and purposes I've never really come out. When I thought it would all be out in the open, and that people would judge me for who I am and who I love... Well, in the face of one of my greatest fears, I couldn't handle it. I was scared, and I panicked. I reacted badly. Instead of seeing all those little faces that reacted wonderfully to the news we were together, I was stuck on the one who didn't, and I made what I thought was my only choice. I have people that rely on me, Mel. I can't just jump into things with my eyes closed and hope for the best."

Mel lowered herself into one of the small sofas, her gaze still on Ruby.

Her feet carrying her from one side of the room to the other, Ruby ran her fingers through her hair and continued. "I got scared. I broke up with you because I was terrified. But, actually, the dean was perfectly lovely. She apologised to me for having to put up with that homophobic witch. She didn't believe Mrs Denzie's story that she'd seen us in the greenhouse having sex. She knows I wouldn't do anything like that. And she has absolutely no issue with us being together."

"Of course she doesn't," Mel said. "Why would you think there might have been an issue?"

"My own stupid assumptions. Fear. Worry that others would see us the way Mrs Denzie did." Ruby perched on the sofa next to Mel and threw her a hopeful look. "I'm sorry."

Mel sucked her bottom lip and pondered the situation. *She really thinks I'm going to forgive her, after the hell she's put me through? The last four days I've been in absolute agony, and all because she's scared of her dirty laundry being thrown out for everyone to see?*

A groan escaped Mel's lips and she rested her forehead in her hand, her elbow on her knee. "So, what, you turn up at my work with a massive banner and suddenly everything is okay?"

Ruby's gaze flicked up towards the banner, and she seemed to deflate at the sight. "You don't like it?"

"It's ludicrous." Mel felt laughter fluttering up inside her and didn't have the reserve to stop it. "Look at the thing. You could probably see the words from across the road."

"That's sort of the point."

Looking more intensely at the banner, Mel allowed the words to penetrate her mind. "You're telling the whole town that you love me?"

"Yes." Ruby's gaze searched Mel's. "I wanted to make some grand gesture. Something that would show you that it's not worth it, losing you to keep my privacy. I don't care who knows, as long as you do. I love you."

Her head throbbed. It was eight o'clock in the morning, and she had been up all night.

"I got here at six because I thought maybe you'd be here. A few people were asleep but they let me in and helped me put up the banner."

"You've been here for two hours?"

"I didn't want to leave before I got to see you."

"Oh." *No one has ever made me a banner before, not even for my fortieth.* Pleasure fluttered upwards and it was as if suddenly she weighed nothing and could fly. In an attempt to keep the soaring happiness under wraps, she pressed her lips together. "So, now you've seen me, what now?"

"I was hoping you'd consider another date." Ruby's voice was small and hopeful, as if she was frightened Mel would just up and leave.

She understood fear—especially when it came to losing the things you held most dear. Ruby loved her job, she loved her family and her house, and it made sense that she would work hard to keep those things safe. Mel wasn't sure what she'd do if someone tried to take her lovely little bungalow away, or Epione. If she had children, she'd feel the same about providing for them. She'd risk her own happiness for their wellbeing. Mel slid her hand along the back of the sofas and wiggled one finger. Taking the hint, Ruby did the same, and their fingertips touched.

"Who's to say you won't get scared again?" Mel asked, her voice catching. "What happens the next time you freak out and break my heart?"

Lines appeared between Ruby's eyebrows. "I don't intend to. But if I do, I'll talk to you. And I won't run away."

Their fingers interlaced, loosely.

Relief settled Mel down into the sofa cushions. "Promise?"

"I'll even give it to you in writing," Ruby said, her bottom lip shuddering at the same time as relief blossomed across her features. She let out a small, watery laugh. "I'll make sure it's in Helvetica. Or Arial."

"Will you?"

"I'll pretty much do anything to make you believe me."

"Including proclaiming to the entire station that you love me?"

Ruby's smile broadened, and she nodded.

"All right."

"All right?"

Mel shifted close so that she was pressed against the arm of her sofa, coaxing Ruby to do the same with a tug to her hand. She reached up to removed Ruby's glasses carefully, then wiped the tears that had gathered underneath Ruby's eyes.

Ruby leaned into her hand, and Mel pressed a kiss to Ruby's forehead.

"For the record, I love you too."

"You do?"

Mel nodded.

Fresh tears spilled over Ruby's cheeks, and they simply sat together. "We're okay, then?" Ruby still sounded unsure.

"Yep. We're okay." Words were just great, but she wanted to seal their exchange with some kind of action. Mel tilted Ruby's chin up and pressed their lips together. It was sweet, soft, and tasted a little salty from tears, but absolutely worth it. When they broke apart, Ruby was grinning through her tears. "Now…" Mel fluttered her eyelashes in mock coyness. "This date you're taking me on…"

# Chapter 24

The following Wednesday the children were off school for half term, so the garden group wasn't running. Ruby had a whole afternoon to herself. She sat in her office, making sure the window was open wide to let in the summer scents and the birdsong, and gathered a stack of second year essays towards her.

*What a week!* Everything that had happened between her and Mel kept pushing into her mind, making her lose her concentration. It was making it difficult to evaluate the essays in front of her. *This is ridiculous. Everything's fine now. I need to get these done.*

When she was half way through a particular essay, where she was convinced she'd seen the phrase 'ethical dilemma' spelt at least six different ways, a knock sounded on her door. *I hope it's not one of my pupils. I need to get these essays marked.*

"Come in."

It creaked open, and a curtain of pale red hair swung through. "Hey."

"Hiya." She stood quickly and moved towards her visitor; Ruby's palm was cupping her cheek before she'd even stopped walking. "What're you still doing here? I thought you were having lunch with your cohort, then going home?"

"I changed my mind." Mel closed the door behind her and pressed a kiss to Ruby's cheek before dipping her head further to kiss her lips.

Ruby hummed contentedly against Mel's mouth, brushing her thumb against her cheekbone.

"Well," she said after they had parted, "it's lovely to see you."

Mel chuckled. "I got that impression."

Her marking forgotten for the moment, they moved towards the sofa. "Coffee?"

"Lovely, thanks."

Mel settled her tall frame on the sofa while Ruby made coffee for them both. Once two full mugs had been carried over, Ruby sat beside Mel, underneath her arm that lay along the back. She snuck up close to her side and nuzzled against her jaw. Then she pulled back and felt heat creeping over her cheeks.

By way of encouragement, Mel curled her hand around from where it sat on the back of the sofa and caressed the side of Ruby's neck.

Murmuring her approval, Ruby rested her cheek against Mel's shoulder. She inhaled, enjoying the scent of Mel's shampoo as it tickled her nose.

"Awfully naughty of us." Mel's breath tickled Ruby's forehead.

"Yes. What if someone walked in?"

"Would we get into trouble?"

Ruby lifted her head and laughed. "No. I am absolutely able to do what I like in my own office." She shrugged, however, and moved away, reluctant but aware that, actually, she was still at work and her students might still be around.

They both grinned and leant forward to collect their coffee cups. Ruby took in the way Mel held hers with both hands and closed her eyes when she rolled the taste around her mouth.

"Mm, thank you."

They sipped for a while in silence. Ruby's heart pitter-pattered as she thought about what she could have lost. *No. Focus. Everything's fine.*

"How are things with Francesca?"

Ruby nodded. "Unsurprisingly not too bad. I think because we both know that she's probably dyslexic, we're both a lot more patient with each other."

"That's really good." Mel placed her hand on Ruby's arm. "I'm proud of you."

Ruby's thoughts flew around for a while, the elation caused by the sparkle in Mel's eyes rejuvenating her. She chewed her lip as she wondered whether this would be the perfect opportunity to ask Mel about her teaching methods.

"Once she gets assessed, she'll get the support she needs. Until then"—Mel went back to her coffee—"you'll just have to give her a bit of space."

The various noises from outside filtered through the open window: birds, cars, the occasional aeroplane. Ruby leant forward and touched Mel's knee. "I was going to ask you, actually."

Mel looked up, interested.

"The way I'm teaching... or the way that I was teaching her. It's obviously the wrong way for her to learn."

"Not the wrong way," Mel argued. "Just…"

"Ineffective, then."

Mel nodded, her hand out, palm up, for Ruby to continue.

"I was going to ask. How do *you* learn? What's the best way?"

"Well, I obviously can't sit and read it in a book."

"What's it like?" Ruby leant back against the sofa, her coffee in one hand and her other hand in her hair. "When you try to read?"

"Well, you know, the words jump about. Even when I wear my glasses."

Ruby nodded.

"Sometimes I'll manage to read something, but it'll just go in one ear and out of the other. And I'll think 'What did I just read?', because it hasn't gone in."

"So, how do you learn things?"

"By watching other people do them. And my listening skills are okay. I have a Dictaphone that I take into lessons, and then I can listen back to what was said, and take better notes when I get home."

Removing her hand from her hair, Ruby reached across and smoothed her fingers against Mel's cheek. As Mel sighed, she drew a tender line from her cheek down to her jaw and then back.

"So, being shown things is helpful?"

"Mmhm."

"So"—Ruby cleared her throat—"so rather than explaining things to you…"

"It'd be better to show me."

Heat crept up Ruby's face but travelled down lower as well. Her whole body tingled, and she was pleased when Mel's eyes drifted closed under her touch. She continued to run her fingers slowly up and down Mel's cheek. She grinned when Mel turned towards her and took the cup from her other hand and set it on the coffee table.

They shifted awkwardly closer on the sofa, and Ruby found she couldn't tear her gaze from Mel's lips. "I want to kiss you. I know we're here, and I'm at work but…"

"I don't understand," Mel said, the teasing evident in her voice. "I think you should show me."

"Ah," Ruby replied, and moved so that they were half an inch away. She closed her eyes. "All right, then."

The door creaked open, and they sprang back from one another. Mel started laughing, her head thrown back on the sofa, as a very wide-eyed Alexander stood in the doorway, his hand still on the doorknob.

"Oh," was all he said.

Ruby downed her coffee, aware her face was bright red and her breathing rather quick.

Mel was still chuckling beside her, her hand over her mouth. She waved with her free hand at Alexander.

He slowly lifted his hand and gave her short and unsure wave back.

"Mel was just going home," Ruby finally managed, grabbing the empty coffee cups and striding over to the kettle. She left them beside it and returned to her own desk.

"Right," Alexander replied, pursing his lips and furrowing his eyebrows. He smoothed down his expertly pressed shirt and tie and sat at his desk, turning on his computer. A shade of confusion was still across his features.

"Come around for dinner on Saturday?" Ruby asked, once Mel's chuckles had quietened and she'd composed herself enough to stand and haul her backpack onto her shoulder.

"Okay. That'd be lovely. What time?"

"Five? Are you off?"

"Yep. I'm free Saturday. On a night shift Sunday too."

"Brill. Meet my fantastic girls."

Mel looked a little scared. "Um. Okay. Do you want me to bring anything?"

"I like yellow."

Mel blinked at her.

"Sometimes it's customary to bring flowers," Ruby explained. "So, if you want to know what colour I like. Yellow."

"Gotcha." Mel grinned and gave her a thumbs up. Then her hands fell to her sides. "Um. Should I bring…" She eyed Alexander who appeared to be very engrossed in something on his computer screen. "Things to stay over…or…"

Ruby's skin started to tingle again. Her head spun… just a little. "Um. Yes. If you like." She shrugged. "I mean. If you don't have to work until the next evening."

"Just in case we… consume so much Zinfandel that…"

A giggle fluttered out of Ruby's mouth. "Um. Yeah."

"Okay."

"Okay."

Mel nodded once. The door creaked as it closed behind her.

Ruby set about organising the essays on her desk, shuffling papers back and forth. She could feel Alexander's gaze on her from across the room. She put a hand to her cheek.

"Things are going well, then?" he asked, idly. When she looked up, he was back looking at his computer screen.

"Well. Yes. They are. Finally."

A pause as he tapped away at his keyboard. "Good. I'm glad for you."

"Thank you."

They went back to their work.

# Chapter 25

Mel stood at Ruby's front door, her backpack—filled with pyjamas and toiletries—over one shoulder. A small bunch of flowers in her other hand. She scuffed a trainer—much neater and cleaner than her usual walking boots—on the front step.

Ruby's front garden was neat. Simple grass and a small tree with an ornate bird feeder hanging from it. The path was straight and neat as well and led up to her front door, to one side of the lawn. *She really doesn't know how to garden; there's not even a potted plant out here.* The town house was three stories high, with a large window in the sloped roof at the top. It was yellow, and the terraced houses were all painted a different but bright colour. Mel liked it—it was like a jolly children's programme. She almost expected a guy in dungarees to come skipping out of Ruby's house, his cheeks painted red and bells on his shoes.

Pushing the surreal image away, she lifted the big brass knocker that gave the front door a vintage look.

The door was answered almost immediately by a young woman in a pair of black cargo trousers and a red T-shirt, her long blonde hair streaked with purple, messy and gathered up into a ponytail. "Hi," she said, her expression curious, but she seemed to decide that Mel wasn't a serial killer and moved back. "It's okay, I recognise you."

Barney skittered into the hallway and yapped at the tall human who had come to visit. Mel wondered if she recognised her from their walk on the beach.

"Your mum's shown you pictures of me?" Mel asked, stepping inside and closing the door behind her. She blinked, having been unaware that Ruby actually had any pictures of her, unless she'd been looking at her social-media accounts.

"Yeah, she showed me a few. Mostly of you bent over some sort of plant."

Mel's eyebrows rose. "She has pictures of me gardening?"

The girl looked pleased, but then shook herself and held out a hand. "Chloe. Eldest daughter."

"Mel. Potential suitor."

Chloe smirked, but not unkindly, and shook her hand with a firm grip. She took the flowers from Mel without a word and moved away, into a room that could be the kitchen from the steam coming out of it, and Mel was left alone with Barney.

She fussed the dog's ears, and Barney sat politely, her tail brushing back and forth on the carpet. Taking the opportunity to look around, Mel noticed a bicycle helmet hanging up amongst a number of coats and handbags on the hooks attached to the wall. Lower down, a selection of shoes, from skater trainers to high-heeled boots, were randomly arranged on a large mat, presumably to keep the carpet clean from any accidental dirt. Three pairs of flat ballet shoes were set neatly to one side, and obviously belonged to Ruby, even if Mel hadn't known what shoes she wore. Ruby's wellies sat next to them, a plastic bag around their soles to keep them off the mat.

The door to the possible-kitchen opened, and Ruby came through, smiling as her gaze locked with Mel's. "The flowers—they're lovely." She was wearing one of her usual T-shirts, a pair of soft-looking jeans, and a stripy apron.

"Yellow, as requested."

Sliding her arms around Mel's waist, Ruby rose on to her tiptoes before pressing her lips to Mel's.

"Hello to you too." Mel pecked her a few times on the lips quickly and tasted sweet wine. She looked at her watch once Ruby stepped away and was holding her hands out for her jacket. "I'm right on time. It's five o'clock and you've already had wine?"

Deciding it was way more interesting in the kitchen, Barney pushed the door open with her muzzle and disappeared through it.

Ruby folded her arms. "Don't judge me. I just had a sip from the bottle I was cooking with."

"You're cooking with wine?" Mel handed her jacket over and stood awkwardly holding her backpack until Ruby took that from her too. It was set on the floor by their shoes. "How very posh."

"It's just bolognaise," Ruby said, her hand randomly gesturing through the air. Then she blinked. "You could taste that on me?"

"It's nice." They both blushed, and Mel closed the distance between them again to catch Ruby's lips between her own.

Footsteps on the wooden staircase behind them broke them apart, and Ruby's other daughter appeared. This one was much more bouncy and didn't have purple in her hair. She was wearing a low-cut top, and a pair of skinny jeans pulled at her curvy frame. "Hey. I'm Jas."

"Jasmine, my daughter," Ruby said.

Jasmine gave Mel a little wave, which Mel returned, feeling unsure. Blonde wavy hair bounced down the remaining steps and into the kitchen. Hushed voices could be heard through the wood.

Ruby stood with a hand to her mouth, her cheeks pink. "Umm. I did advise her on appropriate attire for the evening."

"She looks like she's going out, not staying in with her mum and her mum's boring old girlfriend to eat pasta."

A grin enveloped Ruby's features, and she put a hand up to Mel's cheek, softly caressing her skin. "Aw. Girlfriend?"

"Aren't I?" *Am I? We haven't really discussed that yet.*

"You certainly are, but you're by no means old."

"I'll take your word for it." Mel laid her hand against Ruby's on her cheek. "And for what it's worth, neither are you."

Chloe poked her head around the door and indicated the room behind her. "Shall I give this a stir while you're...?" Her lips twisted like she'd encountered a bad smell. "Saying hello?"

"Sorry, lovely." Ruby shot Mel an apologetic look then turned on her heel to tend to their dinner.

Mel considered the framed prints hanging either side of the door and reached a hand up to touch one. A deer with large brown eyes and at-attention ears stared out from a field of long grass and yellow flowers. The print on the other side depicted a family of rabbits grazing by a hedge. Both pictures were stylish and pastel-coloured and made Mel think of lazy summer mornings. The whole hallway was decorated in a light green, with white paintwork around the three doors.

Pushing the door to the kitchen open, a wave of delicious smells and steamy air hit her. Mel laughed and caught Ruby wiping her glasses on her apron, the skin either side her nose red from where they usually sat. She'd never seen Ruby without her spectacles on before. She looked strange.

Barney was curled up in her basket and wagged her tail a few times as a greeting before sinking her chin back against the wicker.

"Something smells amazing," Mel said as she rounded the table to peek into the large saucepan. Both daughters were sitting at the table; Chloe playing on her phone, and Jasmine had a small hand mirror out, applying lipstick. *She wears lipstick before a dinner at home? Should I have worn make-up and made more of an effort?*

Ruby shoved her glasses back onto her face and blinked rapidly. "That's better. My glasses always steam up if I open the oven too quickly." She pointed down towards their knees. "Garlic bread."

"Yummy."

"We're having the special pasta," Jasmine said, and Chloe rolled her eyes. "It's totally cool for if you want to lose weight. It was recommended in *Heat*."

"The magazine," Ruby clarified.

Mel nodded, then looked around the room, her eyebrows furrowed exaggeratedly. "But that's really weird. I can't see anyone in this room who needs to lose weight."

Giggling bashfully and beaming from ear to ear, Jasmine leant her head on one hand, her elbow on the table. "You're really skinny, Mel. How do you keep so slim?"

"I do CPR for about half an hour per shift," Mel explained, shrugging. "You've no idea how good a workout that is."

"Ever been to a murder?" Chloe asked, a wicked grin on her face. Her eyes flicked to her sister, who pulled a face.

"Ew, Chlo, that's so gross." Jasmine sat up straight and brushed down her top like it had wrinkles in it. An air of superiority floated over her whole body. "And Mel doesn't want to talk about that kind of thing anyway. Do you?"

Mel chuckled and winked at Jasmine before turning her attention to Chloe. "I do on occasion, yes." She leant carefully against the kitchen counter and felt Ruby move up to her side, their arms brushing. "We went to a stabbing last week. Not very nice."

"I'm sure," Ruby said, and when Mel looked at her, she found tenderness filling her eyes. The hand on her arm only added to the warm feeling inside Mel's chest.

"Did the bloke make it?" Chloe asked, her gaze curious but wary. She didn't seem like she wanted to know any details.

"Yeah, he did. He was very lucky."

Chloe's stance relaxed, her face smoothed out, and she went back to looking at her phone.

"Anyway, little 'un," Ruby said, and Mel assumed she meant her youngest as her gaze was directed at Jasmine. "What did I say about your outfit this evening?"

The girls looked at one another and shared a conspiratorial smile. "Um, actually, Mum," Chloe started, but then bit her lip.

"We're off out later," Jasmine finished off for her, flicking her hair over one shoulder to expose dangly earrings.

"*Out* out?" Ruby asked, one eyebrow raised.

"And afterwards, we're staying at friends'."

Ruby looked from one to the other before folding her arms and giving them both a hard stare.

Chloe seemed to curl in on herself, her cheeks flushing crimson; Jasmine was obviously less affected. She just grinned at her mother, pointing one neatly manicured finger from Mel to Ruby and back.

"It's, like, your first night in together, and we wanted to give you some privacy."

"I'm going to Tasha's." Chloe looked like she wanted anything but to admit that the reason they were going out was so that her mother and new girlfriend could be alone. "I'm biking it. And I'll be back before lunch tomorrow."

Jasmine's hand flew into the air in an arc. "I don't know when I'll be back."

"And you're staying with whom, exactly?" Ruby asked sternly, her finger bouncing up and down in the direction of Jasmine's cleavage.

Jasmine put a hand over her exposed throat but didn't seem that bothered. "Laura's. God, Mum, what do you take me for?"

"Girls," Ruby sighed, obviously appeased by their plans. "You don't have to clear off just because Mel's staying over."

Mel's eyebrows hit her hairline. She'd told her children that Mel was sleeping over? *Wow. They really do the honesty thing here, don't they? That's great.*

Jasmine just giggled and went back to applying her make-up. Chloe shook her head and shrugged at Ruby. "It's fine." She set her phone face down on the table and leant forwards on her elbows. "I've been meaning to watch this box set with Tasha anyway, for ages. And we're well due a girly night."

"All right, then," Ruby said, looking like she wasn't entirely sure what to think.

"Thanks, guys," Mel said quietly, and felt Ruby's hand on her arm again.

"Thank you," Ruby said too.

---

Ruby was pleased with her bolognaise, although she'd made it probably a hundred times before, and it always went down well. She shifted in her seat as Mel took her first mouthful.

Mel's eyes closed, and she hummed her pleasure.

She chuckled when Mel tried to express herself around her huge mouthful of tomato-and-onion sauce, which nearly ended with Mel dribbling it down her chin.

"So," Jasmine said, pointing her fork towards Mel. "What do you do?"

"What... what do I do?"

"We know you're a paramedic," Chloe explained. "But what do you do the rest of the time?"

Both sets of eyes looked hopefully towards Mel.

"I like gardening and hanging out with my friends, and I like cycling."

"Oh my God, me too." Chloe looked impressed. "What bike do you have?"

"Just a boring one from Halfords. But I've put better lights on it. And it has a back... thingy." Mel made a rounded gesture.

"A rear rack? I want one of those. Be easier than a backpack."

"They are. And a couple of bungies to hold stuff on it. Great for long journeys."

Ruby wasn't particularly interested in bicycles or their accessories. However, she found she enjoyed listening to Mel talk with her daughters, even when Jasmine cut her sister off and brought the conversation back to the topics she'd brought up.

"Where do you buy your clothes?"

Mel smiled, and Ruby reckoned she recognised her younger daughter's desire to make it all about her. "I buy my clothes from loads of different places. I'm enjoying Burton's at the moment, and the men's department in Next."

"You buy men's clothes?" Jasmine asked, and her wide eyes made Mel chuckle.

"I'm tall, so men's clothes fit better. I also have wide hips and not much up top, so men's T-shirts fit me too."

*I've never noticed she wears men's clothes. They look so good on her.*

Ruby played with the stem of her wine glass and sighed as they chatted, happy to just listen and allow Mel to be the centre of attention for a while.

"You've been a paramedic for seven years, Mum said." Chloe finished the last of her pasta and scraped her plate.

"Yep. Straight after university."

"How was that? Most people that go to uni are like eighteen."

Mel chuckled. "Yeah. Was a bit weird. Luckily the paramedic science lot tend to be a bit older. I think I was the second oldest there."

"Did the younger ones annoy you?" Jasmine asked.

"Not really. I would hope they accepted me into their gang. There were only twenty of us."

"Wow. Mum teaches hundreds of students."

"I know. Her lecture halls are huge."

"What other jobs have you done?" Chloe picked up a piece of garlic bread.

"I've been a teaching assistant," Mel explained. "And I was an ECA before I was a paramedic."

"An emergency care assistant, right?" Chloe asked, her eyebrows raising in curiosity.

"I decided to do the full degree, because I knew I'd want to do further education along the way and I had some money going spare, so why not?"

Chloe lifted her glass of wine, and Mel obliged by clinking her own to Chloe's.

"University was okay, but I really struggled until they discovered I had dyslexia."

"I've got a mate who has that. She got a free laptop when she went into sixth form. Lucky pie."

"Yeah, it's so much easier with a laptop than when you're just writing stuff down. It takes me ages to read things and then when I'm making notes…" Mel shrugged and scrunched her face up.

Chloe poked her bottom lip out but then pulled it back in and nodded. "That must be well tough."

"It can be sometimes. You want to see my crazy glasses though."

"Oh," Jasmine said, draining the half-glass of wine Ruby had allowed her to have. "I've seen those before, on TV."

"You want to see?" Mel asked. Both girls nodded, and Mel gave Ruby a grin and a wink before reaching into her pocket.

When she put her glasses on, both girls hummed their approval. "They don't look that bad," Jasmine said, her fingers on her chin.

"I'm glad you think so." Mel chuckled and put the spectacles away.

Their plates were cleaned with their garlic bread in no time, and when both her daughters decided to clear all four of the plates from the table, Ruby started to feel suspicious. "My goodness, look at that. Who are you and what have you done with my girls?"

"Mum," Jasmine said, her eyes nearly rolling back into her head as a whine left her lips. "Not in front of Mel." She spoke through gritted teeth, and Ruby's eyebrows rose. *Oh, that's the deal, is it? Mel's made a lasting impression on you, hasn't she?*

As Mel was the first woman Ruby had dated that her daughters had even spent time around, let alone been in deep discussion with, Ruby's shoulders relaxed. She leaned back in her chair and watched Jasmine fill the dishwasher, while Chloe rinsed out the large saucepan and wiped the surfaces. As usual, Barney came over and sat down on her podgy bottom, hoping for a treat.

"Garlic and onion, not good for dogs," Ruby stated.

"Makes them die," both girls said in unison.

Ruby watched as they worked—a fairly well-oiled machine. "Thanks, lovelies."

Jasmine sidled up to her mother. "Can I have a lift to—?"

"Nope."

"Oh, come on."

"Really?" Ruby swept her hand, palm up, around the room, and then gestured towards Mel. "Your father may bend at will but I do not. I'm on a date, here."

Jasmine rolled her eyes and huffed something under her breath that Ruby assumed was rude before leaving the kitchen and bounding up the wooden stairs.

"Lauren lives a five-minute walk away," Ruby told Mel.

"Ah. Then she'll have to use her legs."

Chloe finished her jobs in the kitchen and kissed her mother's cheek. Ruby leaned into her and wrapped an arm around her hip to pull her close. Chloe pretended to be embarrassed, but Ruby could tell she preferred a blush over not getting a hug good-bye.

"You off, then?"

"Yeah. I'll text you if my plans change."

"Good girl."

Mel sat up straight in her chair and beamed. "Nice to meet you," she said. "Hope you have a nice time with Tasha."

Chloe grinned and shuffled in her too-long corduroy trousers out of the kitchen. The door swung closed, but Ruby could hear her putting her bike helmet on with a click.

"I worry about those trouser bottoms," Ruby said, tilting her head to one side and beaming shyly over at Mel. "She puts clips on, but they're so long, she gets rising damp."

"I don't remember my flares being that long."

"I don't think they were in the seventies. Not that I'd really remember."

"You were born in…" Mel closed her eyes and then opened them to count on her fingers. "Seventy-five?"

"That's right. Good maths skills, Jackson."

Mel poked her tongue out and waggled her head a bit, which made Ruby snort into her wine glass.

The front door opened and closed as Chloe, and then Jasmine, left.

It seemed very quiet suddenly, eerie almost, and Ruby looked into her wine glass for a while, unsure what she should say.

"So, did you have a plan for tonight, or…?" When Ruby looked up, Mel was sucking her bottom lip and gazing back at her.

"Not a plan, per se, no," Ruby replied. "What do you feel like doing?"

"Backgammon?"

It took Ruby a few beats to work out she was joking. "I was thinking something a little more exciting."

Mel's eyebrows rose, and Ruby blushed.

She dropped her forehead onto her arms and groaned. "You know what I mean," she mumbled into the table.

Mel laughed. "Okay, so, we could sit and talk?"

"On the sofa, please." Ruby stood and rubbed the small of her back. "These chairs are murder."

"Lead the way."

"More wine?" Ruby scrutinised the bottle which had around a third left in it. At Mel's nod, she poured them both an equal measure. *Good job the girls helped us drink it, otherwise we'd be fairly trolleyed by the time we went to bed.*

Bed.

Ruby gulped at the thought and figured it was probably a shame they didn't have more wine. She felt like she could do with another glass.

Barney followed at their heels and stretched out with her legs behind her on the hearth rug, a happy little rumble coming from her chest.

Ruby sat on the sofa and watched Mel walk around the bright room, taking in various framed pictures and ornaments. Once she'd done a full circle, she turned back to Ruby, and pink crept into her cheeks. "Sorry. I like investigating how people decorate their houses. I'm curious, I suppose."

"Do you think how someone decorates their house says a lot about them as a person?" Ruby asked, pulling her feet under her backside and getting comfortable.

Mel settled down on the opposite side of the sofa and faced her, cradling her glass in one hand. "I think it probably does."

"What does my living room say about me?" Ruby asked, a teasing and challenging tone in her voice.

Chuckling, Mel allowed her free hand to creep across the sofa cushion and her fingers curled around Ruby's. "I think the leaf patterns on your curtains mean you're kind, and that you like nature." She looked around. "The pictures of your daughters mean you're family orientated. And that you're passionate about keeping those connections tight." She squeezed Ruby's hand.

Ruby squeezed her back. "Thank you."

Mel grinned and shrugged. "You saw my house. What did it tell you about me?"

"I only saw it for a second."

"You'll have to visit for longer next time," Mel said, leaning her cheek against the back rest and gazing at Ruby.

They were quiet for a while, and the knowledge that Mel wanted to see her again, wanted to spend more time with her, made Ruby's skin feel hypersensitive. She snuggled her back into the sofa and sipped the remainder of her wine, enjoying the fruity taste as it rolled around her mouth. When the wine was gone, they sat forwards to place their glasses on the coffee table.

Mel just smiled across at her, her eyes soft. "So, I feel like I know you, but I don't really know you."

Ruby rested her elbow on her knee when she stretched her legs out along the sofa, her toes poking into Mel's side.

Mel reached to pull off her shoes, placed them neatly to one side, and pulled her feet up too, her fingers linking with Ruby's.

Ruby tilted her head to the side. "What do you want to know?"

"Where did you grow up?"

"Can't you tell?" Ruby asked, her accent thick and Northern.

Mel just hummed.

"I grew up with my mum and older sister in Yorkshire. Dad died of bowel cancer when I was a teenager, so it was just Mum, me, and Maureen."

"That must have been hard?"

"We stuck together, us girls. Dad was okay, but he worked a lot and he didn't have much to do with us. Mum was—still is, actually—a rock. Proper matriarch. Proper scary."

Mel chuckled and nodded.

"I met my husband at university, he was doing English while I was doing my nursing."

"How long were you together?"

"I think Jasmine was... three? When we split up."

Mel's gaze on her was soft, her eyes the deep green of new grass. "Why did you split up?"

"I discovered I wasn't really into men."

"Ah." Mel nodded and grimaced. "Yuck."

"Yeah, it took me a little while, but I got there in the end."

"How did he react?"

Ruby bit her lip and sighed deeply. "He was confused at first, then upset. He thought he'd not done enough for us, as a family, his girls. He felt like a failure. He felt like he'd pushed me away, or something, like it was his fault. I explained to him, several times if I remember, that it was literally a case of 'it's not you, it's me', but it took him ages to believe it."

"How did the girls react?"

"I didn't tell them right away. They were very young; even Chloe was just a bit too young. But I did. Actually, Chloe figured it out for herself, when she was about eight."

Mel squeezed Ruby's fingers again and then let her go so that she could rub her fingertip lightly over Ruby's wrist.

Goose bumps rose wherever Mel touched her. She shivered but shot Mel a beam, hoping she could convey with her eyes that this was okay.

"She asked me, right out, whether I liked 'girls more than boys'." Ruby put quotation marks around the words with two fingers of her free hand. "And I said I did. And she nodded in the most serious way and said that she still loved me, but that she always wanted to meet anyone I went out with."

"And she's been your official girlfriend-vetter ever since?" Mel asked, a twinkle in her eye.

"Well." Ruby put a hand to her cheek. "I'm not saying there has been a whole ream of women knocking at my door…"

"It's okay." Mel tickled her fingertips against the back of Ruby's hand. "I've had girlfriends before you. I'm sure you've had them before you met me."

"Not for a while."

"Ah. Me neither." Mel pushed her shoulders up and seemed a little shaky suddenly. "Not since a woman called Rach. She wasn't very nice to me."

"What happened?"

"I got diagnosed with dyslexia pretty soon after we started going out. And when I told her she… treated me differently. Like a kid, really. Like I was thick as two short planks."

"Blooming heck. No wonder you didn't tell me at first."

"Yeah." Mel cleared her throat. "And then, after convincing me she was absolutely fine with the whole thing, she left."

"For what it's worth, she wasn't worthy of your time."

Mel chuckled. "That's what James keeps telling me. It's had an impact on me though."

Sucking in a long breath, Ruby turned her hand over and spread her fingers so that Mel could draw circles against her palm. *Who knew I was more sensitive there than on the back of my hand?* Ruby felt sunshine-like sensations blossoming from her hand and outwards. She couldn't help the smile that spread across her face.

"So you've… dated women?" Mel asked, her gaze on their hands.

Ruby nodded and hummed, more at the feeling of Mel's fingers on her than as a reply. "A few." She furrowed her eyebrows and studied Mel. "Is that okay?"

"It's… I'm glad."

"Are you?"

Mel swallowed thickly and looked awkward. "I've been a 'first' for someone before. It seems like a really exciting and honour-worthy thing. But it's not."

"The science-experiment thing?" Ruby asked.

Mel nodded slowly.

"Be content with the knowledge, then, that you are not my first. You're not even my second."

Snorting in relief, Mel shifted towards Ruby on the sofa and sank her fingers behind her head and into her hair. Ruby slipped a hand around Mel's waist. They just sat close together, relief and humour flowing back and forth between them, until Ruby wiggled to get more comfortable, one fingertip poking into Mel's belt loop by her hip.

"And now it's your turn."

"Coming-out story?" Mel asked, the humour still evident in her eyes.

"If you like." Ruby rested her cheek against the sofa back and Mel's wrist, content to have Mel touching her in any way she wanted to. Mel's fingers were stationary against her scalp, but her skin was warm, and she was comfortable.

"Well, I was eighteen and there was this girl in my class at school who was really fit. And one night we got drunk together in her parents' dining room and I kissed her."

"What was she like?" Ruby asked, her voice barely a whisper.

"She was sweet and very nice to me. She was on the hockey team, like I was. We used to race up the field together and pass the ball back and forth. Could have won most of the matches with just the two of us."

Ruby giggled and sighed.

"And she kissed me back, right there on the floor. And then I went home and thought my luck was in. Maybe I was gay and now I had a beautiful girlfriend who wanted to kiss me. So I made all these plans, to phone her and arrange for us to be in my house alone so we could... Well, I didn't know what we would do but I figured it was going to be amazing. But she never spoke to me again."

"What?" Ruby said in dismay, sitting up and reaching to stroke Mel's cheek. "Never?"

"Apart from 'pass to me, Jackson', no. She spoke to me on the field, but otherwise, nothing."

"Oh, your poor eighteen-year-old heart," Ruby said.

"Broken and miserable," Mel replied with the back of her hand to her forehead. "I've never got over it."

Ruby laughed and swiped at Mel's hand, catching it to hold in her own. They quietened again, and Ruby sighed. "That's so sad though. Realising you like a girl and then... she just stops talking to you."

"Yeah, I'll be honest I was pretty devastated. And, of course, I couldn't tell anyone. In the end I just got a job, moved out of my parents' house, and got on with life. I didn't kiss anyone else for a long time, a good three years, after that."

"Have you ever been with a bloke?" Ruby found that she didn't feel nervous about asking, and that the smile she got from Mel simply reinforced the fact.

"Nope. It never interested me."

"I suppose there are times when I've wished I hadn't. It was always so... it wasn't great. I just thought that was how it was supposed to be, for the seven years we were married."

"Seven? That's a long time."

"We married when I was twenty-two, and divorced when I was twenty-nine."

"But... the girls."

"The girls," Ruby agreed.

"Must feel like a lifetime ago," Mel said.

Ruby nodded. "I felt so different back then. The girls were little sparkles in a life that just didn't make sense. I couldn't work out why I was so unhappy."

"How did you find out you were gay?" Mel blinked, and her mouth opened wide. "Oh. I mean. You are gay, aren't you?"

"Yes, I reckon so." Ruby chuckled and rubbed Mel's arm soothingly. "I had this dream, about a consultant I worked with."

Mel's eyebrows flicked up once before she seemed to stop herself. The look in her eyes was teasing, however.

"Yes, it was a sex dream, and yes, we were doing some rather... wonderful things in it." Poking a finger into Mel's side and causing her to squeak, Ruby grinned smugly at her. "It never occurred to me before that the reason why I didn't really find any pleasure in sex with my husband, was that I didn't fancy him."

"Big news when you're married."

"I know."

They relaxed again, their faces open and expressions affectionate.

"So now you know me, and I know you." Mel seemed satisfied.

"We do. It's nice to find out about your past, even though your past is pretty miserable."

"Once I'd grown up a bit, and felt confident that not every woman was going to dismiss me if I kissed her, the rest of my time as an out and proud gay woman was okay. Apart from Rach."

"Well, apart from Rach, I'm glad."

"I suppose your story had a happy ending?"

"After the initial confusion and more than a few tears, we worked out what we wanted. The divorce was reasonably quick, for that I was grateful. My ex made it simple, gave me the house, and agreed we'd try to stay friends."

"That's good."

"He finally accepted it wasn't anybody's fault, and left me to my life. The only time we really talk these days is when we need to discuss the girls."

Mel's fingers in Ruby's hair started to caress her, and Ruby inhaled sharply, involuntarily. The fingers stilled, but Ruby made a noise of complaint in her throat, so Mel began again, swirling little circles against her scalp and through her hair.

Humming out her approval, Ruby leant into Mel's hand. "I love having my hair played with."

"And I really like your hair," Mel whispered. "It's lovely and soft and thick."

"Would you think me fickle if I admitted that I dyed it?"

"No. It's a lovely colour."

"I expect I have lots of greys. But I'm not quite ready for them just yet."

"I have loads of greys. But I don't care. I'm kind of looking forward to going properly grey. Better than ginger, right?"

"You're not that ginger," Ruby replied, her hands drifting up Mel's sides to sink into her soft straight hair. She watched as the reddish strands caught the waning sunlight that streamed through her living room window and combed her fingers through them. "I love the colour of your hair. And it looks lovely down."

"Does it? I find it gets in the way." Mel held up her wrist, which had a hair band wrapped around it. "Just in case."

"You never know," Ruby whispered, shuffling closer and bringing both hands up to cup Mel's cheeks.

Mel leant forward too, and their lips met, very gently. They pulled back from one another but stayed close, and Ruby could feel Mel's breath on her cheek.

"It's not really time to go to bed yet, is it?" Mel asked, her cheeks pinking and her voice gravelly.

Ruby sighed and stroked Mel's face. "We could always find a film to watch."

Mel's gaze flicked towards the television that stood in the corner of the living room.

"Um." Ruby's cheeks warmed, and she eyed the television. "The DVD player down here doesn't work."

"Oh." Mel snorted and leant forward to brush her lips against Ruby's cheek. "Well, that's that plan scuppered, then."

"Not necessarily." Ruby clambered off the sofa and held out a hand. "Come on."

Mel looked up at her in confusion. "What?"

"There's one in my room." Ruby beamed smugly. "And that one very much works."

---

Taking Ruby's hand and allowing herself to be pulled up, Mel's face crinkled into a smile. "Your bedroom?"

Ruby chuckled and patted Mel's cheek. "Blimey, don't look so scared." They stood still in front of one another, and Ruby ran her fingers through Mel's hair again. "What do you say to a film in our pyjamas?"

Mel's cheeks flushed more deeply, and she looked away.

"You didn't pack a sexy teddy or something, did you?"

Gaze snapping back to Ruby's, Mel found a glint in her eye and then laughed. "Luckily, no."

"Good. Hot chocolate?" At Mel's nod, Ruby collected their glasses with one hand and pulled her into the kitchen with the other.

Barney got up from her basket and sniffed around them briefly.

"Want to go out?"

The dog wagged her tail and trotted to the kitchen door. Ruby let her out and set their wine glasses down before going to the kettle and flicking it on.

Mel leaned against the kitchen table and allowed her gaze to slide up and down Ruby's body. *So we're going up to her bedroom—okay, I can handle that.* She'd wondered several times how this would go, them sharing a bed. Whether they'd scarper up the stairs and rip their clothes off and devour one another, or whether it would be a little more refined and gentle. She still wasn't sure.

Ruby looked sexy, despite obviously having no intention of doing so, in her tight-fitting T-shirt and blue jeans. Her hair seemed especially glossy, and she smelled fantastic—all flowery and musky and lovely. Cleaner than usual, although Mel was so used to smelling earthy compost on her these days, she wasn't sure which smell she liked better. Perhaps she liked them equally.

At a scrape at the door, Ruby let Barney back in. The dog stretched and climbed back into her bed before flopping down and sighing happily.

As the kettle clicked off, Ruby filled two mugs with cocoa and sugar, then steaming water. She bent down to grab a bottle of milk from the fridge, and her curvy backside was made more prominent. She turned around quickly and grinned as she caught Mel staring.

Mel gulped and flushed yet again, her hand against her own cheek. "I'm sorry."

"You, my lovely, can ogle me all you want." Ruby wiggled her hips as she poured milk into the two cups. "I think we're at the stage in our relationship where we are very much allowed to appreciate each other, aesthetically." Ruby bent down to ruffle Barney's ears on her way past.

Mel took her hot chocolate carefully and followed Ruby out of the kitchen—she remembered to grab her rucksack—and up the wooden stairs, onto a small landing. Three doors stood closed, and another set of stairs led upwards.

"If you prefer a bath to a shower," Ruby said, pointing at the door on the far right, "feel free to use the main bathroom. It's the girls' bathroom, but I do insist they keep it reasonably clean."

"I was wondering whether I'd get a tour of your house," Mel replied, and they went up the second set of stairs.

This floor held a tiny square of carpet at the top and a single door. Ruby swept the door open with an eager flourish, revealing a huge, light room, with a large metal-framed bed on one side, solid wood furniture, and a sloping roof with a window in. The natural light streamed through the window, and the blue sky above them filtered through the glass and spread across the bedroom without a real need for either of the lamps or the main electric light in the middle of the ceiling.

A large print of a naked woman, black and white, hiding her face in her arm while she slept, hung opposite the door. Several smaller pictures, possibly by the same artist, were dotted around. Each one was beautiful, and Mel found herself standing and staring, her rucksack on one shoulder and her cup held tightly in both hands.

As Mel came back to herself and began to admire the whole of the space, Ruby indicated the door that didn't lead downstairs. Ruby had moved around the room, allowing Mel to admire the pictures, and turned on the two lamps, which now cast yellowy light across the mostly white bedroom, making it feel a little warmer.

"My en suite. I have a shower up here, toilet, sink, and the like."

Mel nodded, peeking into the bathroom and noticing that the walls were a pale yellow, Ruby's favourite colour. Her bedroom was white, apart from a few pastel accents of blue and green. It was airy and clean-feeling, and Mel liked it very much.

She set her rucksack at the foot of the bed, not wanting to claim a specific side just yet, and stepped up behind Ruby, who was perusing a bookcase full of films. The television sat on a small table to one side of the bed but near the foot, so that both occupants of the bed could watch it if they so wished.

"What do you fancy?" Ruby asked.

The word "you" was on the tip of Mel's tongue, but she swallowed it back down. "Something light. Not too taxing."

"Plan on multi-tasking?" Ruby asked, with a chuckle.

"Was hoping to get some cuddling in, if that's something you'd enjoy?"

Ruby's face broke into a smile at that and Mel's knees felt momentarily weak. *Will I be able to focus on a film at all, if this gorgeous woman is in my arms?*

Reaching forward with a finger, Mel tapped a film she'd seen before but wouldn't mind watching again.

"Ah, you're an indie film fan, thank goodness."

Mel slid the film out and checked the back. "More an Ellen Page fan, really."

Shrugging, Ruby leant her chin against Mel's shoulder. "The music is great too."

"It's just such a comforting film. I know that sounds weird, a film about a sixteen-year-old getting pregnant."

"No, I understand what you mean. It's a lovely film. Yes, let's have that one."

They took the DVD and their hot chocolates over to the bed and looked at one another. "Um," Ruby began, tapping the DVD case on the table the television stood on, her foot scuffing against her carpet. "I don't mind which side..."

Mel figured taking the lead in this small thing might be a good idea, so she chose the side furthest away from the television. "This is fine with me."

Nodding, Ruby perched on the side of her bed and placed her drink on her bedside table before taking the disk out of its case and turning the relevant machines on.

Mel sipped from her cup, not wanting her drink to go cold, and plumped the pillows behind her. The initial music started, and Ruby sat back too, sitting crossed-legged next to Mel. They watched the beginning credits of the film, the drawn figure walking through her neighbourhood, drinking orange juice. The music was wonderfully familiar, and Mel felt her insides softening slightly.

They glanced at one another and went back to watching the film.

When the long credits were over, they had both finished their hot chocolates. Mel ran her tongue over her teeth and wrinkled her nose. "Shall we get ready for bed?" she asked, and her voice sounded loud in the calm room.

Ruby looked at her for a few seconds, sucking her bottom lip into her mouth, but nodded. She stood and stooped by her chest of drawers, pulling out pyjamas. *How sweet; she's wearing clean pyjamas for me.* With a glance over her shoulder, Ruby disappeared into her en suite and closed the door.

Mel decided it was fair enough. As much as she wanted to undress Ruby herself, revealing each inch of naked skin as she did so, perhaps that wasn't something Ruby was comfortable with just yet. It was new for both of them, and Mel felt like actually, however much she wanted to make love, and yes that was what it would be when they finally did so, she wanted to take her time. Ruby was worth it.

So she clambered from the bed and knelt on the floor to take out various bits and bobs from her rucksack, laying her pyjamas on the bed, and grabbing her toothbrush and toothpaste. She sat on the bed next to her neatly folded pyjamas and waited. Water running sounds carried through the closed door, and Mel was suddenly aware of her bladder complaining. *Good thing we're having a break before we watch the film, otherwise we'd need an interval in the middle of it.*

Emerging with a hairbrush in her hand, Ruby stepped out of the en suite a moment later, her head lowered. She was wearing a purple set of pyjamas—a T-shirt and cotton trouser combination, with a cartoon rabbit on the front.

Openly grinning, Mel looked her up and down and licked her lips. "Sexy," she said quietly.

"Oh, be quiet. The girls got them me for Christmas."

"I'm serious."

Ruby flicked her eyes towards the bathroom, and Mel obediently scuttled inside to clean her teeth and change.

When she pushed the door open, Ruby was sitting up in bed, the duvet around her waist. Her shoulders were pushed up and her hands clasped over her middle. The remote control lay beside her on the bed. Her glasses lay, folded neatly, next to her empty mug.

Mel climbed into bed, having left her toothbrush by the sink for the morning. She marvelled in the way that Ruby's hair looked so neat and soft. Not being able to help herself, she reached up to run her fingers through it.

Ruby shivered. She turned to look at Mel, and some of the tension in her shoulders drifted away. Her dark eyes shone.

Leaning in to kiss Ruby's cheek, then sitting back and reaching for her hand rather than taking things any further, Mel grinned lopsidedly back. "So, you like my bedtime attire?"

Ruby blinked and looked down, squinting a bit without her glasses. Mel had chosen to bring a worn burgundy T-shirt with writing on it, and tartan trousers in a similar colour. Eyes still shining, she trailed them back up Mel's torso and nodded. "Very nice."

"I'm glad you like."

Easy chuckles rumbled through both of them, and Ruby relaxed completely, snuggling her shoulders backwards into her pillows and then resting comfortably against Mel's side.

"Let's get a bit more comfortable." Mel pulled her pillows to rest flat and lay down, holding one arm out. Ruby lay down on her back but grabbed Mel's other hand and pulled it around her waist.

Mel sank against Ruby's side and buried her nose in the thick hair by her face. She made a little noise of affection and Ruby chuckled. Mel lifted her head again and grinned. She felt so soft, so warm. And Mel was suddenly exhausted.

Ruby squeezed her around her shoulders, and her lips trailed gently against Mel's forehead. Then she raised the remote control and turned the film back on.

The sky through the ceiling window was growing dimmer. The only light in the room was the television, and the volume was soft, the voices of the characters lulling and familiar. Mel sighed deeply, languidly, inhaling the soapy, minty-fresh smell that was mixed with Ruby's usual scent. *She must have washed her face as well as brushing her teeth.* Her hair was soft under her cheek, and the patch of skin exposed above the neck of her T-shirt was dotted with dark moles. *I want to join them all up. I wonder if she has them on her belly too.*

The arousal starkly present between Mel's legs felt wonderful and not uncomfortable. It was a gentle ache and didn't intensify when Mel bent a knee up over Ruby's thighs. "Let me know if I crush you," Mel murmured into Ruby's hair, her eyes starting to droop.

"You won't."

"I'm a bit large round the hips though. You might wake up with pins and needles."

Ruby's hand started a gentle caress against her upper arm, Mel's hand curled around her hip. "You're not, and I won't."

"Okay." Mel yawned and tried to smother it with her hand.

Ruby chuckled. "Come on now, snuggle down." She patted her shoulder.

Mel rested properly against her, feeling her against the inside of her thigh, her ribs, under her cheek. She felt great. "Okay."

"Watch the film." Ruby shifted to look properly at her. "You don't even have your eyes open."

"I've seen it before," Mel replied. "I'm listening."

"You're listening," Ruby repeated, her tone unconvinced but unworried. She continued to tickle little patterns against Mel's arm, her fingertips poking under the arm of her T-shirt.

Mel felt her body sinking into the bed and Ruby's embrace. Her breathing slowed, and she tried to focus on the colourful story within the film. Eventually, however, her mind drifted into nothingness, and her last thought was that she'd never been so comfortable in all her life.

---

Ruby listened to Mel's steady and soft snores for more than an hour before she turned the television and DVD player off with the remote. Darkness embraced them.

Her gaze lingered over the sleeping woman, nestled so snugly in her arms, and she decided that was okay. *We could do with taking things steady anyhow. I was so nervous about tonight, and look at us.* Carefully sliding her hand up Mel's arm, she brushed back a few stray strands of strawberry-blonde hair from Mel's freckled cheekbone and tucked them behind her ear. Mel stirred momentarily, but only buried more deeply into her shoulder and let out a long sigh.

Ruby rolled her eyes in amusement. No, it really was okay. In fact, it was perfect. She wanted nothing more than to fall asleep with Mel, and she was getting her wish. She stretched her legs out and got comfortable, Mel's weight resting against her hip, her arm still wrapped protectively around her.

Pressing a soft kiss to Mel's forehead, Ruby closed her eyes and pulled the duvet up a little, so they were properly covered. Traffic sounds, muffled by her thankfully thick brick walls, were the only things she could hear, until Mel made a small noise but didn't wake. Ruby squeezed her gently before drifting slowly into sleep as well.

# Chapter 26

Ruby's eyes fluttered open as the sunlight streamed in through her skylight. She yawned widely and tried to stretch, to make her joints pop and loosen, as usual, but one side of her body wouldn't move. Then the previous evening came back to her like an approaching sunrise, and she smiled, turning her head on the pillow to take in the mass of cherry-blonde hair and the pale face of her girlfriend.

Mel was still fast asleep and in a similar position to last night. Her leg still thrown across Ruby's hips, and her arm still tight around her waist. Her hand had moved, however, and her fingers were curled inside the little valley between Ruby's breasts. If she moved an inch, she'd be effectively feeling her up.

Ruby tried not to giggle at the thought and imagined the look of embarrassment on Mel's face if she woke in such a compromising position. Or perhaps she wouldn't be. Perhaps Mel would touch her properly, intentionally, with a deep look in her eye. A rush of affection and arousal flooded Ruby's body. She shook her head at her own hormones and wriggled a bit, her bladder suddenly coming awake and making itself known.

Extricating herself from Mel's embrace without waking her, Ruby shuffled quietly to the en suite. As she sat on the toilet, she considered her options. Mel would probably want a lie in, as she was on a night shift that night. She remembered them well. Ruby pulled her T-shirt away from herself and sniffed. *I definitely need a shower.* She flushed the toilet and stripped, turning the shower on and stepping under the warm water.

After efficiently washing her hair and body, she felt a lot fresher. She squeezed the water out of her hair before rubbing at it with a towel. After wrapping a dry towel around herself, she tucked it in securely and crept out of the en suite to find some clothes.

"I wondered where you'd got to." Mel's voice was croaky and soft, and the hand that shaded her eyes indicated she had just woken up.

Ruby sat on the edge of the bed and stroked Mel's cheek. "Thought you might want to sleep a bit longer. As you're up all night tonight."

"Hmm." Mel stretched and rolled over towards Ruby, her hand rubbing at Ruby's waist through the towel. "Was hoping for some morning cuddles, actually."

"Were you?" Ruby bent down to kiss Mel's cheek, but Mel shifted and their lips met. "I suppose… a few more minutes won't hurt."

"I plan on stretching out those minutes," Mel replied, reaching up with both hands, and apparently, very much awake now. She tugged until Ruby rested down on an elbow and kissed her again.

Their kisses started out slow and chaste, just presses of lips against lips, until Mel's hands slid around Ruby's towel-covered waist and pulled her even closer. Ruby got comfortable beside her, the towel covering her from armpits to knees, and allowed her fingertips to skim down Mel's neck.

They parted gently, and Ruby gazed down into Mel's eyes. "Good morning."

Mel's eyes twinkled. "Good morning." She stole a glance downwards. "You're not wearing anything."

"I am. Don't you like my towel dress?"

"I take it back. It's beautiful." Mel leant up to capture her lips in a single kiss. "You're beautiful."

Ruby's body tingled all over at Mel's words. She watched as Mel's hand slid up her body, to the top of the towel where it was tucked into itself, holding it in place.

Mel's gaze caught hers, and she narrowed her eyes—a question, permission requested.

Ruby nodded.

Teasing the corner out, Mel allowed it to loosen before slowly pulling it off. There was some shifting around when it got caught underneath Ruby's hip, but eventually Mel reached behind her to place it on the floor by the bed.

Ruby's skin prickled with the chill of her bedroom, beads of water still clinging to her back and stomach. She shivered.

Mel's eyes were wide, and her lips were parted. She guided Ruby onto her back and rested a warm palm against her shoulder. "Okay?" she whispered.

"I'm okay," Ruby replied, swallowing and bringing one foot to the bed, wrapping an arm around her own naked stomach. She took a deep calming breath and let it out slowly, turning her head on the pillow to watch Mel as she looked at her.

Mel's gaze started at her shoulders and travelled downwards. It was as if each area of skin she looked at she touched as well, causing goose bumps to rise in her wake. Her hand did eventually rise from the duvet, and Mel caught a droplet of water from the side of Ruby's breast.

"This is really unfair," Ruby said, shivering at Mel's touch.

"Why?" Mel seemed regretful suddenly, and her gaze shot back to Ruby's face.

"You're fully clothed."

Letting out a sigh that could only be of relief, Mel nodded. She sat up, and Ruby enjoyed watching Mel cross her arms over her chest and whip off her T-shirt, then wriggle out of her pyjama bottoms.

The scene made her mouth water. Mel was lean, and her skin was dusted with freckles the colour of a sunset. Her breasts were small and her hips wide, but she seemed in proportion, as if she'd been sculpted, carved from porcelain. Her legs seemed to stretch for miles, and the hair at the joint of her thighs was a deep strawberry-blonde, just like the hair on her head.

"Crikey," Ruby said, conscious that her accent was strong but not caring.

"Not exactly what you expected?" Mel's voice was soft, and her gaze rested across the room, on the empty backpack that hung on the back of a chair.

"What? Are you joking?" She deliberately drew her gaze from Mel's toes all the way up to her eyes. "You're gorgeous."

"Really?"

"If we're comparing bodies, what about these?" Ruby stretched back and ran her finger over her lower belly, across the silver lines that marred her skin.

"Stretch marks?" Mel asked, furrowing her eyebrows in concentration as she shifted into a sitting position and looked closer. She ran her own finger against one of the marks, which made heat flush down Ruby's chest.

"They are. From Jasmine."

"None from Chloe?"

"She's always been my favourite of the two."

Mel laughed and leant down to press a kiss next to her finger. Ruby gasped and arched back involuntarily. When Mel sat back up, she looked smug.

Feeling like she wanted to throw something at her, Ruby huffed and reigned in her nerves. "They're ugly."

"They're wonderful. Like the scars of war."

Unable to do anything but smile at that, Ruby took Mel's hand and tugged her down.

Mel lay atop the covers and leaned on one elbow above her. "I've delivered a lot of babies," she admitted.

"Aren't you supposed to grab them and go, if they need to be in hospital?"

"You're right." Mel poked her in the side. "For once. But if birth is imminent, you have to stop the truck. I actually had a baby born on the stretcher before we got inside the truck once. Most paramedics go through their lives without having to deliver a baby. Lucky buggers."

"I can imagine."

"Anyway, I never heard more swearing and screaming than I have with women in labour. Even people who are in immense pain from injury tend to keep the language appropriate. So, when I say 'the scars of war', I mean it. I can't think of anything so trialling or scary as giving birth." She kissed Ruby's collarbone and then pressed her nose and mouth to her skin. "I think you're a hero."

Again, Ruby was lost for words. *This doesn't happen very often. I must be chilling out in my old age.* Opening one arm, Ruby wrapped it around Mel's shoulders as she lay snug against her side.

"So, now we're here," Mel whispered against her neck.

Ruby chuckled. "That's right. We are."

Tiny fireworks pattered against her skin as Mel ran her fingertips across Ruby's stomach and upwards. She closed a soft hand against her breast at the same time as she captured Ruby's lips with her own. Ruby's body sang, and she held Mel's head in both hands, pushing her long hair back to keep it out of the way.

Mel growled low in her throat as Ruby's bent knee wrapped around her, and Ruby groaned back as their bodies finally came together, with Mel rolling on top of her. She pushed her other thigh between Mel's and Mel removed her hand from her breast, needing to lean on her elbows to keep herself up.

Her skin tingled all over again as Mel's body slid against hers. Ruby trailed a hand down the soft skin of her back, kissing her with the passion that was building inside her. Moisture pooled between her legs. *It's been a while since I've made love with anyone.*

Mel's skin against hers felt glorious, and her breasts were firm, her nipples hard and dragging against her wet skin. The thigh between her legs pushed upwards with the perfect amount of pressure, and Ruby gasped again, squeezing Mel's hip with her thigh.

Mel broke the kiss, her breathing shallow. "I'm… I'm a little older than you."

"I know that," Ruby replied, tilting her chin upwards, eager to continue what had begun.

"It's just that…" Mel swallowed. Her eyes darkened. "I'm in the throes of the menopause and…" Her cheeks reddened, and her eyes drifted away.

Without changing their position, Ruby reached up and stroked Mel's cheeks. Her arousal sat back as Mel's discomfort became more important than her own, or even Mel's, potential orgasm. "Talk to me. I want to know."

"I'm shy."

"You're blooming well *not* shy," Ruby whispered.

That pulled Mel's lips upwards and she brought her gaze back to Ruby's. "I mean about... the stuff that's going on with me."

"I'm a nurse. Have been for a while."

Mel leaned on one elbow and caressed Ruby's cheek. "Okay. It's not as if I don't trust you. I just…" She inhaled deeply and nodded once. "My brain is… very much into this." She looked down and even gave a figure-of-eight hand gesture to emphasise her point. "But sometimes, it takes a while for my body to catch up."

"That's all right." Ruby pulled Mel's lips to her own with a hand on the back of her head and kissed her, briefly. "I can deal with that."

"Can you?"

"Of course. Stop worrying." Ruby kissed under her jaw and then pulled back to smile at her, hoping she could project enough reassurance through her gaze. "Tell me how you feel. Let me know if I'm going to fast or…" She pressed her thigh up between Mel's legs and was pleased about the shudder that went through Mel at the contact. "Or too slow."

"Okay." Mel nodded, and winked at her. "I knew you were kind really, when I first met you."

"Hm." Ruby sucked Mel's bottom lip and felt her resting her weight properly back against her.

They kissed for a while, and Mel's tongue pushed softly at her lips until she parted them and allowed her access. Their kisses became deeper, and more delicious, but remained slow. Ruby drew circles against the skin of Mel's back, tracing around her shoulder blades and each vertebrae. When she touched an apparently particularly sensitive spot, Mel pushed her hips downwards and let out a shaky breath.

The thigh between Ruby's legs was becoming insistent, and Mel was beginning to roll her hips slightly in a slow but regular rhythm. The friction was sending lightning bolts from her centre to the rest of her body, and she could feel the wetness building in her engorged sex.

*She feels so good, her skin against mine, her body on top of me.* Ruby moaned as a wave of arousal swept over her, and she hooked her foot around the back of Mel's calf. She was on fire, and the heat increased as Mel lifted a hand to her breast, her fingers rubbing and teasing her nipple until it stood out.

"Show me." Mel's breath tickled her cheek as she whispered to her.

"What?" Panting, Ruby blinked up at Mel, who looked slightly unsure.

"That's how I learn best," Mel said, and a glint of humour cut through the uncertainty in her eyes.

Ruby laughed and took her hand as Mel rolled from her. Mel settled next to her, her free hand holding up her head, her elbow on the bed. Ruby's skin prickled, the warmth of Mel's body having so far covered her all over.

"Is it?" Ruby cocked an eyebrow, and Mel simply shrugged. Ruby let out a fake-frustrated sigh and held onto Mel's wrist as she led her fingers down her neck. She pressed the palm to her breast, Mel's fingers cupping her flesh and the heel of her hand pressing against her nipple. "You were, by the way, doing just fine before."

Mel looked smug again.

"But if you insist."

She led Mel's hand in circles around one of her breasts, then across to the other, giving it the same treatment. Mel's fingers took over, rubbing at her nipple in small spirals, causing trickles of pleasure to swarm southwards. Ruby dropped her hand to the sheets, closed her eyes and moaned, her shoulders pushing into the bed as her ribs pushed upwards.

When the caresses subsided, Ruby opened her eyes again and found a pair of green eyes shining down at her. She took Mel's hand again and pushed it down her midline. "Touch me," she murmured, keeping her hand on Mel's wrist but giving her some reign over her own movements.

Mel rested her head on Ruby's shoulder and kissed underneath her jaw before sliding her fingers down and through Ruby's pubic hair.

Her whole body tensing in anticipation, Ruby felt like she was teetering on the edge of a cliff, waiting with bated breath for Mel's fingers to make contact.

Pushing past her hair, Mel slipped her fingers between Ruby's outer lips, and they both gasped as she found wetness and warmth. Ruby parted her legs and took her hand away from Mel's, lifting it to thread her fingers into Mel's hair. She groaned when Mel found her clitoris and started to rub back and forth, very gently and very slowly.

Ruby tugged, and their lips met again, teeth nipping and tongues sweeping. Sliding one hand down Mel's body, she took hold of her hip and tugged her there too, hard enough to Mel to break the kiss and look down at her. "All right?" The circles stopped between her legs, and Ruby nearly cried.

"On top of me," she said.

Mel nodded and knelt between her legs, lying down against her as Ruby raised her knees and tugged at her hip again.

*Yes. She feels so good.* Their breasts brushed, and Ruby nearly came from that. She was glad she didn't.

Mel continued to look down at her, her gaze full of uncertainty.

So Ruby took her wrist and guided her down a little. She tapped the back of her hand and Mel, thankfully got the message, sliding one, then two, fingers inside her.

"Oh," Ruby gasped, her body adjusting to the feeling of Mel inside her, the way her fingers curled and pressed and made her back go warm.

Beginning a slow rhythm, Mel leant down to suck on Ruby's shoulder as she moved her whole body with the thrusts of her hand. Ruby wrapped her legs around Mel, squeezing her with each thrust. Her heart hammered against her ribs, and her breathing was laboured. It was fantastic, brilliant, amazing, and she never wanted it to end.

Then Mel brought her thumb forward and touched that tight bundle of nerves, and Ruby let out a sound she didn't even recognise. Her hips surged upwards, her fingertips digging into Mel's scalp as her orgasm overtook her and tiny pops of light erupted behind her eyelids. Her whole body felt full of electrical charge, buzzing and breaking and reconnecting as the pleasure pushed all other thoughts away.

It was intense, and for a while her body was not her own, thrashing about beneath Mel's. When it faded, Ruby was lying in a heap underneath Mel's strong body, her internal muscles still contracting around Mel's fingers.

The puffs of air tickling her cheek were warm and quick. Ruby gave Mel a last squeeze with her thighs, and she withdrew. Ruby's insides missed her the minute she was gone. She expected Mel to roll from her, but she didn't; she simply stayed resting against her, between her legs, her fingers curling into the duvet cover.

Stretching her arms above her head, Ruby let out a long hum of contentment. She blinked at the sunlight streaming through the ceiling window. The smell of sex was sweet in the air.

Mel's lips brushed against the skin of her shoulder before trailing up, smoothing along her jaw, up her cheek, and finally to kiss her gently on the lips. When she pulled away, she was beaming widely, her eyes full of something that resembled wonder.

Ruby caressed her cheek and grinned back up at her, a giggle bubbling up and out of her. "Looks like you're a quick learner."

"I've had plenty of practice," Mel replied, pushing Ruby's hair, still damp from the shower, back from her face.

"Have you?"

Mel shrugged, and Ruby patted her hip to indicate she could dismount. Mel chuckled and climbed back to Ruby's side. "You all right?"

"Yes." Ruby turned to face her and snuggled her cheek into the pillow, bending her knees and curling up. "Just... give me a moment."

"Your wish is my command." Mel trailed a gentle hand up and down Ruby's side as she closed her eyes.

Ruby was determined to stay awake but needed a few minutes to recover. The sunlight from the window warmed her skin, and her sex pulsed with aftershocks that were slowly ebbing away and being replaced with the sated feeling of calm.

As her body relaxed, Mel's hand slowed to come to rest against her waist. Ruby sighed and opened her eyes, reaching forward to cup Mel's cheek. "How're you doing?" she asked on a whisper.

"Me? How are you doing?"

"I'm well and truly done," Ruby said gently. "I meant…" She flicked her eyes downwards. "How are you doing?"

A flush crept into Mel's cheeks. "Okay."

Ruby took Mel's chin in her fingers and tilted her back up to look into her eyes. "Truly?"

"I'm…" Mel rubbed her thumb against Ruby's waist and furrowed her eyebrows, twisting her lips.

"So, what do we do? What can I do to help?" Ruby pushed Mel over onto her back, and Mel lay with her legs tight together.

"Um…I suppose the usual stuff."

"Maybe you should show me?" Unsure where her sudden ability to flirt had come from, Ruby batted her eyelashes at Mel in jest.

It had the desired effect, and Mel laughed. "Why not?"

Ruby held out a hand, flexing her fingers in preparation, which brought another chuckle from Mel's lips. Resting her cheek on Mel's shoulder, Ruby kissed her neck, brushing her lips in little trails across her skin, finding particularly large freckles to poke with the tip of her tongue. She spent a long time kissing Mel's neck and then her shoulders, trying different things: running her tongue in little circles, biting gently with her lip-covered teeth, and humming against her. When her mouth moved down, to caress the swell of one small breast, Mel sighed and shifted a little.

Encouraged, Ruby rubbed her nose and lips against Mel's skin, the soft flesh smelling like almonds. The freckles that dusted Mel's cleavage looked like cinnamon, and Ruby couldn't help lapping the skin there to see how she tasted. *She doesn't taste like cinnamon, but she still tastes delicious.*

Mel lifted a hand to sink her fingers very carefully into Ruby's hair. Her fingertips tickled her scalp in little circles.

Ruby looked up to catch Mel's eye. "This nice?"

"Very," Mel replied, and Ruby was glad to see the anxiety had all but disappeared.

Satisfied that her cleavage tasted like heaven, Ruby honed in on a pale pink nipple, rubbing her cheek against it first, causing it to pucker, then taking it into her mouth. *She's not had kids, so I suspect she's more sensitive than I am.* She was gentle, rolling her tongue around and around.

Mel's hand tightened in her hair before she seemed to catch herself and relax her fingers.

Murmuring her enjoyment, Ruby continued to lap, suck, and tease her nipple, until Mel started to fidget her hips around. She made quick work of giving the other nipple the same attention and then lifted her head to lock her gaze with Mel's once more.

A look passed between them, one of tentative fondness and trust. An intense desire to be even closer consumed Ruby, and she pressed her lips to Mel's. Then she lifted her hand into the air.

"Show me."

Mel complied, taking Ruby's wrist as Ruby had taken hers, and trailing it down her midline, between her breasts, around the soft hair surrounding her navel, and closer to her impending goal.

Mel's lower hair was soft; softer than Ruby's. She traced little circles, tangling Mel's pubic hair a little with her fingertips.

Taking a deep breath, Mel allowed her legs to fall open and rested her feet on the bed. She swallowed, and her eyes drifted away, but she blinked hard and brought them back. The green of her irises was deep, like the leaves of Ruby's clematis, growing steadily up the shed.

Something was growing inside Ruby: A tight ball of dancing warmth, like a fireball in her chest. It was red and orange and wonderful. Was it love?

Mel guided her hand between her legs and sighed, a shiver passing through her.

A smile blossomed on Ruby's face, and she couldn't help shining it down into Mel's eyes. "You're wet," she whispered by her ear.

Mel shivered again and then relaxed back. "Phew."

Ruby pressed her lips against Mel's ear and stayed close, her fingers resting stationary against her slick sex. "It's nice to know I did that," she said, and then chuckled softly. "Unless you were thinking about Ellen Page."

"Who's Ellen Page?" Mel turned her head on the pillow and gazed deeply into Ruby's eyes.

They kissed, slowly and thoroughly, until Mel's hips twitched a few times and her hand where it held Ruby's wrist squeezed.

"Okay." Mel nodded ever so slightly.

Ruby nodded back and then dipped her fingertips lower, gathering wetness and relishing moan that rumbled out of Mel. She made long sweeps, from top to bottom, keeping it steady in case Mel needed her to. She kissed her nose then her lips again and closed her eyes, focussing solely on kissing and touching Mel.

Mel's ribs started to expand more quickly, and her hips began to circle. When Ruby looked down, she took in the flush that had crept up from Mel's ribs to her forehead, the dilation of her pupils so that the green almost disappeared, and the white of her knuckles as her free hand clutched at the duvet by her hip.

When Mel squeezed her wrist again, Ruby took this as an indication that she wanted more, and so concentrated on Mel's clit, circling one way, then the other. Mel moaned and pushed upwards, so Ruby caressed with more pressure.

Mel grinned at her through her arousal. They kissed messily, until Ruby pulled back.

"Do you want me inside you?" she breathed, needing to ask, wanting to do whatever Mel wanted her to do.

Mel shook her head on the pillow.

"Okay. Is this okay?"

Squeezing her wrist, Mel slid her fingers down to cover Ruby's hand and to press her harder. She moaned, her ribs expanding and contracting in time with her hips. Then she led Ruby to make large sweeping circles, using all her fingers, against the whole area where her clit was nestled.

Ruby moaned too, the feeling of Mel's wet sex against her hand almost too much. It made her dizzy; Mel's little noises of pleasure, the way her body was so flushed, and the way her hips rocked back and forth, it was almost too much. She could barely see. She pressed her lips and nose against Mel's neck and tongued her skin, murmuring pleased noises of her own as Mel's hips sped up.

She knew when Mel was close. Her voice had shifted up an octave, and her body was taught as a tourniquet. Ruby slowed her hand, kissed Mel's cheek gently, and waited until she opened her eyes. "It's okay," she said. "Just relax. I'm right here."

And Mel did. She seemed to steel herself, and as she exhaled, her muscles softened and her hips rested back on the bed.

Ruby started touching her again, slow circles that sped up as Mel's moans became more frequent. Then Mel held her breath and came with a rush of renewed wetness, and Ruby pressed her hand against her sex, her lips against her neck, and held her tight.

---

Mel's head hit the pillow, and she tugged on Ruby's wrist, pulling her arm around her waist. Her hips twitched occasionally, but otherwise her body was floppy. Her gasps slowed, and eventually her heart calmed its hammering.

She felt sweaty and a bit achy but wonderfully sated. Her skin prickled as the cool air from the bedroom touched her skin, and she flapped a hand towards the duvet in a meagre attempt to reach for it.

Ruby sat up, and a minute later the duvet was cuddled around them both. Ruby was back against her shoulder.

Mel extricated an arm and slid it around her, her fingers trailing half-awake circles against Ruby's back. Her eyes fluttered closed, and she was vaguely aware of Ruby chuckling beside her.

When she came back to herself, she opened her eyes and found a mound of dark hair, so she sunk her nose into it and squeezed Ruby around the shoulders. She smelt wonderful, like soap and life and sex. Like Ruby.

Ruby rolled away a little and caressed Mel's cheek.

Mel felt her face flush with shyness, but happiness overtook the feeling, pushing the shyness away and plastering a grin onto her face.

Ruby made a long sighing noise in her throat, leant down to press her lips against Mel's cheek, and then returned to looking at her, her eyes shining with affection.

"I like this new way of learning, and teaching." Ruby pushed her shoulders up and grinned. "Perhaps I'll utilise these new methods in my lecture theatre."

Mel's laugh was loud and throaty, and they both jumped as a knock sounded on the door. She pulled the duvet up to her chin as Ruby snorted into her shoulder.

"Mum? I don't want to come in if you're naked." Chloe's voice was tinged with uncertainty.

"You might have to give us twenty minutes, then," Ruby called back, her hand pressed to her mouth as she tried not to laugh.

"Okay. No probs. Do you want some coffee putting on?"

"You're an angel," Ruby replied, and they both relaxed as footsteps on the wooden staircase faded away.

Mel rolled her eyes and shot Ruby a look. "What the hell time is it?"

They both looked at the large wall clock to their left, and Mel was surprised to see it was nearly midday.

"Crumbs." Ruby's gaze stopped by the door before she turned back to Mel. "Well, that's the morning gone."

Shrugging, Mel rolled out of bed. "That's about right for me before a nightshift."

"But we weren't sleeping. Are you going to be okay?" Ruby stood, and Mel was amused to see her legs appeared rather shaky.

"I'll be fine. I'll catch a few hours when I go home." The realisation that she would have to leave settled over her like a chilly fog, but she pushed it away. *Of course I've got to go home. That's where my uniform is, and Epione will be hungry.* She pointed into the en suite. "Mind if I go..." She looked down at herself, noted the discomfort between her legs, and felt heat rising in her cheeks. "Clean up?"

"You go ahead. Use whatever you like."

Showering quickly, and finding a folded towel obviously left for her on the side of the sink, Mel wrapped herself up and twisted her hair into a small knot. She couldn't be bothered to dry it, and it was so thin it would dry itself in an hour. She stared at herself in the mirror above the sink and smirked. Then she moved back into the bedroom, her gaze on her feet.

"I took a leaf out of your fashion-advice book."

Ruby looked up from tucking her duvet in neatly, a smirk crossing her face. "It looks better on you than it does me."

"I very much doubt that." Mel stepped up to her, and Ruby stood up straight, brushing the backs of her fingers down Mel's cheek.

She was still naked from the waist down but had pulled her pyjama T-shirt over her head. It fell just to the tops of her thighs. Mel passed her palms over Ruby's sides, resting her hands on her hips and leaning in to kiss her.

Ruby patted her cheek. "We should get downstairs for that coffee."

"Great idea."

Ruby trotted off into the en suite, and Mel took in the way her slim waist curved into soft hips, swaying a little as she walked. Mel wondered whether it was for her own benefit. A fond warmth spread through her chest as she relived the feeling of Ruby's skin against her own, and the noises Ruby had made as Mel had touched her. The warmth expanded into the rest of her body; even her fingertips tingled with it.

# Chapter 27

They emerged into the kitchen with clean bodies and fresh clothes. Ruby noticed that Mel stared at the floor quite a bit, but that coy happiness tugged her lips and crinkled her eyes.

"Did you sleep okay?" Chloe asked, pouring three mugs of coffee—her best china, Ruby observed—and then bending down to get milk.

"Yes, thank you," Mel answered for both of them before Ruby could chastise her daughter. Something about Chloe's nonchalance made Ruby both amused and wary. *Is she going to say something inappropriate?*

"We watched a film."

Chloe looked up sharply, her eyes wide as saucers, but then relaxed. "That's nice." Her bottom lip disappeared between her teeth, perhaps to hide a smile. "Nice first date."

"Not our first," Ruby said without thinking. She blinked. "I mean, we had a picnic date."

"We did." Mel was lingering by one of the kitchen chairs, her fingertips caressing the back.

Ruby took pity on her and patted the chair. The scraping of wood on tiles seemed loud in the quiet kitchen.

After taking the mug that Chloe handed to her, gratefully, Mel seemed to shake herself inwardly. "Did you have a nice time with...?" Her eyes flicked from side to side. "Tasha?"

Apparently impressed, Chloe nodded. "Yeah. Had a nice time." Then she looked back at Mel.

Ruby considered her eldest daughter with pride. She hadn't had many women sleep over in the years between her divorce and now, and it must seem new. *But at least she's happy for me.*

They drank their coffees and chatted about this and that. Ruby made them toasted sandwiches for lunch, which Mel ate with gusto. That made Ruby grin, although she tried to hide it. *Sex obviously makes her hungry. I'll have to remember that.*

The door banged open and a scampering sound reached them. Barney pricked up her ears and got out of her bed to greet Jasmine, who looked as if she'd run all the way. "Morning!"

Ruby lifted an eyebrow but resolved it quickly by rising to hug Jasmine. "Afternoon. How was your evening?"

"Great. Everyone had fun."

"*Everyone?*"

Jasmine blushed. "Oh. I mean we had fun. And Laura's sister was there too, just in her room, you know?"

"More on this later," Ruby said, pointing at Jasmine.

To her credit, Jasmine lowered her head. After a moment of guilt, she smiled, however, and turned to Mel. "So, what did you watch?"

"*Juno.*"

Jasmine stuffed her hands in her pockets. "Good film. Funny."

"Yeah, it's sweet. Kind of..." Mel twisted her lips. "Comforting."

"I like indie films too," Chloe said.

Ruby took in the way Jasmine stood, her hands in her pockets in a strangely similar position to how Mel often stood. It made her chuckle inwardly. It seemed like both her daughters were comfortable with the fact that she was dating Mel now, and that sometimes Mel would stay over.

It was still a slightly baffling concept to Ruby herself, if she were honest.

---

The garden on campus was growing steadily, leafy green filling every area they'd planted things. Ruby was getting used to the terminology too: cuttings, fertiliser, suckers, tubers, and embryonic leaves. Mel was a great teacher; she was patient with the children and spoke to them in a way that didn't seem patronising. They seemed to really respond to being treated like small adults. Ruby couldn't help watching her, without the worry of a certain school teacher picking up on every little glance.

She had no idea what had happened to Mrs Denzie, only that she was no longer bringing the children to campus. A new teacher, Mr Stephens, had been sent to replace her, and he seemed a much better fit. He pretended he knew nothing about plants, and although the pretence was obvious to Ruby, it wasn't to the children, who delighted in teaching him the knowledge and skills they had learned so far. And he seemed oblivious, or otherwise unconcerned, with any affection Ruby and Mel held for each other. It was a massive weight off her shoulders.

Ruby felt content with that part of her week. Wednesday-afternoon gardening had begun again after Easter, and the kids were ecstatic with how the plants were thriving under their care. Michael was on top form every week, carefully running mini groups himself regarding the care of tomato plants, and how long they would take to produce fruit. Ruby thought perhaps she'd make him a certificate to acknowledge his hard work. Chelsea continued to help the shyer children and seemed to know instinctively when they needed assistance. Becca's onion had grown the tallest leaves, although she appeared unsure whether this meant the bulb would be the biggest. Such scepticism in a nine-year-old!

Frank's potato plant was most impressive. His leaves were so huge they weighed down the entire plant and he'd had to borrow some canes to prop them up. His chubby fingers were careful as he tied the thick stems to the canes, and his eyebrows furrowed in concentration. *I wonder what certificate I can make for him.*

The entire garden had surpassed Ruby's expectations, especially those she had held at the beginning. Mel's bright enthusiasm seemed to permeate the plants and make them thrive; or perhaps it was the "extra special" feed they were giving them each week. Whatever it was, everything was going to plan, and so far, nothing had withered. Ruby found herself in the garden on days that were not Wednesdays, checking the plants for slugs and plucking off any suckers from the tomatoes. *Maybe I'll try to grow something in my own garden. I think Chloe would enjoy helping me with that. Jasmine too, perhaps.* She sat for long minutes, drinking coffee and gazing lovingly at her clematis, secured firmly to the side of the shed. *Mel bought that especially for me.* The flame-like flowers had opened, and they stood proudly in the sun. Ruby loved it.

# Chapter 28

The boot of her small Mini Cooper full of sandwiches, packets of crisps, and random donations from the various shops she'd sent letters to, Ruby pulled into the car park with a thrum of excitement making her whole body tingle. *Today is the day. The fruit of our labours.*

Chloe went immediately to the boot, hauling platters of sandwiches into her arms, her face alight and her trousers, as usual, dragging on the dusty concrete.

Jasmine ignored her and folded her arms, until Ruby shot her a look. She rolled her eyes and took several bags of crisps from her mother.

"Thank you, lovely," Ruby sang, as if Jasmine had intended to help all along.

They made their way through reception. Ruby noticed Chloe lingering by the various leaflets detailing each course before she blinked hastily and followed her down the corridor and back out into the sunshine.

The children and their selected family members and friends were already there. Francesca, fresh from her assessment and looking a lot less tired, stood slightly awkwardly near the shed. Various other students and lecturers from the university had also arrived. So had Mel, and Ruby couldn't help the grin that swept onto her face as she took her in. Gone was her usual gardening attire of walking boots and old jeans. She was dressed in a buttoned-up blouse, dress trousers, and shiny boots. Her hair was neat but down, the ends fluttering in the breeze. Ruby thought she recognised the outfit from the first time she had met her, all those months ago, in the canteen of the university. *How we hated one another. And now look at us.*

The urge to go up to her and kiss her full on the lips was strong, but she pushed the feeling away, aware of the large group of people occupying the space. Michael was holding court, apparently giving a guided tour of each section of the garden. As he reached the sunflowers, yellow as the morning sun, and stretched his small hands upwards, a hum of amazement drifted through the sunshine. *They really have done such a good job.*

Jasmine and Chloe set the food on the long tables Mel had brought from her garage and then went to join James and his girlfriend, Jade, who were standing with Chelsea's parents and blatantly raining praise down on the small girl.

Ruby took it all in. The garden was lush and green, with flowers all over, and a few remaining potato plants amongst fresh earth, left behind after last week's harvest. The onions had been pulled up a couple of weeks ago and were now tied in seven bunches, ready to be taken home by the kids who had cared for them. Flowers sparkled from each bed, nasturtiums and poppies, and smaller sunflowers, and marigolds. The bursts of colour made the whole space look luminous, warm, and friendly.

Suffice to say, the entire student population of the university had begun using the space to socialise a lot more over the last few weeks. Ruby had never seen it so busy; sometimes she'd had to shoo people out when the kids had been hard at work, unsure whether they would want to be watched or not.

The greenhouse was full to bursting with fruit, most of which still needed to be harvested. Michael led the Tomato group and their respective followers into the greenhouse, and his gestures told Ruby he was giving them the all-clear to pick what they liked. Chelsea noticed and skipped over to the greenhouse too, her group, responsible for pepper management, following at her heels.

Onion and Potato groups sat on the grass, enjoying the sunshine. Mr Stephens had helpfully taken it upon himself to take the harvested vegetables home to wash, cook, and mix with mayonnaise and chives. The potato salad bowls were laid out on the table, and Ruby was amazed at how much food there was. Her mouth watered, and her stomach groaned. *Oh goodness, I didn't have breakfast.*

A warmth behind her made her turn, and a pair of shining green eyes met her own. Mel grinned and passed a hand over the scene before them. "Quite a turn out."

"You're not wrong." Ruby laid a palm over Mel's upper arm and leaned in close. "Is the whole of the county here?"

"Just about." Mel's gaze left her. "Um. Would you mind just… giving me a hand to grab some stuff from the shed?"

With a raised eyebrow, Ruby watched as Mel walked over to the shed, her hand resting on the door as she turned back. Mel beckoned to her.

Ruby rolled her eyes and walked purposefully across the grass. Someone wolf-whistled, and she turned around, her arms folded and her face stern. "Just getting some… something."

Whoever had whistled remained anonymous, but Ruby reckoned it was probably James.

Mel pulled the door open and held it open while Ruby stepped inside. The shed was dark except for the small window, which had taken on a mucky and more than a little opaque look. It faced the university building, rather than the rest of the garden, and they were quite hidden from the party. The door creaked closed behind them.

Ruby turned around. "What're we—"

She didn't have time to finish her sentence. Mel crushed her lips to Ruby's and wrapped her arms around her. Ruby faltered momentarily but regained her senses in time to kiss her back. She murmured wordlessly and gripped Mel's shoulders.

When they broke the kiss, Mel's hands remained at Ruby's waist. "I'm sorry. It's unprofessional, I know. But dear God, woman, can you see what you're wearing?"

Ruby looked down at herself and furrowed her eyebrows. "I can."

"That top," Mel said, indicating the floral wrap-around top with short sleeves currently adorning Ruby's top half. "And those jeans."

Ruby looked down further and frowned, shaking her head. "This is sexy to you?"

Mel caressed her hips with her thumbs and nodded, the blush creeping across her cheeks visible even in the dim light of the shed.

"In that case, I'll wear it every day."

Mel smiled. "Sounds good to me." She kissed Ruby again, more softly this time, her tongue running teasingly along her bottom lip.

Ruby started to melt into the kiss, but her brain took over after a few seconds. "Ahem. We have work to do."

"Oh, um, also… I passed all of my assessments."

"That's wonderful. So it's just your portfolio to get back now, and then you'll be a fully-fledged ECP?"

"Come over later to celebrate?" Mel asked. Her gaze shot down again. "And don't change your outfit."

"Okay," Ruby said. She stroked Mel's cheek and stepped away, brushing down her clothes as if they had dirt on them. She looked about her and grabbed a long-handled fork, handing it to Mel before she took up another for herself.

When they emerged, several grins greeted them. The kids, apparently, were not naïve, and even some of the parents were giving them knowing looks. Ruby ignored them and threw herself into pulling people together. *It's fine if people know we're together. I don't need it to be a secret anymore.*

Everyone gathered on the lawn, a sea of beaming faces all focussing on Ruby.

She plunged the fork into the ground, as if she had a flag that she was using to claim a newly discovered country. Her heart thudded with speed, and her palms were clammy. But she could feel Mel standing close to her; not so close as to be noticed, at least by those that didn't know them, but close enough that she could feel her support and warmth. *She's right there, and I don't need to be nervous.*

"Welcome, everyone, to Sutton Primary's very special garden party." She introduced herself, then Mel, and finally the garden. She spoke about the different areas, and the flowers and fruit and vegetables. She talked about the care each group had taken into looking after their respective plants and how everything was now ready to eat.

"But, before we tuck in," she continued, "I have a few certificates to give out." Fumbling in her briefcase, she pulled out a wad of A4 sheets, all laminated by Alexander the day before. "Becca Robinson, you get the award for the most sensible gardener. You helped everyone who needed it. I'm very proud of you."

Becca came forward, shock and pleasure shining from behind her black fringe.

"Frank Marshall. For growing the best potatoes, and the tallest sunflower I've ever seen."

Frank's pink face popped out from behind a taller boy, and his podgy fingers clasped his certificate to his chest.

"Chelsea Smith. You get the award for the most improved gardener. You've learned a lot this year, well done."

The blonde girl skipped towards Mel and Ruby and waved her certificate in the air, amid her own glee.

"And to my right-hand lad, Mr Michael Harrison. You've been a great help, and you get the award for the best leader. Most likely to become Prime Minister, I reckon."

A huge cheer, from parents and his teammates alike, rose throughout the garden as Michael walked up proudly. He shook Ruby's hand, then Mel's, and then turned to his adoring fans, his certificate held high above his head. The cheering became a roar, and he laughed into the sunshine.

Once the noise had dissipated, and Michael had re-joined his family, Ruby stood with her hands clasped. "I'd just like to say a final thank you to Mel. She didn't have to help on this project, but she did. She's taught me more about gardening than all the kids put together I think, and for that I am eternally grateful." Ruby turned to Mel and beamed at her.

Mel blushed as red Ruby's clematis flowers, leaning proudly on her pitch fork, and took in the kids before her. "It was a pleasure."

Everyone clapped, and Ruby leant close to her ear. "I couldn't have done it without you."

"I know you couldn't," Mel replied, laughing.

Ruby stuck her tongue out briefly but then caught herself. *Not very professional.* She pulled the pleased but professional mask back on and swept her hand towards the tables full of food. "Please, tuck in, everyone."

Michael launched himself towards the tables, and the rest of the children followed, grabbing plates and forks and crisps and cupcakes. Francesca stood close to Chloe, and Ruby noticed their gazes meet and a shy conversation begin, although they were too far away for Ruby to hear. *That's good. Maybe Chloe will be a good influence on her—they're only a year apart.*

Ruby and Mel stood back, nodding modestly to a few parents as they came up and thanked them. The band that James had arranged—a few of his mates—had set up in one corner and were beginning to play. Some of the children took their food over to the band, and their knees began to bend in time.

James and Jade approached them with impressed looks, and James clapped Mel on the back. "Get you, all teachery and stuff," he said.

Mel smacked him around the head. "Shut up, pea brain."

They laughed like naughty kids until Mel quietened and pursed her lips, eyeing Ruby with embarrassment. "You've met my crewmate, James."

"I have," Ruby replied, pulling the memory of their amusing drinks together the week before to the forefront of her brain.

James gathered Ruby up in a bear hug that knocked the air from her lungs. He rubbed her back and let her go. "You've done a brilliant job. Both of you."

"Yeah. It looks amazing," Jade said.

"It was a joint effort," Ruby replied.

Mel beamed at her.

"And I totted up the donations. We've already made over a hundred pounds."

"That's amazing." Mel was gaping. "That helicopter can fly another day."

"Are you going to have some of these sandwiches, Mum, or what?" Jasmine tottered over to them on her high heels and stood with her hands in her pockets.

Ruby looked her up and down, and then took in Mel, who was standing in exactly the same way.

Mel must have noticed the fact, because she pulled her hands out and instead folded her arms across her chest. The black shirt she wore pulled a bit across her small breasts, and Ruby had to look away. *I thought when you slept together some of the allure was supposed to fade? Perhaps not.*

Ruby focussed on her daughter. "You worked very hard filling those sandwiches with ham. Do I look like someone who passes up an opportunity to taste your culinary delights?"

Jasmine nodded in satisfaction and stepped up to Mel. "Um. I made you some with pickle, because I know you like pickle."

Mel's lips twisted as she tried not to smile. "Oh. Thanks, Jas."

Jasmine seemed to almost burst with joy and hopped away across the grass and back to the food. She turned back to them and pointed to a plate.

Rolling her eyes, Ruby took Mel's elbow and steered her towards the other end of the garden. "Looks like you have an admirer."

"Can I help it if she thinks I'm amazing?" Mel asked.

James and his girlfriend were running the tombola, with Jasmine handing out prizes. Becca won a stuffed monkey, and Frank bagged himself some delightful perfume. They swapped prizes, and everyone laughed.

The kids and adults all filled their bellies, then Michael and Chelsea went into the greenhouse with empty bowls which had contained crisps, to pick the remaining tomatoes and peppers.

They brought them outside to flurries of applause and handed them around for people to taste. The juice from many chewed tomatoes dribbled down chins for the next few minutes, and Chelsea flapped at her mother, who was chasing her around the garden with a napkin.

Ruby took the tomato she was offered, and the sweet tangy fruit exploded in her mouth as she bit down. She placed a hand over her chin to catch any juice and closed her eyes, humming out her pleasure at the delicious fruit. She swallowed. The pepper she tried next was crunchy and sweet as well, and she was glad that Mel had not insisted they grow hot chillies, as it would have meant they wouldn't have been able to eat them straight from the plants.

A warm body rested against her side as Ruby swallowed her mouthful of pepper, and Mel's arm slid around her. "This okay?" Mel whispered.

"Yeah. It's okay." Ruby sighed, the warm sun on her cheeks, the children chasing each other round the garden, and the parents relaxing on blankets, in lawn chairs, and picnic benches. *It really is okay.*

She watched Jasmine stuffing crisps into her mouth and Chloe rolling her eyes at her, drinking from a water bottle and eating very little. James kicked a football he had brought around the far side of the garden with some of the children, and his girlfriend even joined in, her laughter ringing through the summer air as he picked her up by the waist and prevented her from tackling the ball from him.

Mrs Denzie had not been invited to the party.

His sandy hair shining gold in the sunshine, Mr Stephens approached them and gave them both a thumbs up. "Great work, you two."

"Thank you, sir." Ruby tilted her head graciously.

"Sir? You must be kidding. It's Jeffery. Did you see my wife?" He pointed into the crowd. "She's currently keeping young Chelsea amused."

Ruby and Mel both looked over a few heads, and Ruby caught sight of a pretty woman with grey hair and a friendly posture listening intently to Chelsea as she gestured emphatically.

"We're just glad they all had a great time." Mel's hand stroked Ruby's waist gently.

"They did. That they did." Jeffery smiled at them both. "Michael told me in class last week that you guys were together."

Ruby looked at Mel and then nodded.

"Good for you. Not the gay thing; that's a non-issue with me. But being open about it. I know it can be hard."

"Sometimes." Mel's tickling hand started up again. "But not when you're being open to a bunch of fine young people. And these guys really are." She chewed her lip, and she looked out over the class.

Ruby followed her gaze. She rested her cheek against Mel's shoulder and felt Mel's arm around her tighten.

"I'd like to apologise." Jeffery continued. "Not on behalf of the school. They've... Well, they've dealt with it." The look he gave them told Ruby he didn't think this was quite good enough but that he had no control over the situation. "On behalf of humanity. Off the record, I've never liked her."

As he walked briskly away, back to his wife, Ruby laughed and shook her head.

Mel continued to stroke her waist with gentle fingers.

A lot of people bought the vibrant flowers the kids had cut from the garden. Ruby had to insist they leave at least *some* for the bees and the butterflies, reminding them all that the flowers would provide essential food for them. The sunflowers remained too, and Ruby was eager to see the birds begin to harvest the bulging seeds once they appeared in autumn. The band, having finished what they had come to play, started to pack up. The clanking and banging of their equipment carried over the kids' good-byes to one another.

As the last parent left, pulled along by a skipping child with an arm full of flowers, Mel kissed Ruby's cheek and guided her into a gentle hug.

Her professional facade dropping finally, Ruby pressed her nose into the warm cotton covering Mel's shoulder and looped her arms around her neck.

They ignored the whooping from James behind them and the groan from Chloe.

"Get an actual room," Jasmine said, her embarrassment outweighing her urge to impress Mel.

"Bugger off if you can't handle it," Ruby said, cuddling her close as Mel's chuckles vibrated through her.

They still had a whole lot of mess to clear up: napkins and paper plates and half-eaten sandwiches littered the tables. But for now, Ruby was snug and safe in Mel's arms, and nothing else really mattered apart from that.

# About Jenn

Jenn Matthews lives in England's South West with her wife, dog, and cat. When not working full-time as a health-care assistant at a mental health rehab unit, she can be found avidly gardening, crocheting, writing, or visiting National Trust properties.

Inspired by life's lessons and experiences, Jenn is a passionate advocate of people on the fringe of society. She hopes to explore and represent other "invisible people" with her upcoming novels.

CONNECT WITH JENN
Website: www.jennmatthews.com
E-Mail: jenn@jennmatthews.com

# Other Books from Ylva Publishing

www.ylva-publishing.com

# Hooked on You
## Jenn Matthews

ISBN: 978-3-96324-133-8
Length: 281 pages (98,000 words)

Anna has it all – great kids, boyfriend, good teaching job. Except she's so bored. Perhaps a new hobby's in order? Something…crafty?

Divorced mother and veteran Ollie has been through the wars. To relax, she runs a quirky crochet class in her English craft shop. Enter one attractive, feisty new student. A shame she's straight.

A quirky lesbian romance about love never being quite where you expect.


# Major Surgery
## Lola Keeley

ISBN: 978-3-96324-145-1
Length: 198 pages (69,000 words)

Surgeon and department head Veronica has life perfectly ordered…until the arrival of a new Head of Trauma. Cassie is a brash ex-army surgeon, all action and sharp edges, not interested in rules or playing nice with icy Veronica. However when they're forced to work together to uncover a scandal, things get a little heated in surprising ways.

A lesbian romance about cutting to the heart of matters.

# All the Little Moments
G Benson

ISBN: 978-3-95533-341-6
Length: 350 pages (139,000 words)

Anna is focused on her career as an anaesthetist. When a tragic accident leaves her responsible for her young niece and nephew, her life changes abruptly. Completely overwhelmed, Anna barely has time to brush her teeth in the morning let alone date a woman. But then she collides with a long-legged stranger...

# L.A. Metro
(The L.A. Metro Series – Book 1)
RJ Nolan

ISBN: 978-3-95533-041-5
Length: 349 pages (97,000words)

Dr. Kimberly Donovan's life is in shambles. After her medical ethics are questioned, first her family, then her closeted lover, the Chief of the ER, betray her. Determined to make a fresh start, she flees to California and L.A. Metropolitan Hospital. When she meets Jess McKenna, L.A. Metro's Chief of the ER the attraction is immediate. Can either woman overcome her past to make a future together?

***The Words Shimmer***
© 2019 by Jenn Matthews

ISBN: 978-3-96324-243-4

Also available as e-book.

Published by Ylva Publishing, legal entity of Ylva Verlag, e.Kfr.

Ylva Verlag, e.Kfr.
Owner: Astrid Ohletz
Am Kirschgarten 2
65830 Kriftel
Germany

www.ylva-publishing.com

First edition: 2019

No part of this book may be reproduced, scanned, or distributed in any printed or electronic form without permission. Please do not participate in or encourage piracy of copyrighted materials in violation of the author's rights. Thank you for respecting the hard work of this author.

This is a work of fiction. Names, characters, places, and incidents either are a product of the author's imagination or are used fictitiously, and any resemblance to locales, events, business establishments, or actual persons—living or dead—is entirely coincidental.

Credits
Edited by Andrea Bramhall and Amanda Jean
Cover Design and Print Layout by Streetlight Graphics